THE RISING OF 15 THE SHIELD HERO

Aneko Yusagi

Motoyasu Kitamura

Itsuki Kawasumi

Ren Amaki

Ruftmila

Fohl

Raphtalia

Naofumi Iwatani

Atla

Raph-chan

THE Rising OF ⑮ THE SHIELD HERO

Table of Contents

Prologue: A Problem with Bandits

"You rabble! Fall in!"

"We'll try!"

My name is Naofumi Iwatani. Originally from Japan, I was summoned here to this world to be the Shield Hero. As you might expect, that's all a pretty long story, and right then I really didn't have the time to reflect on all the details.

I'd just finished breakfast with the group from the village that was under my control and was about to lay my orders on them. We'd finally finished the cleanup from a series of events that had seemed to both take forever and be over in the blink of an eye. And so here we were.

The disturbance in Q'ten Lo coming to an end was all well and good, but that had then led to a smaller disturbance in Siltvelt involving the pain-in-the-ass process of me having to display my authority as the Shield Hero. By which I mean it had taken longer than expected to get back to the village.

It had been tough, sure, but as a result, various problems were also actually on the road to improvement.

"Everyone take your regular posts and complete your duties as normal! That's all!" I used my best commanding voice.

"Roger that!" The replies were full of energy. The residents of my village certainly had a lot of that. Too much, perhaps.

"Mr. Naofumi, what's the policy for today?" This question was from Raphtalia, a girl who I treated much like my daughter. She was the official representative of the village, as well as the Heavenly Emperor—that is, queen—of Q'ten Lo, the nation we'd just been off invading. Going from being a slave to the ruler of her own nation? Talk about bettering yourself!

Not to mention, she was the holder of a very special weapon—a katana from another world—known as a "vassal weapon."

Damn, I mean, taking in her entire history, she might even come out looking better than me.

Today, she was also wearing the miko outfit that served as the symbol of our invasion of Q'ten Lo, and it really was super soothing on the eyes.

"Yeah, about that. There was all that hassle in Siltvelt too, right? So I'm thinking of sorting through all the spoils from Q'ten Lo and Siltvelt," I informed her.

"So we should just train on our own?" Raphtalia asked. That sounded like a pretty good idea, but I couldn't help feeling I was forgetting something . . . In that moment, Ren, Itsuki, and Rishia, having finished their meal, came over.

"Naofumi!" Ren, the one calling my name, was the Sword Hero, summoned from a different Japan than the one I came from. His full name was Ren Amaki. The other guy with him,

Itsuki, was the Bow Hero, and just like Ren and me, he too had been summoned here from a different Japan. His full name was Itsuki Kawasumi. Rishia was a heroine-level, emotional roller-coaster of a girl who always followed Itsuki around.

Ren continued, "Eclair said that she and Queen Melty have something they want to discuss with you, Naofumi."

"What?" I didn't have time for that.

"Sounds like there's been some trouble with bandits recently," Ren explained.

"Is that true?" First I was hearing of it.

"Yeah. While you were off invading Q'ten Lo, we carried out the trading that you ordered, Naofumi, so quite a lot of new information has come into the village," Ren explained.

"That reminds me," Keel reported, as though it was the most natural thing in the world. "We met with quite a few bandit attacks while we were off trading."

"Why haven't these reports been reaching me?" I inquired.

"They've been fought off so far, so they haven't really been a problem. And you've been busy yourself, Naofumi. Right?" Ren offered.

"Hmmm." I guess that made sense.

"These attacks are starting to stand out though, so we're wondering if you have any good ideas," Ren continued.

It was true that our trading had really been taking off recently. Spirit Tortoise materials had become pretty trendy, and with me managing the trading of them, the economy of Melromarc was really starting to improve quite nicely. Seeing as I'd been away, everyone had likely been getting sloppy with making reports. These attackers had only just come to the village too.

This reminded me of the accessory merchant in Zeltoble. Always an excitable fellow, he had eagerly explained how, with the appearance of the Spirit Tortoise, people were now much more sensitive to the threat of the waves and much more keen to spend their money on protecting themselves. He'd sworn that getting in now was the route to quick money.

Perhaps it was only natural, then, that the success of merchants such as him would also give rise to bandits preying on them. Currently the Four Holy Pillars—the Adventurers' Guild, Trade Union, Band of Knights, and the Church—supported each other and maintained the economy. Meanwhile, thugs and killers were banding together to attack merchants and villages for their own profit. Handling such violence was surely beyond the means of those operating the trade in slaves and accessories. They had power, perhaps, but at their core they were nothing more than black-hearted merchants, dynamically opposed to those who relied only on violence and would never listen to reason.

They likely had some plans in place, but still I'd have to act.

What this meant overall, anyway, was that the chain of events since the appearance of the Spirit Tortoise had led to a fall in the general public safety of Melromarc.

"We'll have to go big on this one. Wipe them all out," I concluded.

"But how?" Ren asked.

"I do have one idea," I said, and it brought a grin to my face.

That very same day, I visited the place I'd been thinking of—a farm set up for the rehabilitation of criminals. I took Ren, Raphtalia, and anyone else with me who looked like they might be useful in a negotiation.

"Now do you see? I've got a very special, very large job just for you," I explained.

"N-no thanks! I've made up my mind. Once my dues have been paid, I'll go back home and stick to the straight and narrow!" This from a bandit who, after numerous encounters with me, was now being managed here by Ren. I was trying to convince him to take pride of place as a key player in my plan. However, perhaps truly regretting his deeds from the past, the man continued to reject my offer.

"You actually don't have the right to say no," I pointed out.

"Whatever you may say, I'm working hard, right now, to make a go of a normal life! Please don't mess things up for me!" The man was indeed making an effort. I couldn't deny his desire to turn over a new leaf.

That said, I didn't give up on trying to win him over.

"I won't. Don't worry. But at least listen to what I have to say. I'm not asking you to do anything crazy for me—nothing too insane. There's plenty in this for you too." Honestly, I had quite a lot of respect for this guy. He'd taken his licks, plenty of them, and still stuck it out as a robber.

He was unlucky for sure, but he was also lucky enough to have gotten away with his life.

"First," I continued my pitch, "I'm going to let you class up, level up, and everything." The punishment this guy had received from the state was a level reset and to work in developing the land. That meant he was currently level 1. With no means to fight he was just like a slave anyway, simply working off his sins.

Of course, seeing as he actually was a slave, if he ran his slave seal would activate and kill him. So he also had to live with that hanging over him.

All of this stuff certainly made keeping criminals in line easier than in my world.

"Next, and I don't even know where you come from, but I'll send some money to your family. Help them out a bit. You are being hired by the state, after all. Give your folks back home something to brag about, for once."

"Gah!" That seemed to have worked, at least a little. He was paying more attention to me now. A thief with no abilities or connections had a chance to receive support from the state. Of course he was giving it some thought.

"This will be a good deed if it goes well." I went for the kill. "I promise a significant reduction in your sentence."

"Naofumi, you look positively maniacal," Ren observed.

"Shut up. This is called plea bargaining!" I shot back.

"I don't think that's quite right," Ren corrected me.

"Then what? A decoy investigation?" I retorted.

"He's a decoy?" Ren still didn't sound convinced, giving me a suspicious glance.

"I appreciate the offer, but still—" This bandit wasn't having any of it.

"Come, come, don't rush to a decision. You must be hungry. Here, let me feed you." The dish I produced was, of course, a cutlet rice bowl famous in Japan for its use in interrogations. My recollection might have been fuzzy on that. Anyway, the exact ingredients couldn't be obtained in this world, so I'd cobbled it together from stuff that looked the part.

The robber said nothing, but his stomach growled for him. Looking at the food—my trump card—he gave a swallow.

He'd been stealing things for a living, after all. He'd likely never really eaten nice food.

"It's not poisoned," I assured him. "Go ahead. I'll have one of my slaves eat a little first, if you want." I'd brought Keel along for just this reason, and I placed some of the almost-cutlet-and-rice onto a small dish and had her eat it.

"Bubba Shield! This is delicious! Give me more!" she yapped.

"Just wait," I replied. "If he doesn't give me the nod, you can have it all."

"You'd better not nod, nasty, bad person!" Keel quickly quipped.

"Keel!" Raphtalia admonished. Yeah, I guess taunting the guy to get him to reject my offer just because Keel wanted to eat more herself was worthy of reprimand.

"You've twisted my arm then! I'll eat! I'm eating!" Phew. With that, the robber started to eat the cutlet rice bowl I'd prepared for him.

"W-what is this?" He reacted at once. "It's delicious! I can't stop! Like mom used to make, but so much better—" Keel, the little puppy, looked on with jealous eyes as the robber, actual tears streaming from his eyes, greedily stuffed the food into his mouth.

Ren was looking at me with a really odd expression on his face. Like I cared.

"Of course, it doesn't have to be you. I'm sure there are some other faces here I recognize." I put the pressure on as the robber finished off the meal. Now that his stomach was full, he'd probably be more inclined to listen to what I had to say. Now I just had to close the deal.

This kind of negotiation was fun. It looked like a good way to burn off some of my recent stress.

"If you do the job that I'm asking you," I continued, "I can see my way to making you more food." I held all the power in this particular negotiation, anyway. As I'd already alluded to, if this guy wouldn't give me the nod, I could easily find someone else who would.

"Whatever you promise, I just can't sell out my comrades—"

"Filo." I called in my big gun. This particular robber had a specific trauma in his past of having been beaten black and blue by the so-called "bird god."

Of course, she wasn't actually here. Filo was currently with Melty, who had been posted over in the neighboring town.

"Okay, okay! You'll set me free if I can pull this off, right?" Man, he caved quickly! Was he really that scared of Filo?

"Of course." I was magnanimous in victory. "I think I can agree to that." Of course, his freedom was contingent on him even wanting to leave this job behind once he got started.

"Naofumi." Ren's mouth hung open, as though he had something he wanted to say.

"What?" I didn't have time for it. "If we fight all these bandits one group at a time, there's only so much we can achieve, right? We need to rip them up from the roots."

"I'm sorry, but . . ." Raphtalia, silent until now, finally spoke up. "You're really going to make someone try to atone for his past by going back and doing more bad things?"

"I'm not sure I'd call them 'bad,' you know." I smirked.

My plan was to use this individual to investigate the real reason why bandits were on the rise in this nation while at the same time improving public safety. If the heroes were going to increase the light, it stood to reason that they should also manage any darkness created by that light. How many people were there in this entire world? Who would guess that one of those heroes was pulling the strings on one of those bandits?

Even if some did, I had nothing to fear, with almost all of the four holy heroes now among my forces. Reflecting on it for a moment now, I realized that my standing had really changed dramatically.

"You can start by gathering those comrades you spoke of." I started to outline the plan. "Then go on to expand your forces. Of course, I don't want you attacking any of *my* merchants."

"How are we meant to make a living if we don't attack merchants? What do you think bandits do?!" There was desperation in his voice.

"Did I say don't attack anyone? Actually, there's quite a few merchants I'd love for you to attack." I gave a wicked grin. There were numerous villainous merchants at work who didn't belong to the Trade Union and happily ignored territories and regulations. Picking apart the causes of this bandit problem, I had been told on the way here that merchants like these were actually in league with the bandits. And behind both groups were a bunch of moderate anti-shield nobles. Thinking about it, I did recall a bunch of puffed-up peacocks giving me the eye.

"Harvest those evil merchants who ignore the rules," I commanded. "Do that and I'll provide you with financial support."

I should mention that, before coming here, I went to Zeltoble via portal and completed negotiations with the accessory dealer. He'd been very excited and said that he'd definitely name me as his successor.

I really didn't understand what made this guy tick.

"I can't tell the difference!" he said, sounding desperate.

"I've got you covered," I assured him. "I'll keep you fully apprised of the routes taken by my own merchants and the others who you aren't meant to attack. You select any other wagon to strike, and just take the cargo from evil merchants."

And so bandits of justice were born—only stealing from evil men. Of course, in this equation "evil men" were determined by the Shield Hero.

This plan should maintain the peace for at least a little while.

"And then? What do we do with the stuff we steal?" my new bandit leader asked.

"Good question," I pondered and stroked my chin. "You *could* bring it to me, but then again it would be a hassle if it gets traced back to me. Use half to pay your underlings and give the other half to poor people and villages. Then the world at large won't see you as evil. As for the nation . . . well, just look at me."

"Is this really something a hero should be doing?" he questioned. This from a bandit! There was always someone pulling the strings behind every large organization. That was just the way of the world. I'd join forces with the queen if I could and wipe out the trash trying to hide from me too.

"I'll have the heroes patrol, making it look like we're clearing the bandits out. You can emerge as a cunning boss with a good nose for a target. If any of your men oppose you or start causing trouble, have them attack one of my merchants. We'll take them out for you, without it looking too suspicious," I added.

"Your conditions aren't bad. It's not like I can turn you down either. Very well," he replied.

"Then we have an agreement." I grinned.

And that was how I successfully became a patron to a bunch of bandits.

"You're black-hearted, truly," Ren offered. "I don't know what Itsuki will say about this once he returns to normal."

"That's why I left him in the village, so he wouldn't see it," I said smugly. "Seeing as you're working with Eclair to keep the peace, Ren, you needed to see this stuff."

"Very well," he grumbled. "It isn't easy making money, is it?"

"I'm not sure that's the takeaway from all of this," Raphtalia said, obviously not happy with this turn of events, the result of which was that a major new organization, the "Chivalrous Bandit Guild," if you like, had now appeared in Melromarc.

If we could control the bandits at the state level, it would be best for everyone. It just meant another layer had been added to those shadows we couldn't discuss with the common folk.

When our negotiations with the bandits finished, we returned to the village via portal.

Soon I would need to go and report to the queen of Melromarc. With everything that had been going on, I hadn't visited her at all recently. As I considered these things, I looked over a ledger containing the profits and other details from the trade during our invasion of Q'ten Lo.

"Wow," I exclaimed. Keel's sales were incredible. The monster that pulled Keel's wagon for trading—a large caterpilland—was looking over at me. Ah, whatever. I decided to offer Keel some praise.

"While we were away from the village, it seems you've been working very hard, Keel. Well done."

"Bubba?" she asked.

"Mr. Naofumi has suddenly started to praise you. Be careful," Raphtalia warned.

"I will," Keel agreed. All it took was one compliment

from me and Raphtalia immediately thought I was planning something.

You reap what you sow, I guess. I'm one dark individual most of the time.

"She's been working hard, so I was just offering some praise. I'm even thinking of giving a reward," I explained.

"Cook me a meal then, Bubba! Something even more delicious than the food back there!" Food was the reward she wanted from me? That was always what Filo went for too.

"Very well," I agreed. "I'll make you a delicious dessert, maybe." I thought of a dessert because we'd achieved the production of honey using a mutant species from a bioplant I'd been researching with Rat. I could experiment a bit while cooking something up.

If that failed, I'd use some of the luxury sweeteners that Siltvelt had offered up. I'd given them a lick and found them to be a little unique, but definitely sweet.

I headed to the kitchen, and Keel came in to watch excitedly. Once I started cooking, everyone in the village got like this.

"That does smell good. It looks delicious," Raphtalia offered.

"Bubba! What'cha making?" Keel asked excitedly.

"Just shut up and watch," I barked. "Ah, I have to adjust the heat . . . I need it as low as possible." I heated the hotplate and then created the batter by mixing wheat obtained through trade with monster milk from a ranch in the neighboring town managed by Melty. I'd also separated the fat from the milk to form cream and whipped it up. I added the honey to that to make it sweeter. Oh, and I needed some fruit too.

As I continued cooking, my slaves and even monsters started to gather, lured in by the smell.

Was there going to be enough?

"Right." I spread the batter as thinly as I could across the hotplate, flipping it quickly to cook both sides. I placed the finished articles on a separate table, arranged them with fruit, topped them with cream, and then wrapped them up.

"All done," I proclaimed.

"Right. I thought you were making crepes," Ren muttered upon seeing the finished food.

"Yeah. I had a part-time job in a food court, so I know how to make them," I explained.

"Part-time job, huh? There's a concept that takes me back," Ren mused.

"Have you ever had one?" I asked. He had been hooked on Internet games, after all, which meant that he'd probably needed all the money he could get his hands on for in-game purchases. Those kinds of games could cost money to play. That or you could make better progress if you paid. If things got serious, those weren't the kind of charges you could cover with an allowance. You'd need to at least get a part-time job to raise funds.

"Nope," was his flat reply. "Although I wanted one." Ren was a high-schooler, after all. His school, or maybe his parents, probably didn't let him work. My younger brother was already attending a school that didn't allow the students to work.

Me? I'd been working my butt off since I was in high school, desperate for cash. I think you can guess why.

With that, I gave my first experiment to Ren. This was a popular dessert in Japan, so Ren was probably best positioned to evaluate it for me.

"Delicious. A little different from what I'm used to, but not enough to bother me," was Ren's verdict.

"Ah, ah! Are they really good?" Keel's eyes sparkled as she looked on.

"Here, this is a thing from my world called a crepe," I said and gave the next one to Keel.

"A crepe? I've never heard of this. A food from your world, Bubba?" she asked and sniffed at it, eyes wide. At the moment she was in human form. She'd been in dog form a lot recently. According to her, although it consumed magic while she was transformed, it heightened her senses and made her lighter on her feet (paws?), which was convenient for all sorts of things in daily life.

Keel took a big bite out of the crepe. "I've never tasted

anything like this," she managed to say around her stuffed cheeks. She kept on chewing, wagging her tail and wriggling her ears. "It's delicious."

"Glad to hear it," I said. Thanks to Keel's comments, the rest of the villagers and the monsters were all displaying a desire to try one.

I started to cook more, but then, "So delicious! crepes rule!" Keel started yapping while running around.

"Don't fall over," I warned her. Almost at that same moment, Keel took a tumble!

"Hey. I've seen that bit before, somewhere," Ren commented.

"That's a coincidence. Me too," I realized. She spilled the crepe across the floor. "I think it was ice cream though."

"It was shaved ice for me," Ren said. "A bit dated now, but I definitely saw it." Looks like classic comedy was the same even in a futuristic and otherworldly Japan with VRMMO games.

Keel. The life of the party.

"Uwah! The crepes Bubba made! Noooooooooo!" Clutching her head in her hands, Keel shouted and looked at the scattered crepes, tears in her eyes. If she wanted them so badly, I'd have to try and do something. But did I have the materials?

I wasn't even sure there'd be enough for everyone else in the village.

Keel was looking intensely at the crepes on the floor.

Another demi-human slave extended an arm to help her up, but it was like she couldn't even see them.

A moment later . . . she ate one?!

Possessed by something perhaps, Keel turned into her dog form and started to gobble up the crepes from the floor.

"Keel! What are you doing?" Raphtalia dashed over and warned her to stop. Others from the village were pointing at her in surprise. "You'll make yourself sick!" Raphtalia was almost wrestling with the dog.

"Let me go! Bubba made these for us to eat! I can't let them go to waste!"

"Stop it!" Raphtalia wasn't giving any ground. "He told you himself not to eat food from the ground!"

"I'm still going to eat them! Move! I need to eat these crepes! Uwaaaaaaah!" Even when she was pinned down, Keel's feral eyes still scanned her surroundings as she reached for the scattered crepes.

Man. Did I slip something addictive into the batter by mistake? I'd have to let Rat know that the honey was a failure.

"Calm down! Here, you can have mine," Ren offered.

"Really?!" Keel perked up at once.

"Sure." Ren's selfless act finally brought the situation to a close. I was still having trouble understanding why Keel had got so carried away. At least Ren seemed to be getting more comfortable in the village.

Eventually Ren returned to my side. "Naofumi, all the kids in the village really love you, don't they?" he said with a slightly perplexed look on his face.

"Nah, that's just the honey. It must have come out as a narcotic," I explained. "I'll stop us from making any more."

"I don't think that's it," Ren replied. "Please, don't stop. Everyone is looking at you with such emotion in their eyes . . . Please, keep making it!" Ren said, flustered, looking at the slaves. They were all looking at me; that was true. I still suspected narcotics, but that wasn't confirmed. Very well, then.

"Something smells nice." Drawn by the smell, Raphtalia's cousin came in, accompanied by Wyndia. Wyndia was the guardian of a dragon called Gaelion. She loved monsters. Alongside Rat, she was in charge of managing the monsters in the village.

To add a further note, she was also the daughter (well, stepdaughter) of a dragon that Ren once defeated. But she didn't exactly bear ill will toward Ren. Actually, if Ren started to get pessimistic, she wouldn't hold back in trying to pep him up a bit.

Raphtalia's cousin, meanwhile, was the kid who had been raised into the leader of the forces opposing us in Q'ten Lo, the nation we had recently visited—and then conquered. The same race as Raphtalia, he had a face that really reminded me of his cousin when she was younger.

Ostensibly, he had been executed. But in actual fact we'd

brought him here to the village. One difficulty was that he hadn't learned the Melromarc language yet, so he could only really talk to me, Raphtalia, the heroes, and those who knew the languages of the demi-human nations.

When he was Heavenly Emperor, he'd honestly been a bit of a fool, including putting out a dangerous proclamation against harming monsters. In the end though, the silly laws he had enacted actually helped us take Q'ten Lo far quicker than expected.

The real fools had been the corrupt politicians beneath him, anyway.

A selfish bitch called Makina, apparently originating from Siltvelt, had really held the reins of power in Q'ten Lo. But we'd successfully managed to take her down.

Anyway, to get back to Raphtalia's cousin, he had also very much liked a certain type of monster—filolials. However, after learning the true terror of monsters, he came to regret his past actions. That said, he was still very curious about monsters and was very interested in Raph-chan in particular. I wondered if I could make effective use of Raph-chan to lure him over to my side.

"Hey. Do you want some too?" I asked them both.

"Yes." Raphtalia's cousin took a crepe and started eating. The expression on his face was just like when I gave Raphtalia food when she was small.

"Can I ask you why you've got such a gentle look in your eyes?" Raphtalia asked with the same tone she normally used for a snide comment at my expense. What did I say this time?

"I was just remembering when you were small," I explained. "I felt a bit paternal for a moment there."

"I'm not sure I like that reason . . . by the way, Mr. Nao-fumi," Raphtalia continued coolly and placed her hand on her cousin's shoulder. "Seeing Wyndia just now reminded me of it. You do know my cousin's name, don't you?" From the look in her eyes, you'd think Raphtalia was interrogating me.

The reason for this was, for an extended period in the past, I had privately called Wyndia "valley girl." I'd eventually had cause to mention this to Raphtalia and the others, and she'd made the same face that she was making now.

My answer to this question was as follows.

"No idea."

The only information I had on the kid was that he was the former Heavenly Emperor of Q'ten Lo and Raphtalia's cousin. I'd never heard his name and was getting along just fine without it.

"If you don't tell him your real name, he'll give you a silly nickname!" Raphtalia desperately explained to her cousin.

"That's right!" Wyndia joined in. "I almost ended up being renamed 'valley girl'!"

"Mr. Naofumi," Raphtalia rounded on me. "What do you

currently call him in your head?"

"Raphtalia's cousin," I replied curtly.

"Look! He's sinking to just describing you already! Hurry up or you'll end up as nothing more than 'cousin'!" Raphtalia was practically panicking.

"O-okay, I'm . . . Ruftmila," the kid managed. His name sounded similar to "Raphtalia." I guess they did come from the same country.

"Fair enough. I'll call you Ruft," I decided. I still thought "cousin" would be enough. "Should we use a totally different name when folks from Q'ten Lo are around?"

"No weird nicknames!" Raphtalia was adamant about that one point.

"Raph," Raph-chan chirped. Ignoring Raphtalia, I passed Raph-chan my absolutely best-made crepe. And with that, my dessert-making was finished.

"Ah, I forgot. That woman and Gaelion were asking to talk to you, Shield Hero," Wyndia announced.

"That woman" would be Ratotille, an alchemist well-versed in monster lore who had joined us from Faubrey. Gaelion was a dragon, as previously explained.

"Okay, no problem. I need to talk to them about managing supplies and other stuff anyway," I replied. She might have completed her investigation into the unique ecosystem of Q'ten Lo and prepared materials on it in her lab here in the village.

"In that case, Naofumi, I'll go and explain what's been happening to Eclair and the others. Just give me a call if you need me," Ren said.

"Sure thing. Have a word with Atla and those guys too. Tell them it looks like I'm going to be too busy to come and train today." My duties piling up, there was no time for that stuff. So best to just shut that down right away.

"Sure thing. Although I can't promise Atla won't come charging after you," Ren warned.

"I know how to handle her. Taunt her a little for me. Tell her to overcome that recent terrible performance with more training," I suggested. In Siltvelt, Atla had caused a bit of trouble. They'd been completely tricked by illusions created by an enemy and hadn't been much use. It seemed to be really getting to Atla in particular, and she was sticking to her training rather than perving on me. That should keep her off my back for a while anyway.

"It's a shame we weren't there," Ren commented. He and his party had been on the move when the problems occurred. There hadn't been time to call them back, but there was also nothing to be gained by worrying about that now.

"In either case, we need to take some steps to prevent that from happening again," I said. "You and Itsuki not being there wasn't the issue." It was an issue that we'd let our attacker get away, but this wasn't the place to say that. Other than the Shield

Hero, the holy heroes could be pretty difficult to handle.

"I'll go and see Rat right away," I said. "I'll catch you later."
Splitting up from Ren, I followed Wyndia and Ruft toward Rat's lab.

Chapter One: Birth of the Raph Species

"What do you need from me?" I asked, entering a room in Rat's lab. As always, bizarre monsters were bobbing in their culture tanks.

"Raph?" Raph-chan waved at a monster inside one of the tanks, and the monster went right ahead and waved back.

"Kwaa." So Gaelion was here too.

"Ah, Count," Rat greeted me. "I've got some exciting reports for you."

"Like what?" I'll be the judge of what was exciting.

"First, a progress report. Concerning the sakura lumina trees, there's no way to cultivate them. I don't understand the reasons, but they wither the moment you put the cuttings in the ground," Rat explained.

"I see." That was a shame. They were so beautiful. I'd asked Rat to try planting them here, thinking we might be able to make the village famous for the trees. The sakura lumina were endemic to Q'ten Lo and could provide all sorts of convenient abilities. I'd thought it to be something of a waste if they could only be used in Q'ten Lo.

"Working with bioplants really demands the cooperation of you, Count, and the other heroes," Rat explained. Among the bioplant expansion functions there was "formulation." It had shown up after messing about a bit. Maybe we could use that to prevent the sakura lumina from withering.

"Sure thing," I replied. "Should I just do that now?"

"Hold on, hold on. I've got other things to report that I'd like you to listen to first," Rat said.

"Huh? Like what?" I'm a busy guy.

"Wyndia, dear. Go get them ready," Rat ordered.

"Okay," Wyndia responded and left the room.

"Ah, good. She's gone." With the departure of the girl, Gaelion started to speak.

"Why do you only talk when Wyndia isn't around?" Ruft asked, tilting his head.

"Keep that to yourself," I told him. "Gaelion's got his own rules for doing stuff. Don't tell Ren either, okay?"

"Okay," the kid replied.

"I'm sure Wyndia would love it if you'd talk to her," Raphtalia offered. Neither her nor Ruft had parents, so they likely felt that more keenly. In any case, Gaelion was raising Wyndia as her foster father and had decided that not talking would be best for Wyndia. It wasn't really our place to make comments.

"Come on then. What's going on?" I tried to keep things moving along.

"You already know that Dragon Emperors can obtain further strength and knowledge by obtaining Dragon Emperor fragments, correct?" Gaelion asked.

"Yeah." I had some idea of that, not only from the events in Q'ten Lo but also from the Demon Dragon trouble we'd had when Gaelion first joined the party.

"In order for me to become stronger, it is vital that we defeat Dragon Emperors—dragons—and obtain more fragments, but concurrent with that, there's other information that might be prudent to share with you," Gaelion explained.

"Like what?" I asked.

"The knowledge of a class-up to break the level 100 cap should be among the lost fragments. Along with lots of other useful information, I should think," Gaelion continued.

The "level 100 cap" referred to the phenomenon in this world that affected most everyone apart from heroes, causing their development to stop at level 100. People from this world normally stopped at 40 but could then continue on to 100 after a class-up. I vaguely remembered being told something about that around the time I purchased the hakuko siblings, although some of the Siltvelt demi-human species, such as the hakuko, had a limit of 120.

I'd been thinking if we could have everyone pass 100, that was something we should definitely investigate. I hadn't expected to receive hints about it like this though.

"You've been involved in so much trouble I've not had much chance to talk with you," Gaelion explained.

"I mean, it's definitely an issue, but is that all you want to say?" I replied. To be honest, it certainly wasn't a problem for me, and Raphtalia wasn't affected by this system either. Ren, Itsuki, and S'yne were all categorized as heroes, so no problem for them either. When I thought ahead, sure, it was knowledge that I wanted. It just wasn't a priority at the moment.

"First things first. Now the filolial isn't nearby, I can remove the lock on your shield, at least to a certain extent," Gaelion continued.

"Huh?" What was going on now?

"The lock placed by the filolial queen. You don't remember this?" Gaelion quizzed. A lock? I might remember something like that when I placed the Demon Dragon materials into my shield. Was that what he was referring to?

Hold on! Don't tell me that the reason I couldn't bring out dragon-type shields was because of Fitoria's cowlick? Unlocking the filolial series had sealed the dragon series away? Dammit, Fitoria! What was she playing at? Especially after having made a request from me! That was going to place a limit on my abilities. What was she trying to say? She had dibs on me?

She might as well have taken a piss on me! Marking me, like a dog marks a tree!

"You have a core inside there, remember?" Gaelion continued. "At the right level, most of the genealogy of dragons should be available to you."

"I see." It kind of made sense. I just hadn't been a high enough level for most of them. So the dragon core overlapped with Fitoria's cowlick? Like in a game, there was only two options.

I'd been thinking a lot recently that I really wanted someone to make it clear whether this was reality or a game.

"Bring out your shield," Gaelion suggested.

"Okay. Let's try it." Then Gaelion sent something, like his thoughts, to my shield. It felt like the whole thing flickered and sparked.

A number of locks were released.

Conditions for the Dragon Leather Shield were unlocked.
Conditions for the Dragon Scale Shield were unlocked.
Conditions for the Dragon Meat Shield were unlocked.
Conditions for the Dragon User's Shield were unlocked.
Conditions for the Dragon User's Shield II were unlocked.
Conditions for the Water Dragon's Shield were unlocked.
Conditions for the Water Dragon's Vassal Shield were unlocked.

Interesting. The stats looked pretty high across the board. The name "dragon" really meant something. The ability-up multipliers were also pretty high. The unlock conditions were around level 50.

Fitoria! Gah, she'd really done a number on me!

Oh? Dragon User's Shield also had Dragon Growth Adjustment (small), which meant collecting more Dragon Emperor fragments would further heighten the adjustment to Gaelion's abilities.

"I can also provide the other heroes with Dragon Emperor weapons. That's another reason I want you to collect the Dragon Emperor cores," Gaelion explained.

"I'd have loved it if you reported all of this sooner," I quipped.

"That Demon Dragon really stirred things up in my head. It's taken a while to get all my knowledge back in order," Gaelion said. It had affected him even more than I'd thought.

"So the plan is to give the protection of the Way of the Dragon Vein to all heroes," Gaelion said.

One immediate problem was to get Ren and Itsuki to learn the Way of the Dragon Vein. I'd finally managed it myself. But I really needed them to learn it before the Phoenix battle.

"I can also provide a class-up adjustment via my protection," Gaelion added.

"About that," Rat said, cutting in. "Most of the monsters in the village have hit the growth limit of level 40. I could have made arrangements with the state to perform class-ups, but I really need the Count's permission, now don't I?"

"Definitely nice to be asked," I commented.

"Your monsters are keen to become stronger, Count," Rat continued. "They want a special class-up, like the others from the village."

"They've received the protection of the filolial queen, correct?" I sometimes had trouble keeping track of this stuff.

"Ah, that Filo cowlick class-up," Rat recalled. "That counts as a protection, does it?" Filolials had all sorts of different abilities, but yes, I had thought it was a protection.

"I don't know the conditions to trigger it," I admitted. "But it is related to class-ups." Some people might consider it a nuance.

"Having a hero nearby is one of the conditions," Gaelion revealed. "The power of the earth is also involved, expanding potential." The power of the earth—also known as experience.

If that was where it came from, then it should also bring power in a good way to one's own status magic.

Gaelion continued, "A class-up is an expansion of strength. Of course, receiving the blessings of the heroes can further increase those abilities, but that's not the point I'm making."

"So what is?" I asked.

"You can't place the filolial blessing on monsters," Gaelion said. "It should go without saying, but you know what the filolial can do, correct?"

"Hmmm." That gave me pause. They had to want nothing more than to become strong. A tricky proposition. Sadeena,

Atla, Fohl, and the others had already had a class-up performed by Filo.

"The monsters want to become stronger too," Rat assured me. "In order to protect this world. They even want to help in the fight against the Phoenix."

Another "hmmm." I hadn't really cared for them much myself recently, so I was surprised to hear they were pushing so hard.

"Some of them cry at night, wanting to see you, Count," Rat lamented.

"Why would they do that?" I inquired.

"You used to care for them in the mornings, right? They all love you, Count," Rat explained.

"I do understand how they feel. Mr. Naofumi is quite considerate when it comes to taking care of people," Raphtalia chimed in with a somewhat lamenting tone. Yeah, she had a point. Filo, and even Gaelion, did seem to easily take a liking to me. In Kizuna's world, Ethnobalt had been pretty friendly with me too.

"Raph?" Raph-chan spoke up.

"Huh?" Gaelion looked at her and made a strange noise.

"What was that all about?" I asked.

"No, it's nothing," the dragon dismissed it.

"Let's get back on track, then," I suggested. "You've called me here because you want to help with class-ups, is that it?"

"That's right. Considering what we have coming up, it can't hurt to do what we can now, right?" Gaelion reasoned.

"Sure," I agreed. So much other stuff was going on, but the date for the revival of the Phoenix was also drawing closer. I'd started the whole plan to raise the village slaves to prepare for the waves in order to restore Raphtalia's homeland. That had been successful, and now we could even call in further reinforcements from places like Siltvelt and Q'ten Lo. But I still wanted to make the villagers stronger than anyone else.

So why not have some monsters among them too?

"The reason you had Wyndia go out was to prepare to bring in those you want to class up," I realized.

"That's right," Gaelion confirmed.

"You can get around quickly, can't you, Count? The classups should finish pretty quickly too, right? Shall we sit down and dig into the sakura lumina problem after that?" Rat suggested.

"Sounds good," I agreed. "Let's get moving. Raphtalia, you'd better get ready too."

"Very well. We'll use a Scroll of Return?" she confirmed.

"Yeah. I have to say, this particular procedure goes a lot easier with you, Raphtalia," I said. Raphtalia's katana, which was a vassal weapon from Kizuna's world, had a transport skill called Scroll of Return. It allowed the user to jump to the last registered dragon hourglass. She'd registered it really recently, so we'd be able to travel at once. I could also increase the number of people she could take with her by using Portal Shield.

"Can I go with you and watch what happens?" Ruft asked, worry on his face. He had Raph-chan in his arms, both of them looking at me.

"Sure, no problem," I assured him. It looked like he was gradually becoming a true monster lover.

With that, we headed to the monster stable where Wyndia was already making preparations and I popped the big question.

"We're going to class up! Anyone who wants to get strong, come forward!" My question was greeted by a cacophony of affirmative roars and growls, with almost all the monsters in the stable taking a step forward. Damn! They completely understood me. Even my village's usapil stepped forward. That beauty was getting pretty big. Big enough to ride, even.

In any case, it looked like all of them had a taste to get stronger.

"This is really going to give our combat strength a boost," Raphtalia commented.

"I guess that's a good thing." I was hedging my bets. Most of these guys had grown up pretty wild. Would it even be possible to incorporate them into battle strategies? We'd have to give that side of all this some thought as well.

Without further ado, we departed.

Taking the monsters along, we arrived at the Melromarc dragon hourglass and explained the situation to the soldiers placed in charge of it.

"Thinking about it more carefully, we might have been better off doing this in Siltvelt," I realized. After all, the dragon hourglass was a facility used for class-ups, meaning people who had received permission from the state could very well be coming in and out.

Furthermore, Melromarc had long been a humanist nation. That was changing a little, thanks to my own activities. But it might still cause a problem if we kept other adventurers or national guards waiting while we performed class-ups for a veritable horde of monsters.

For that reason, it might have been better to do this in Siltvelt.

The problem there was requests had to be made very carefully or they might start to ask for strange things in return. The potential for that definitely added some pressure. The trouble we'd had in Siltvelt on the way back from Q'ten Lo, being forced to display the authority of the Shield Hero, was still fresh in my memory.

Still, they should also be starting to prepare for the fight with the Phoenix, so I'd like to think they wouldn't be making any more annoying demands.

"That's no problem at all," one of the Melromarc soldiers responsible for the dragon hourglass replied to our request, smiling while he did so. "Speaking strictly from the state of national affairs, you'd probably find somewhere like Zeltoble more receptive to performing class-ups for monsters, but here in Melromarc, we certainly aren't going to refuse aid to a hero."

Hmmm, nice. I knew the queen was doing some things on our behalf.

"You and your party are fighting to protect the peace of our nation," the soldier went on, "and the famine has been resolved. Why, if someone did try to turn you away, they'd need to be slapped down as a rightly ungrateful so-and-so!"

"You think? I mean, that works for me." I wasn't about to touch that.

"Rumors have already been spreading that you're going to start dealing with the robber problem too," the man continued. "I take it this is part of that?"

Raphtalia murmured to me quietly, "I think he's getting the wrong idea about this. Are you okay with that?"

No, not really . . . although on second thought, from a trade perspective that actually wasn't incorrect.

"It'll be a pain to correct him," I whispered back. "The monsters do pull the wagons, so overall he's not wrong. Let's just roll with it."

"You don't have it easy, do you, Count?" Rat sympathized. "Having to handle all these different jobs, day after day."

"If you think that, you might help out more," I jibed.

"I am helping out! Now, monsters, we're going to class you all up, so form up into a line." That was all it took from Rat for the monsters to form an orderly line.

The Melromarc soldier was so surprised he could only stand there blinking.

"Your monsters really are very tame, Shield Hero," he commented.

"Yeah. I guess so," was all I could say. They weren't on the level of Filo, Gaelion, or Raph-chan, but they did listen very well. In Japanese terms, it would be like shouting "line up!" and having a bunch of cats and dogs understand the meaning and fall into line.

"Kwaa," Gaelion offered.

"Right, Gaelion," I ordered. "Go ahead and perform a special class-up on each of them."

"Kwaa!" the dragon confirmed.

"We're counting on you," Wyndia offered. Proud to be asked, Gaelion beat his chest and then climbed up on top of the dragon hourglass. We'd discussed all of this beforehand, after all. The monsters were going to give it their all too. Just like with the slaves, we were letting the monsters themselves decide the direction to take with the class-up.

"Let's get started," I said. With the help of the soldiers, we started the class-up ritual using the dragon hourglass.

First came the largest of the caterpillands—the one Wyndia had protected. It looked to have pretty low latent potential. How much stronger could a class-up make it?

According to Wyndia, when it had been attacked, it had felt terrible about not being able to do anything but just watch. I'd seen it looking at me too. It clearly wanted to get stronger.

The magic circle started to sparkle as Gaelion started to incant magic atop the dragon hourglass. I'd been present at class-ups numerous times. Just like normal, the sand in the dragon hourglass started to give off a faint light that then passed into the magic circle.

I hold ownership of all the monsters. That meant the directions in which they could be classed up appeared before me. I could choose for myself here, but my policy was to leave it up to the individuals themselves. They could do this multiple times by using level resets, but still it was a major element that would have a massive impact on their lives.

I checked the possibilities hovering before me. Yeah, they were pretty different from the choices I had with Filo. It was a caterpilland that we were about to class up and it looked like it could turn into a variety of different monsters.

Those included simply the advanced form of the caterpilland and also a monster called a butterfland. That was the direct class-up cluster.

Checking more carefully, I saw there was a status item called "required attributes," and if the numbers within that range were satisfied, then the races it could class up into would also increase.

"Kwaa!" Perhaps Gaelion was lending his strength, because there was another item that shouldn't really exist.

I checked it more closely to see it had pretty high stats across the board. It was an item leading to a complete upgrade monster cluster with a slight lean toward magic.

So this had to be the special class-up.

A filolial would surely choose the complete upgrade, but what decision would this monster make?

An option appeared: select "reject" and allow the monster to choose for itself?

I confirmed it. That was what I wanted to do.

"Raph!"

"Ah!" Ruft gave a shout as Raph-chan leapt out of his arms.

"Huh?" I was surprised too. Raph-chan entered the magic circle, and it looked like she was incanting magic just like Gaelion. Her tail was all shiny and puffed up!

Raph-chan tottered along and climbed up onto the head of the caterpilland. The outline of the caterpilland started to blur.

"Hey . . . I have a really bad feeling about this," Rat interjected.

"Raph-chan, don't get in the way!" I shouted.

"Raph!" Raphtalia shouted.

For some reason, Raph-chan's entire body started to glow.

"Uwah!" I had to shield my eyes because it was so bright! There was normally some shining going on during a class-up, but it was pretty surprising that Raph-chan was glowing too.

Even more bizarrely, there was smoke rising, centered around Raph-chan and the caterpilland. Well, Raph-chan did have something like levels. Due to the further variability provided by Shikigami power-up and through our fighting in Q'ten Lo and other places, she had become pretty strong.

Still, she really needed to wait her turn.

I was about to caution her again when the smoke cleared. I narrowed my eyes.

"Raph!" Everyone there looked on with stunned expressions on their faces, hardly able to breathe due to what we were all seeing. Even Gaelion's mouth was hanging wide open in shock.

There were now two Raph-chans.

"W-w-what's going on here?!" Raphtalia was the fastest to recover and react verbally.

"Kwaa!?" Gaelion also gave a shout, confusion in his eyes.

"What's happened to Raph-chan?" Wyndia, brow furrowed, was looking at me.

Hey! I didn't make this selection.

The other animals all started to give roars and growls of approval and support.

"Which one is the caterpilland?" Wyndia asked, to which the Raph-chan-like monster on the right—the one with a pattern around its face that looked a bit like a compound eye—raised its hand and gave an energetic "Raaph!"

Then it leapt up into the air and its body transformed into . . . a large Raph-chan—really—but with a tail like a caterpillar. So it was a slightly unpleasant-looking monster, like a combination of Raph-chan and the caterpilland.

"Raaph!" The former-caterpilland looked pretty pleased with itself. Raph-chan herself struck a victory pose and then pointed at the caterpilland, but I guessed it was fine to just ignore her. I checked her stats instead.

It looked like Raph-chan had managed a class-up herself.

All her stats had more than doubled, and she'd acquired various new abilities . . . maybe? I didn't understand much of the details and would have to look into it later.

"Raph!" Raph-chan then performed some kind of magic on me.

Shikigami has mutated and skills have expanded! C'mon Raph acquired!

Oh? She'd acquired a strange-sounding new skill.

"Awesome! We've got more like Raph-chan now!" Ruft's eyes glimmered as he rushed over to the former-caterpilland.

"Raaph!" The new monster just stood there and took Ruft's eager stroking.

So what about the abilities of the former-caterpilland?

I checked them, and yeah, they had all seen quite a boost.

Gaelion slid down from the dragon hourglass, crashing face-first into the ground.

"This is . . . amazing, right?" I postulated.

"Raaph!" The former-caterpilland posed like a bodybuilder for a moment and then turned back into its Raph-chan-like form.

"Hold on, hold on. Just what's going on here, Shield Hero?" the soldier asked.

"A very good question! Mr. Naofumi, just what is all this?" Raphtalia, face pale, grabbed me by both shoulders and started to shake.

"I don't know. I mean, it looks likely that Raph-chan got involved in the class-up somehow," I ventured.

"That part is obvious! I want to know why things turned out like this though," Raphtalia raged.

"I mean . . . monster class-ups can be pretty involved, with massive changes in appearance or even reverting to their ancestors. But even I couldn't have seen this one coming. Seriously, Count, spending time with you brings one surprise after another," Rat said. With that, she started her examination of the former-caterpilland.

The other soldiers responsible for the hourglass all looked pretty stunned too. What had just happened *was* pretty stunning, after all!

"Hmmm," Rat pondered and plucked a hair from the former-caterpilland, took out a device, and started to test it. "Now grow big."

"Raaph!" As ordered by Rat, the former-caterpilland turned again into its large Raph-chan form.

I had to admit, that form was really something.

After multiple tests and examinations, Rat turned back to me. Raphtalia was still yet to really calm down. She kept looking back and forth between me and Raph-chan. Finally, perhaps looking to just escape from reality, she grabbed her head in her hands and shook it, practically hysterical.

"I don't have the facilities here to make a more thorough analysis, but I can tell you that Raph-chan's characteristics are on full display here," Rat reported. "The ability to transform like that . . . Transformation properties have been seen in filolials and dragons too. It must have an ability of that type."

"So you don't know the exact reason, but it's safe to say that in the same way as Filo and Gaelion, Raph-chan had some effect on the class-up transformation pattern?" I asked.

"Raph!" Raph-chan nodded at my question.

"And this means she did it regardless of the consent of the former-caterpilland?" There was an edge to my question. I'd have to caution Raph-chan quite strictly if that was the case. It wasn't fair to decide something so important against the will of the one experiencing it.

"Raph, Raaph!" The former-caterpilland waved its hands, making clear the answer to my question was negative.

"You chose this?" I asked the former-caterpilland. "You could have had a dragon class-up and you chose the Raph-chan one?"

"Raaph!" The former-caterpilland nodded at my question.

"I see," I acquiesced. "If that's the case, so be it."

"No! So be nothing!" Raphtalia was still trying to caution Raph-chan, but the pair of them looked pleased as punch and just ignored her.

"Raaph!"

"Stop that! This is nothing to be so proud of!" Raphtalia chided.

"Raaph . . ." Ah, they did look a little depressed by Raphtalia's anger.

"Just look what's happened to it!" Wyndia clutched her own head, stunned, and looked down at the ground. I could understand her point of view. She had doted on that caterpilland, and look what it had turned into now.

That said . . . I couldn't help myself . . .

"Wonderful!" I exclaimed. I mean, simply put, this meant there were now more Raph-chans, right? The newcomer couldn't beat the original, of course, but I still saw this as a victory.

"Amazing!" Ruft seemed just as happy as I was. Heh, it

seemed we agreed on this. We were definitely going to get along.

"There's nothing wonderful about this either. Please, some-how, can't you heal it?" Ah, Raphtalia had quickly recovered and now came at Rat and me with this.

"You say 'heal,' but this isn't a sickness. The monster seems to have accepted—indeed, chosen—this outcome. I'm afraid there's nothing I can do," Rat explained.

"I still don't see a problem with it. It's like having a second Raph-chan," I said. And that was my take.

"I don't like it. I'm still resistant to having one Raph-chan around. Now there are two of them!" Hmmm. Raphtalia seemed pretty stubborn on this issue. I mean, maybe I could kind of understand. It was like a creature that was already a replica of her was now replicating itself. A bit weird.

The roars and growls from the remaining monsters were starting to become more pronounced. They were getting tired of waiting, clearly. Realizing something, Raphtalia gave a start, turning even paler as she looked first at the other monsters, then at Raph-chan, and finally at me.

"Hold it," she said, her voice quivering. "You're not telling me that all of these monsters want the exact same class-up, are you? You can't be?!"

"What do you say, guys?" I asked, pointing alternately at Raph-chan and then the now nearby Gaelion to see which of them they wanted to pick.

All of them as one turned in the direction of Raph-chan.

It looked like, if it were possible, they had a preference for Raph-chan.

"No way! Stop this! I'm not allowing this, not at all! Mr. Naofumi!"

"I mean, we have to respect the individual rights of the monsters, right? I reckon if they can't do the Raph-chan class-up, some of them won't even do it at all," I reasoned. At this cunning piece of leading, many of the monsters voiced their agreement.

"You should just choose for them, Mr. Naofumi!" Raphtalia insisted.

"That's not fair. Look, it's already happened once—" To be quite honest about it, I didn't mind this turn of events. It was like having more Raph-chans. "You've said it yourself in the past, haven't you, Raphtalia? You'd like more Raph-chans around with all her convenient skills."

"I might have said that," Raphtalia admitted. "But actually seeing it happen, I've realized I don't like it!"

"Why not?" Ruft backed me up. Good boy!

"Raph?" The original Raph-chan also tilted her head.

"Don't you understand?" Raphtalia rounded on Ruft.

"Hmmm, well, I like how lively things are getting. It makes me feel less sad," Ruft admitted.

"Just think for a moment what it would be like to see a

horde of monsters that look just like us. You see what I mean, right?" Raphtalia pressed.

"Yeah, I do," Ruft agreed. "It sounds like loads of fun."

Raphtalia proceeded to slap her hand to her forehead and look to the sky. She clearly thought she didn't have a single ally.

"I can't believe this," she moaned. "Mr. Naofumi won't listen. Ruft won't listen. There's no one here to take heed of my words."

But hold on. I could be pretty flexible when I needed to, and I wasn't doing this to Raphtalia on purpose.

"I'm sorry, Mr. Naofumi!" With that apology, Raphtalia snatched up Raph-chan and touched the dragon hourglass.

"Ah, Raphtalia!" I shouted. Where was she going?!

"Mr. Naofumi, this alone—this one thing—I simply have to prevent!" she announced. She was so worked up. "Return Dragon Vein!"

"H-hey, hold on. You can't just—" Before I even finished, Raphtalia was gone. Taking Raph-chan with her, she'd gone off to heaven-knew-where. Hmmm . . .

Even as I thought that, however, an icon floated into my view.

It was an icon like a Raph-chan face from the expanded items for the Shikigami.

The text read "C'mon Raph."

"C'mon Raph." Couldn't hurt to try it.

"Raph!" With a pop, Raph-chan appeared in front of me. It was a skill that allowed me to summon Raph-chan anywhere!

"Raph!" Raph-chan started posing, clearly happy to have made her escape. Then she touched the dragon hourglass. The sand inside it glowed slightly in response.

Raphtalia, meanwhile, having now lost Raph-chan, didn't come back.

Had Raph-chan just done something to prevent Raphtalia from returning?

Both the Scroll of Return and the Return Dragon Vein were performed using a dragon hourglass. Therefore, making adjustments to the dragon hourglass could prevent them from being used. Where had Raphtalia gone off to though? And then the monsters started to make noise again! They were looking at us intently.

"They want to class up quickly. They want to become stronger. That's what they are all saying. What do you think?" Wyndia asked, holding onto the sleeve of my shirt.

Rat, for her part, just put her hands in the air and gave a bemused "don't look at me" look.

Ruft's eyes were sparkling as he clearly wanted to class up them all into Raph-chans.

Personally, I still had issues with rejecting their wishes and forcing them to take a normal class-up. I also felt really bad about doing this to Raphtalia, but . . . there seemed no other way out of it.

I also loved the idea of having loads of Raph-chans around!

"Right, you rabble!" I commanded. "You need to persuade Raphtalia once she gets back, understand?" The monsters all provided agreement with whatever noises they could.

With that, we completed the class-ups for all the monsters before Raphtalia made it back. Gaelion? He just slumped dejectedly in the corner. After all that explanation he gave, in the end none of them had wanted his own class-up.

"Raph."

"Raaph."

"Tali."

"Lia."

"W-what's happening here?" Having finished the class-ups, Raph-chan touched the dragon hourglass again and Raphtalia came back. Then all the Raph-chan-like monsters crowded around her and started to make noises that I presumed were intended as "persuasion."

Since she was surrounded by Raph-chans on all sides, I did want to try and throw her a bone, but I also didn't want to throw myself onto that particular grenade. So all I could do was silently watch.

"Ignoring for now the fact that they all seem to have cries based on my own name . . . seriously, Mr. Naofumi?!" Raphtalia was near breaking.

"I know you don't like it, but what choice did we have?" I countered.

"I'm not accepting that! This is all your fault, Mr. Naofumi! Seriously, I'm even thinking of running off to Kizuna's world." It was that bad? I knew she hated it, but I needed her to put up with it for the sake of my greater ambitions.

"So, Count, how are we going to handle these monsters?" Rat asked.

"What do you mean?" I replied.

"The name for the race of this monster," Rat clarified.

"Rat! Is that all you're really worried about?" Raphtalia cut in. She really was steaming mad. It was too late to back down now though. This was our reality. We just had to get her to compromise somewhere.

"What I mean is that there's enough monsters here to be considered a new species. If we don't decide on at least a provisional name, things are going to get confusing." Rat raised a good point.

"Okay, based on their calls, let's go with Raph species, Raaph species, Tali species, and Lia species. How about that?" Simple was best, I decided.

"You can't just ignore me, Mr. Naofumi! We're not finished here!"

"Raph."

"Raaph."

"Tali."

"Lia."

All the monsters that were now like Raph-chan turned moist-looking eyes on Raphtalia.

"Uwah." Raphtalia backed down.

"Nothing is confirmed yet, so we don't have to divide them up so specifically," Rat added.

"Okay, in that case, the first one was Raph-chan, so 'Raph species' will be fine," I declared.

"Very well," Rat concurred.

"So many Raph-chans! Say, Shield Hero, could I have one?" Ruft asked.

"Yeah, we've got so many, so why not? But not Raph-chan!" I replied.

"Thanks!" the kid said.

"Please stop ignoring the real issues here!" Raphtalia was still having problems.

"How did it all come to this . . ." Wyndia wondered.

"Kwaa . . ." was Gaelion's only contribution. In the end, Raphtalia grudgingly accepted the situation at the supplication of the monsters who had all become the Raph species. Ignoring the complaints of Wyndia and Gaelion, we all returned to the village—and further chaos.

Chapter Two: Territory Reform

"If we're going to be counting monsters as combat strength, this monster stable is going to start getting a bit cramped," I announced. Having arrived back at the village, I checked over the monster stable.

"You're going to add even more monsters? No more turning them into Raph species!" Raphtalia was adamant.

"I've discussed that with Wyndia already. If we did turn all monsters in the village into Raph species, it would definitely cause some diversification issues," I explained.

"That's the only problem?" Raphtalia asked, pointing. In one corner of the monster stable, the filolial, Filo's Underling Filolial #1, was trembling in terror. On the other side, Gaelion was adopting the same pose. The entire village monster stable had been completely taken over by the Raph species. They weren't unfamiliar with the Raphs, but those two still stood out.

Add Filo, and that made three, although Filo did have a room in my house in which she slept and ate—actually, she spent most of her time at Melty's place.

Enough about Filo anyway. This was a problem with monsters.

After this, Wyndia had proposed keeping other types of

monsters in the village for the sake of diversity. It seemed Rat was of a similar opinion. While the Raph species was an interesting subject to study, just that species alone wasn't going to further her research.

Then, having discussed the cause of this turn of events, we decided it was apparently rooted in me caring for the monsters, although I'd only been doing that in the mornings . . . In any case, they had started to look jealous due to me doting on Raph-chan. And they all started wanting to become like her.

They'd also had sufficient latent strength, so it was two birds with one stone.

The dragon power-up, meanwhile, only had a weak effect unless the monster was already pretty strong. And just like the Raph species, in the case of monsters it could often lead to blending in some dragon elements. It was a bit like turning them into a vassal, I guessed.

"With that in mind, we're going to have Ren, and maybe Itsuki, start caring for some monsters—registering monster crests," I explained.

"Hmmm." Raphtalia still didn't sound completely onboard.

"We should also make a filolial monster stable," I added. The stress from all these Raphs was going to drive the poor creature into the ground.

It was scared, right? That was what that meant.

At that moment, a soil maintenance worm-like monster

called a dune popped up from the ground. It hadn't taken part in the class-up bonanza so it was still just a normal dune.

Now it seemed like it was conversing with the Raph species.

"That's not going to happen," Raphtalia snapped, quick to shut that down too. She glared at the dune and it went back into the ground.

Then it headed over to Gaelion.

I asked Wyndia about it afterward and was told that dune types preferred dragons.

"Right now," I said as I got things straight in my head. "I guess we'll build a temporary monster stable at the bioplant." The sun was starting to set, but we had to make the most of the time we had. There was no time to be managing materials. Then I had another thought. "Hold on . . ."

"What now? You're not planning on using Raph-chan for something else weird, are you?" Raphtalia immediately turned suspicious eyes on me again. I was really going to have to cut back on the Raph-chan joking around for a while, or she might explode.

I was a jerk, sure, but I wasn't a *complete* jerk.

I really wanted to explain that the reason I liked Raph-chan was that it was an expression of my feelings for treasuring Raphtalia like my own daughter.

"The Shield of the Beast King that I picked up in Siltvelt not only has beast transformation support, but it also has a skill called Territory Reform. I tried it out and a map appeared with the area around the village glowing. Is that strange?" I asked.

"Hmmm," Raphtalia pondered as she took a moment to think about my question. This was totally different from the Raph-chan issues, after all.

"In either case, I guess the best thing we can do is just give it a try," I suggested.

"I mean, sure. But what's brought this on now?" Raphtalia inquired.

"I forgot about it, okay? We only dropped in on the village when we brought Ren back. After that, we went right back out to Siltvelt and then Q'ten Lo," I reminded her.

"You're right. There wasn't really time to test it, was there?" she agreed.

"Of course I'm right. So let's test it right now," I proclaimed. In the instant I thought of it, my viewpoint was shifted up into the air. But I could still see normally too. It was like . . . double vision.

I reckon this could really bring on a case of motion sickness. It had never happened to me, but some people started feeling really ill while playing games that displayed images like this.

"I have what looks like an aerial view of the village," I explained.

"Like what you'd see when riding on Gaelion, correct?" Raphtalia clarified.

"Yeah, like that," I affirmed.

"The Bow Hero mentioned that he has a skill which allows him to scout out the surrounding area from a higher vantage point," Raphtalia recalled. Itsuki said that? I mean, he was the Bow Hero. It wouldn't be strange for him to have a skill that allowed him to search for distant targets. That sounded like quite a convenient skill too.

Maybe I'd have him make us a map.

"This is something else—a skill called Territory Reform," I reminded her.

"That does sound different, doesn't it?" she agreed.

"Yeah. This is coming from a shield found in the single nicest room in all of Siltvelt too, remember? Taking the shield power-up method into account, maybe it is influenced by faith too?" I pondered.

"I guess that's a possibility . . ." Raphtalia didn't sound entirely convinced. Anyway, I checked the items in my field of vision.

Move, Place, Remove, Create, Combine.
Offering Points.

What was all this? I tried moving the cursor that had appeared. It seemed I was able to select different buildings. If I could select them, did that mean I could move them? I gave it a quick try, but a warning message appeared: there are people inside the building. The "remove" command sounded dangerous too. And I was sure the same warning would appear.

In that case, I selected the command "place."

Then a separate option appeared, but there was nothing I could select.

Hmmm. This was all very much like a game I'd played a bit in the past.

I tried selecting "create."

That opened up a list of the possible buildings that I could create from the materials I possessed—the materials in my shield. It looked like creating stuff also consumed something called "offering points." Meanwhile, "combine" looked like it was linked to building modification. I could also confirm links to skills.

Just what I thought.

I used some of the materials I had obtained to create and place a wooden bench in front of the monster stable. With a puff of smoke, the bench appeared.

"W-what's going on now? A bench suddenly appeared!" Raphtalia squawked.

"It seems this is a skill that allows buildings and objects to be placed in villages within your territory," I explained. It couldn't have come at a better time either. We'd wanted to expand the monster stable, and this allowed for a more detailed setting than one simply produced by the bioplant. You could also make detailed adjustments, shifting things around after an initial placement, and even set an intended placement area.

What I needed to build was a generic building for filolial use—the kind a horse might use—like you'd see on a ranch. You could even set the room layout and indicate the number of them. I'd left the camping plant settings up to Rat, but this was super convenient.

Huh? There was even some flavor text.

Medium-sized terrestrial monster stable (bioplant produced).
A building used for raising monsters—may have to be adapted to suit specific types but can cover the basics for most surface-dwelling monsters.

With that, then, I placed a camping plant seed into my shield, and after selecting "create," I created a monster stable. After that, I slapped it down next to me.

Huh? With a rumbling sound, the monster stable grew up from the ground. Okay. It was exactly where I placed it. Without getting too carried away, I put another one down too.

"I-it feels like you're doing something pretty incredible here," Raphtalia commented.

"I don't think this shield can ever surprise me again,"

I replied. After all, we were talking about a shield that could take bioplants and use plant manipulation to transform them, completely harmlessly, into completely beneficial things!

That said, placing too many things or moving too much stuff around was quickly going to use up all the offering points. I didn't know how to get more of those yet either, so I had to be careful.

Thinking that, I checked the "combine" item to saw that plant manipulation and other skills were linked. The sakura lumina branch I had quietly placed inside the shield and the bioplant could be combined together. Rat had said that trying to plant them just caused them to wither right away. Combining them with bioplants, however, applied a growth modifier. Why not give it a try?

Modified sakura lumina (unbranded)
Sakura lumina with a boost in vitality provided by bioplant elements—can access the Dragon Vein, heighten the power of the Earth Vein, and create a defensive wall.

That was more like it! It looked like it had some really beneficial abilities. I indicated a place in the village for it to grow.

Warning: it cannot be placed there.

But just as I started to think it was a plant restricted to Q'ten Lo after all, the warning text scrolled down.

When creating a Dragon Vein defensive wall, please place multiple trees at the same time around the desired perimeter.

A defensive wall?

"Mr. Naofumi, what are you thinking? You placed the monster stable here, didn't you?" Raphtalia, obviously, couldn't see what I was doing.

"Yeah, now I'm trying to plant some sakura lumina," I explained distractedly.

"They did have beautiful flowers. I wanted to bring some back myself, but you talked about it with Rat earlier, didn't you? She said it failed," Raphtalia continued.

Yeah, it was a good bet that this wasn't going to work.

Still, I tried placing multiple trees surrounding the village, including near the graves for Raphtalia's parents. Then light started to spill from the shield, and with a gentle glow, sakura lumina slowly started to appear.

"What's going on? What is it?!" Keel and the other villagers emerged from the buildings with gasps of surprise.

"Don't worry," I calmed them. "I'm just testing some new powers."

"Raph!" Raph-chan touched one of the growing trees. When she did that, light passed along the ground between Raph-chan and Raphtalia and the sakura lumina, which burst into blossom.

"So beautiful!"

"They're shining!"

"Amazing!"

These and similar calls rose from among the villagers. Yeah. This had really brightened up the village.

I took a moment to check the sakura lumina that had grown.

Perhaps it was thanks to the bioplant influence. I'd only just planted them and yet they were already fully grown trees. It looked like I'd smoothed over the problem of getting them to grow. They were also emitting a barrier that seemed to protect the entire village.

"Count!" Rat dashed over amid the hubbub. "What's going on now?"

"Well, I used a new ability," I explained. "It looks like placing the sakura lumina to encircle a specific area allows them to grow like this."

"Is that so?" Rat looked around. "You've made some pretty big changes in a single day."

I couldn't disagree. Now we had a monster stable full of Raph species and sakura lumina growing around the village.

"These are all so significant. I'm not sure I can keep up," Rat said with a sigh and then scurried back to her research.

"Right. As we first planned for today, we need to organize the materials we brought back from Q'ten Lo and Siltvelt," I said.

"With all these distractions, it's already night!" Raphtalia opined.

"Don't be like that," I said with a grin. And so, after preparing the evening meal, we set about sorting the materials.

After that, prior to bed, I conducted some accessory-making research in my room.

Thanks to the Raph species, our countermeasures for things like status effects were proceeding toward a resolution, but there was still a pile of other problems.

The principle facing me right then was how to enhance the accessories for Raphtalia, Ren, Itsuki, and myself. As I was working on the issue, I heard Raphtalia and the others battling with Atla outside.

"R-Raphtalia. Brother. I just want to go and see Master Naofumi! Move aside," Atla stated.

"No," Raphtalia replied.

"Never," replied her brother.

"Raph!" barked a horde of Raphs.

"Raphtalia, what a cowardly move! Increasing the numbers

of your race like that!" Atla was aghast.

"I'm not party to this increasing. Trust me!" Raphtalia retorted. She didn't sound too broken up about it now though. "All of you Raph species, you know what to do, right?"

"Raph!" came a horde of Raph replies.

Although I also caught myself thinking that it sounded like fun too, it really was getting noisy out there.

As I had that thought, Raph-chan arrived in my room. Ruft was with her. Even among the large number of new Raph species, I knew this was the original Raph-chan right away.

"Raph."

"Hey. What's up?" I asked.

"Well, Shield Hero, I was thinking . . ." Ruft trailed off.

"Okay, I see what you want," I said. It wasn't hard. The kid was feeling lonely, and so he didn't want to sleep alone. Also, he wanted to ask all sorts of questions about the Raph species. Heh, looked like my plan to draw Ruft into the Raph-chan alliance had achieved success.

"Raph," Raph-chan cried. She had been asserting herself since her arrival. Was she holding something—a ball?

I cautiously took it from her, and she adopted a pose telling me to put it inside the shield. So I gave it a try.

Conditions for the Raph Shield were unlocked!
Conditions for the Tali Shield were unlocked!

Conditions for the Lia Shield were unlocked!
Conditions for the Attacking Raph Shield were unlocked!
. . . etc.

Just to see what it was like, I checked out the Raph Shield.

Raph Shield 0/20 C
<abilities locked> equip bonus: Raph species growth adjustment (small), Raph species attack order 1 (limited period), Raphtalia and Raph species abilities adjustment (small)
Mastery Level: 0

I'm not even sure where to start with this. "Limited period?" What was that supposed to mean? Not to mention raising the abilities of specific individuals. This thing was crazy!

Still, I relied on Raphtalia the most out of everyone, and so I was certainly not opposed to her getting stronger. It looked like unlocking them would be pretty quick too.

"What's this? I feel a slight boost in my strength . . . and that gives me a bad feeling about this!" Raphtalia was already reacting from outside the house.

"Right. What do you want to talk about then?" I turned back to my visitor. "What do you want for Raph-chan?"

"Well, Shield Hero, do you think she could get bigger like you said before? Like those others that started out as different monsters?" Ruft asked.

"You've got a keen eye, kid. I like how you think. You're right. We do want a massive Raph-chan, don't we?" I'd requested S'yne make just such a thing, actually.

"Raph!" As the two of us stroked Raph-chan, and as though making our every wish come true, she suddenly grew bigger!

She was now around the size of Filo in her filolial form. About the same size as the former-caterpilland from earlier in the day. Then she relaxed on the floor, tapping happily on her chest to show off her new size.

What was this? Was I hallucinating? I didn't care if I was. I just wanted to touch her.

"Uwah!" Ruft seemed to be in a similar position.

"Right, let's stroke her," I said.

"Yeah," the kid agreed. As we proceeded to do so, I quickly began wanting to just snuggle up and sleep on her like a pillow.

"Raph." Raph-chan happily returned our affection. Ah, what a strange sensation. Such reassuring relaxation! "Raph!" Raph-chan seemed to be enjoying it too.

"Mr. Naofumi! We've successfully captured Atla. The Raph species actually seems pretty useful! So I'm thinking—" The door clattered open and Raphtalia came in just as Ruft and I

were hugging the now huge Raph-chan.

"What the hell is going on in here?!" Raphtalia glared at me, eyes squinting closed. I felt something like a cold gust of air.

"I was just talking about Raph-chan stuff with Ruft, and then Raph-chan went and turned into exactly what we asked for, so we were just enjoying the moment—" I explained.

"Being honest about it doesn't get you off the hook!" Raphtalia exclaimed.

"Raph?" Raph-chan seemed puzzled.

Hahaha! Wow, this massive Raph-chan really was the best. I wanted to use her like a bed, sleeping on top of her tummy.

"When did you and Ruft become so friendly, anyway?" Raphtalia probed.

"You saw it, didn't you? We bonded over Raph-chan," I replied.

"The Shield Hero is nice to me and playing with Raph-chan is really fun," Ruft added.

"We're best buddies now, aren't we?" I said.

"Yeah!" he agreed.

"You're heading into this far too casually! Do you have any idea how difficult it is to be friends with Mr. Naofumi?" Raphtalia scolded. What was her problem? It was almost as though she was suggesting he shouldn't be my friend. We have the same interests. Of course we were going to be friends!

Ruft might have been our enemy during the ridiculous Heavenly Emperor ruckus, but he was also Raphtalia's cousin. By talking to him we'd come to an understanding, which was why we were here together now. His so-called allies had only been using him. He was quick on the uptake. Being related to Raphtalia had also created a good first impression. Then, after introducing him to Raph-chan, he'd agreed with me about how cute she was after everyone else wouldn't listen, however hard I talked her up!

People I could talk to about stuff like this, like a friend, rather than someone like Atla who worshipped me—these people were a precious commodity.

"Ah, you two. I was just starting to think the Raph species could be useful, and then I have to walk in on this. Please, stop treating Raph-chan like a big pillow," Raphtalia said.

"If you're willing to go that far, Raphtalia, very well," I acquiesced. In the future we'd just have to cuddle with her when Raphtalia wasn't around.

"You too, Ruft," Raphtalia admonished.

"Yeah, okay." He didn't sound happy about it either. When Ruft and I moved away, Raph-chan turned back to her small size.

"We've managed to get Atla under control anyway, so you're safe for tonight," Raphtalia reported.

"Okay," I replied. It seemed the Raph species had access to

illusion magic. While illusions didn't have much effect on Atla generally, it seemed that piling them on in numbers was enough to contain her. Was she now happily seeing illusions of being with me?

I was going to start feeling sorry for her if we used this too much.

"That said, it's a scary thought that Atla may well soon learn to overcome the illusions," Raphtalia commented.

"It is Atla we're talking about, after all," I agreed. Not only was she a genius, but she quickly adapted if the same attack was used against her repeatedly. Constant adaptation was therefore required; the only advantage was that pitting oneself against her naturally increased one's own skills.

She would surely overcome the illusion attack, eventually.

"I need to put further efforts into our current, biggest problem—learning magic," Raphtalia said.

"How about training the Raph species in magic at the same time? They seem to have the same magic qualities as you," I suggested.

"Uwah. I'm not keen on that idea, but I guess that's what we need for the future," Raphtalia admitted.

"We could do with raising Ruft's level a bit too," I added.

"I have to defeat monsters?" Ruft looked a little troubled by that.

"Yeah. You were the Heavenly Emperor, so you understand

this much, right? You can't protect anyone without strength. So you need to learn what it means to fight," I explained.

"Uwah . . ." Ruft looked at Raph-chan. He definitely had some resistance to defeating monsters.

"Monsters are living things too, but humans and monsters are in different groups. We're part of the human group. I understand that you like monsters, but unfortunately we can't prioritize them over humans," I explained.

"Okay," Ruft finally managed. "I'll try . . . my best." When I thought about what it had been like when Raphtalia was smaller, I knew it might be hard for him. But I wanted him to learn those same lessons—the gravity, the weight of life. Experiencing fighting for his life against monsters would definitely help him to mature.

"Once you reach level 40 I'll perform a class-up on you too," I promised.

"Sure! I want to try a class-up!" Ruft said eagerly. Heh, that hooked him. I guess it was due to his age. Keel and the other younger ones had been happy to hear about a possible class-up too.

As I thought about the future, Ruft looked at Raph-chan. "Raph?"

Ah! So that was it!

"I want to do a Raph-chan class-up!" Ruft exclaimed.

"Hmmm. That sounds wonderful," I replied.

"You're planning something strange again, aren't you?" Raphtalia interjected. "We don't know what will happen if a human does that!"

"What? If Raph-chan performs my class-up, I might become like Shildina, able to turn into a therianthrope. Or maybe I could turn into something like Raph-chan!" Ruft postulated excitedly.

"That really does sound wonderful!" I exclaimed. Once we confirmed it worked with Ruft, then we could do the same thing with Raphtalia, although due to the katana vassal weapon, not only would a level reset be difficult, but it wasn't clear if she could even class-up.

In any case, I was rightly impressed with our former Heavenly Emperor. He had an eye for things that the common folk just couldn't see.

"No, it isn't! Stop it at once!" Raphtalia still wasn't having any of it.

"Raphtalia," I admonished. "I can't condone you standing in the way of Ruft's future."

"Mr. Naofumi," Raphtalia shot back. "What will you do if Ruft ends up like a Raph-chan?"

"I'd love him and cuddle him to bits," I replied without hesitation. "And then I'd ask if you can't do the same thing."

"I never should have asked, should I?" Raphtalia despaired. What was her problem, really?

"Right!" I just decided to ignore her. "This means I really need to put some time into leveling you up, Ruft!" I wasn't planning on actually having him take part in the Phoenix battle, but I still felt like throwing my full support behind leveling him up as much as possible before it happened.

"I'll do my best!" Ruft enthused.

"There's no need for that! Ah, honestly . . . this is the point where Sadeena would normally step in. She always knows what to say to convince you," Raphtalia lamented.

"She said she was going to show Shildina the oceans around here," I recalled. "I bet they are holed up in her secret base, wherever that is, sharing some wine." Anyway, Sadeena didn't "convince" me at times like this so much as "persuade" with prejudice.

"She's going to drink Shildina under the table again, I bet," Raphtalia predicted. I couldn't deny the likelihood. When the two sisters were together, Shildina was always trying to prove herself and always ending up with a terrible hangover the following day. Was it time to seriously think about separating them?

As we talked, there came a knock at the door. It was a bit late for a visit from anyone who wasn't already here.

"Naofumi, we're coming in." That was Melty.

"Master, I'm home!" Which meant that was Filo. The two of them came in.

"Hey, if it isn't Melty. Been a while!" I played it light.

"It really has been. You don't come to see me at all either, Naofumi," Melty complained.

"I've been pretty busy, you know," I explained.

"I understand that much. Still, I wasn't especially happy with your answer to the issue I had requested the Sword Hero to ask you about." With that, Melty looked at Ruft.

"Good . . . evening," the boy managed in the Melromarc tongue.

"So nice to see you," Melty replied, a bit out of character for her. "So this is the kid with the connection to Raphtalia?"

"Yeah, this is Ruft," I explained. "He doesn't know much about the world yet, so I brought him to the village to learn more. Hey, this is the perfect opportunity. Melty, can you teach him everything he'd need to know as a leader? Like, how to be an emperor? Stuff like that?"

"Huh?" The boy seemed surprised.

"It's important for you to play with monsters and make lots of friends, but among everyone I know, Melty here knows the most about the duties of royalty and the stuff they need to know. Thinking about the future, having Melty teach you that stuff seems like the best idea," I explained to him.

"That's what you think about me, Naofumi? Honestly! Not that I mind. He'll have to learn the language first, of course," Melty agreed.

"Okay. I understand." What a good kid! "Thank you for

agreeing," he managed again in the Melromarc tongue and gave a bob of his head. Melty returned a smile, suggesting she wasn't entirely unhappy about the situation.

"Well, if there's anything you want to ask, just come and find me. I'll make time to help. If you know the language of the demi-human nations, you can use that for now, until you get used to things here," Melty told him. If I recalled correctly, she could speak all sorts of languages.

Ruft nodded, looking a little surprised.

"Anyway, Melty, did you just drop by to say hello?" I asked.

"That was part of it, but not all. My mother is very busy with preparations to fight the Phoenix, and so I've got a message from her for you," Melty explained. "Even that's not the main reason though." With that, Melty and Filo looked at each other.

"Filo," Melty prompted.

"Okay! You see, Fitoria is really mad, wondering how much longer you're going to keep her waiting," Filo revealed. Before our invasion of Q'ten Lo, and immediately prior to heading to Siltvelt, Fitoria, the queen of the filolials, had made a request of me via Filo and Melty. But I'd wanted to prioritize Raphtalia's problems at the time, so I'd put it off until later.

Still, maybe it wasn't wise to piss off one as selfish as the queen could be. I wasn't sure we could beat her either, if it came down to a fight.

"Yeah, of course. With the Q'ten Lo invasion and everything, it kinda slipped my mind," I admitted. "So that's why you're here?"

"Yeah," Filo responded.

"I was coming to talk about that ahead of Filo. It has become a bit of a problem in Melromarc," Melty added.

"What's that mean?" I asked.

"Well," Filo started. "There have been some dangerous filolials around in your country recently, Master, who won't do as they're told."

"Huh?" I was puzzled. What was she talking about? This was the request for me?

"I've heard similar stories myself, and so I thought maybe this is what Filo—I mean Fitoria—wanted you to solve, Naofumi," Melty added.

"Hmmm." I wasn't sure what to make of it, but if our neighbors had also been hearing about this, they had to be creating quite a problem.

"To be more accurate, they are filolials who act like mountain bandits, attacking wagons carrying off goods and stuff like that," Melty continued. "We did tell the Sword Hero to tell you about it, but it seems it just got turned into an issue with mountain bandits . . . Robbers, basically."

"I mean, that's the short of it, isn't it? Robbers based in the mountains, thus mountain bandits," I surmised. Ren was pretty straitlaced, but from this description, it had just sounded like a problem with robbers.

"It seems they are robbers that only appear at night. They prey on merchants or adventurers who are using a wagon, challenging them to a fight and then taking that wagon if they lose," Melty explained further.

"Taking their cargo? That does sound like a problem," I sympathized.

"That's not what I said," Melty corrected me. "They leave the cargo. It seems they only want the wagons."

"What?!" That did surprise me. What could they want just with wagons? More like "mountain wagon collectors." Quite aside from anything else, what were people doing driving wagons around at night?

It was an issue involving filolials anyway. That explained why Fitoria would make this request.

"They've become pretty famous at being quite odd mountain bandits," Melty continued. "In a few rare cases, the wagons have come back all beaten up, but also packed with treasure. Needless to say, the 'victims' have been quite happy about that. There are even some merchants who are now purposely looking to get targeted."

"Hold on a moment. What the hell is going on then? And—" I finished my thought in my head. If this was the issue that Fitoria wanted help with, then . . . "You're telling me filolials fight over wagons?"

"Yes. That's what I've been told," Melty confirmed. Uwah! So she wanted me to resolve some kind of turf war? If these were wild filolials, they weren't going to go down without a fight.

"The loser has to give their wagon to the winner," Melty explained. "Also, if it's the season of love, they can only find love by defeating their opponent." What were they, hermit crabs?

Hmmm, in any case, I made the promise, so I had to go. I just couldn't help but feel there was something else to all this. Surely Fitoria could handle some filolials herself.

Or maybe she couldn't. Not these particular ones.

When I thought about it, maybe there were other wild filolial queens apart from Fitoria. What if a second filolial queen was giving orders in her human form, seeking to expand her territory? Maybe, like the queen of Melromarc, there would be all sorts of problems if she reproached them herself. So she was trying to send in a hero to clean up for her. I had to review the situation.

"This sounds like getting involved in a turf war between Fitoria's faction and another filolial queen, or something like that." My assessment made Filo's cowlick stick up on end.

"Yes, that's pretty much it. But she said that you and I would be able to handle this quickly, Master. So that's what she wants us to do," Filo explained.

"What choice do I have then?" I groaned. "I'm tired, but if they only appear at night, maybe we should go right now."

"It's already late, so even if we leave right now, I'm not sure we'd encounter them tonight," Filo said. "I should receive word soon with likely locations for them to appear too."

"Tomorrow night then," I replied. "Although I can't help feeling we are going to get caught up in a whole pointless conflict."

"Alright, alright. Filo did help out a lot in Q'ten Lo too," Raphtalia pointed out.

"I guess," I acquiesced. Ruft, meanwhile, was still a little scared of Filo, so he was sitting a little distance away, hugging Raph-chan while he listened to us talk.

Filo, perhaps aware of the distance he was still giving her, was looking at him with a slightly troubled expression on her face.

Maybe Melty could bridge that gap. Would the day come when the pure filolial-lover Melty finally became friends with Ruft, the boy who had pursued filolials purely in the world of books and pictures? Hah! Ruft already belonged to the clan of Raph-chan. Too late to try to convert him now, Melty!

"Mr. Naofumi, what are you thinking about? You've got that wicked smile on your face again," Raphtalia commented. I ignored her.

"About this request from Fitoria," I asked instead. "Are you coming too, Melty?"

"Huh? Well . . . it's also a problem for Filo, so I think I'd better tag along," she reasoned.

"Sure thing. Tomorrow, then. We'll sort a time out later, but Melty, Filo, you two come along too," I ordered.

"Okay," Melty agreed.

It would probably be fine with just that many, but a bit more muscle also wouldn't go astray. Who to take though? If I called S'yne into action, she'd probably come . . . Ren would probably want to be with Eclair. If Melty was going to leave the town tomorrow night, it would be best to have Eclair act as governor in her place. In either case, Melty would have to teach her the ropes. It was best to place Eclair close to Ren.

Itsuki, meanwhile, came as a set with Rishia. Oh, and that reminded me, I still needed to send him to read the tablets on the Cal Mira islands. Okay, I'd have them go and do that. He also had lots of memories with Rishia there. That was where they had split up.

Now that their relationship had been renewed, a trip there could also be an indicator of a second chance.

Ah whatever. I'd just take along whoever was around at the time we set out.

And with that, we called it a night and everyone else returned to their respective bedchambers.

Before I got into bed, however, I continued with my accessory-making.

A short while after I got underway, there came another knock on the door.

Raphtalia should have been asleep by now, preparing for the long night tomorrow. So who else might be knocking at this time of night?

I opened the door to find Fohl standing there.

"What?" It was a few hours past pleasantries.

"I want to talk with you a little—just the two of us," he explained. Hmmm. This sounded like nothing more than another massive pain in my ass.

We left the house and stood together in the village square.

"So? What's this about?" I still didn't have the patience for this.

"I need you to stop dragging Atla into your dangerous battles!" Fohl's resolve was firm, and he even thrust his fist at me as he spoke. "I've been feeling this for a long time now! These battles are just too reckless!" The shame of it was I couldn't deny it. Thinking back on everything that had happened since coming to this other world, I'd been caught up in all sorts of trouble and had many one-sided struggles forced upon me. I'd long been expecting someone to show up with the very complaints that Fohl was now voicing.

"I have to protect Atla with my life if necessary!" Fohl exclaimed.

"Your sister seems pretty fixated on me though. Can't you help keep her under control?" I asked.

"You have no interest in Atla?" Fohl replied after a pause.

"However I answer that, you're going to get mad. What answer could satisfy you, really?" Heh, I really got to the heart of that one.

"Uh . . ." Fohl had no reply.

"Why do I have to keep saying this? I'm not interested in romance. Atla is like . . . If I had to classify it . . . she's like my child." Just like I considered Raphtalia my daughter, I was starting to feel like Atla was an adopted child who just liked to chase around after me. I'd even started feeling the same thing about the village slaves, recently.

Romantic love? Nope, I certainly wasn't feeling anything like that at the moment.

"I mean, I feel the same about you, I guess," I continued. "You need to just fight hard and make sure to protect her yourself. If you can even keep up with her! Hah! As the one training you to fight the waves, maybe it's not my place to say that."

"I don't need you to tell me to do that!" Fohl came back, still aggressive. "I'll defeat the waves and whatever else you want me to, if it means Atla doesn't have to fight. That's a promise!"

"Fine, fine. You don't want me having Atla fight the waves, is that it? Then that's what we'll do," I conceded.

"Huh?" Fohl sounded dumbstruck.

"What's so puzzling about that? I'm not going to drag people who don't want to fight into battle any more than I'm going to ignore a plea to spare someone from having to fight. That's just not me right now. You don't want Atla involved in dangerous battles, right?" Sure, I'd put her in some pretty dangerous situations, but if this was what Fohl wanted, then I could choose to keep her out of the wave battles.

"Are you sure?" he asked.

"If you can cover the gap she leaves, sure. And whatever Atla says, you're the one who's going to have to stop her. I'm not getting involved in that," I asserted. Fohl looked down at the ground for a moment, thinking. Then he looked back up.

"Very well," he accepted. A little easier than I expected. "I think I understand maybe a little what Atla sees in you. Not that I like you any more for it myself."

"Whatever. Just keep your precious sister's rampages under control, you hear?" I commanded.

"I will," he managed after another long pause. "I'll become strong enough to stop her. You'll see. Until that time, I'll be counting on you." Hold it! Counting on me for what? I really didn't like the sound of that last part.

Immediately after that, Fohl hurried away into the glooming darkness.

Chapter Three: Spirit Tortoise Shell

It was the following day, just after breakfast.

After giving my orders to everyone, I decided what to do for the day. Training was going pretty well. I was making progress with life force too. S'yne knew a lot about the topic, so when she had the time, I was having her teach me and Atla.

"Naofumi." Ren, also having finished his breakfast, came over to me.

"What's up?" I asked.

"We need me to learn some smithing, right? So I'd like to see the weapon shop guy and his master if possible," he said. Yeah, I'd forgotten about that. I'd introduced him to them when I took him over to Q'ten Lo. It would be a good chance to request some things from the old guy too.

"Okay then, today we'll go and see them in Q'ten Lo," I decided. "We can't afford to leave the Melromarc store closed for any longer." Worst-case scenario, we'd end up bringing Imiya's uncle back with us.

That reminded me. There had been some developments with Imiya. While I was away from the village, the accessory dealer had paid a visit, looked at some of the accessories that Imiya made, and given her some advice. If he thought she was worth teaching, that meant she had some real skill. He knew she was my underling too.

When I found a moment, I'd try and chat with her about how to make better accessories.

With that, we used Raphtalia's Return Dragon Vein and headed to Q'ten Lo.

In the capital of Q'ten Lo, Raphtalia was the Heavenly Emperor—basically the queen—and so she couldn't just stroll around the streets. So we had her wait in the castle. Just Ren and I headed over to Motoyasu II's workshop.

"Hey! What're you doing here, kid?" The weapon guy came out to greet us. As for Motoyasu II . . . Hold on! He was forging away with a serious look on his face. That seemed unprecedented! Imiya's uncle was working as his assistant too. He was carrying in what looked like a vast volume of water . . . no, holy water. Above it all, some members of the Q'ten Lo clergy were chanting away constantly in the corner. It was totally crazy, to be honest.

"How's it going with you?" I asked.

"I'm improving a lot, thanks to my master," the old guy replied.

"That's great to hear," I complimented him.

"You've done a lot to help me out recently. I'm sorry for all the trouble, kid. Really, I am," he said gruffly.

"Hey, you always do so much for us," I pointed out. "No need to worry about it. What about them?" I looked over to Imiya's uncle and Motoyasu II.

"My master is just reforging that cursed sword for the Sword Kid. Tolly and I are in the middle of helping him out," the old guy explained.

"Got any plans for the store in Melromarc?" I prodded gently.

"Hmmm." The old guy crossed his arms and gave it some serious thought. The whole setup for forging was really great here in Q'ten Lo, that much was true, but I doubted that was keeping him from wanting to leave. After all, he just had to ask me and I could move everything around.

"You're worried about letting your master off the leash again, aren't you?" The old man nodded at this perceptive comment from Ren.

Yeah, I had already guessed as much. If I took the old guy away now, his master would probably jump for joy.

"That said, leaving things as they are probably isn't going to be much better. He's going to run up a tab the first chance he gets," I surmised.

"He really is incorrigible, isn't he," Ren agreed.

What to do with the creepy letch once the old guy and Imiya's uncle finished their training was definitely something I needed to think about.

"Anyway, we can worry about that later," the old guy said. "It's not like me or Tolly have finished our training yet anyway."

"You haven't?" I asked.

"Just a little more and I think I'm really going to have something," the old guy enthused. "Although there's still a lot more beyond that too." So he was coming up to a milestone at least. Hmmm.

In any case, we needed all this cursed gear to be purified.

"I don't want it to sound like an afterthought, but we've also got some weapons we made using the Spirit Tortoise materials. After all the hassle recently, go ahead and take them with you," the old guy said, truly sounding apologetic.

"So you solved the problem?" I queried.

"Yep, that's right. I asked my master about it, and seriously, he solved it so damn quick. All that worrying on my part just seemed silly. It really makes me think, you know, I've got a long way to go yet," the old man replied. He was so skilled though. I had to wonder at his humble personality sometimes. "The Q'ten Lo bigwigs said they'd pay, so no need to worry about that," he continued.

"Hey, that's a big help," I said gladly. Just as we finished that exchange, Imiya's uncle found a break in his work and came over. Hmmm, he also looked a bit thinner.

Then he went into the back room with the old man. They clattered back with all sorts of gear in their arms. There was a shield among the pieces and some armor too.

"That dragon of yours brought the core on over. That let us complete this armor for you!" The old guy beamed. It looked a lot like the Barbaroi Armor that I'd worn in the past. However, after a closer inspection, a tortoiseshell-colored material had been added to the metal parts. The slightly darker coloring had been made brighter too.

Barbarian Armor + 3
defense up: impact resistance (large), slash resistance (large), fire resistance (large), wind resistance (large), water resistance (large), earth resistance (large), lightning resistance (large), absorb resistant (medium), HP recovery (low), magic recovery (low), SP recovery (low), EP recovery (low), magic power-up (medium), dragon territory, earth vein protection, dragon element, four holy beasts power, Spirit Tortoise power, magic defense processing, automatic self-repair, growth power

It had so many effects on it that it made my head spin a little. The curse from when it was the Barbaroi Armor was gone too. I could already tell, just from a glance, that it was better than what Romina had made. No, more like an enhancement to one of Romina's pieces that had ceased to function.

"Can I give it a try right away?" I asked.

"Sure thing. Show us what it looks like!" the old guy enthused. I took the armor and got changed in the fitting room. While feeling familiar and well-worn, it also had a new feeling to it. It felt a bit strange. Still, although the coloring was different, the design wasn't changed much.

"How is it?" I asked the old guy.

"Looks like you've come back to yourself at last, kid," the old guy replied.

"Yes . . . I'm not sure it's my place to say this perhaps, but for a hero it might be a little . . . Ah, sorry, it's nothing," Imiya's uncle started and then thought better of it. I mean, he wasn't wrong. The old guy always seemed pretty pleased with it, but when I first saw the armor, the first thing I thought of was a thug from some apocalyptic future. But just putting that same armor on made me feel stronger. The old guy made it—someone I entrusted implicitly—making it the armor I felt I could rely on the most.

Raphtalia had said she wanted to become my sword. The old guy had given me this armor. Modifying this Barbarian Armor really did make the best armor.

"Now I just have to think about the shield. After copying it, what to do?" I wondered. It was another piece the old man had taken the time to make for me, after all. Maybe hang it up on display in the storehouse?

"I think I've got an idea of what you're thinking kid, from

the look on your face. But am I mistaken? You look like some blue-blooded collector who just found his next trophy." Ulp. I guessed I'd have someone equip it.

With that I gripped the shield, and with a sparkly flash, weapon copy was activated.

Weapon copy activated!
Conditions for the Spirit Tortoise Shell were unlocked!

Connecting with the Spirit Tortoise Heart Shield!

Spirit Tortoise Shell (awakened) 80/80 AT
<abilities locked> equip bonus: skills: S Float Shield, Reflect Shield,
special effects: gravity field, C soul recovery, C magic snatch, C gravity shot, vitality boost, magic defense (large), lightning resistance, nullify SP drain, magic assistance, spell support, growth power
special equip effect: comet shield (Spirit Tortoise)
mastery level: 100

So it had blended with the Spirit Tortoise Heart Shield? It looked like an enhanced version of that. Its shape was also different from the original, strengthening the idea of it being a mixture with the Spirit Tortoise Heart Shield.

However, it looked like it couldn't use Energy Blast.

It was still incredible. It was like it had all the best parts of the Spirit Tortoise line of shields. Overall, it was better than the Demon Dragon Shield too. I thought I should be making this my main shield in the future.

"S Float" was likely "Second Float Shield." That would make it a semi-passive skill that created a floating shield, like E Float. Considering other "Second Shield" examples, it probably made a second shield appear or something like that.

What about Reflect Shield though?

Based on the text and the games I knew of, it might perform a counter based on a percentage of the damage taken, but that would be worthless against weaker enemies.

Also, what was this "growth power" that I sometimes saw? Yeah, there were quite a few effects here that I didn't really know what they did.

The special equip effect comet shield (Spirit Tortoise) also caught my eye. I'd caused trouble for the old guy by testing things in front of him before, however, so I'd put that off until later.

"It looks like you've copied it, but hasn't its appearance changed quite a bit?" the old man noticed.

"Yeah, it's because it's a Spirit Tortoise shield," I explained. "I've got all these bonuses which make it transform." Ost's blessing was still in effect. I was happy to make use of it.

"Here, Sword Kid, one for you too. This is the Spirit Tortoise sword created by my master," the old man said.

"Huh? Spirit Tortoise sword? We saw one of those in Zeltoble," I recalled.

"Yeah, about that," the old man started.

"What?" I prompted.

"We reckon the Spirit Tortoise piece you saw in Zeltoble was one made by my master," the old guy finally explained, his face looking pained. "Once, when he was looking for some spending money, my master used some rare materials to make a sword, and it seems those were Spirit Tortoise materials. He only told me once he got a good look at these materials."

What? So the sword we saw in that auction had been made by Motoyasu II?

"In the least, I'm yet to encounter a blacksmith other than the two of us who can turn Spirit Tortoise materials into any kind of workable weapon. I think that has to be the case," the old guy continued sheepishly. I mean, Motoyasu II was exceptionally skilled . . . but had that piece traveled all the way from Q'ten Lo?

I probably should have pressed for more information, but Motoyasu II looked hard at work and I didn't want to disturb him.

"Hmmm. Ren, how about your curse?" I asked.

"Yeah, it feels a lot better, thanks to you guys, Naofumi.

I don't think the sword will snap or anything like that," Ren answered.

"My master made that especially sturdy, just for you, Sword Kid. Should be fine," the old guy added. Without further ado, Ren took hold of the Spirit Tortoise Sword.

"Wow!" He was impressed at once. "It has incredible sharpness. I just copied it, and the quality is so high. It has some bonuses on it!"

"What! Even those effects are reflected in the copy?!" I failed to contain my surprise.

"Yeah, the level required for transformation has been significantly dropped, and there's a pretty big bonus on the sharpness. It looks very easy to use too. It's like an order-made weapon with all sorts of effects on it!" Ren said, sounding very pleased.

I hadn't seen the same kind of stuff with the Spirit Tortoise Shell though. Mine had been a special transformation realized solely by the link with the Spirit Tortoise Heart Shield. So why didn't it have these other bonuses?

I looked at the old guy, and he was embarrassedly scratching at his head.

"I'm sorry. When you compare things made by my master with the Spirit Tortoise Shell, I'm ashamed of how poor it looks," he lamented.

"Hmmm. In that case, in light of the further growth I

expect from you, I think it best I leave the Spirit Tortoise Shell with you. Right?" If he could enhance the Spirit Tortoise Shell further, it would only make me stronger too.

"I'll make it just like the weapon the Sword Kid just got," the old guy vowed.

"Good. I believe in you," I replied.

"Right, what else? Ah, my master also made weapons using Spirit Tortoise materials for Raphtalia, S'yne, Filo, Rishia, and Atla," the old guy confirmed.

"That lecherous dog. He only made weapons for the women? The size of his balls!" I was almost impressed. He'd likely only made the sword for Ren because he sensed a kindred spirit.

"Anyway. Come by again soon," the old guy told us.

With that, we carried the gaggle of new weapons back home with us.

Once we were in the village again, I looked at the sword Motoyasu II had made for Raphtalia.

Spirit Tortoise Katana

Its specs were too high. I could only see the name. I seriously needed a shield that would raise my appraisal abilities.

I had Raphtalia copy it anyway. She quickly started swinging it around, reporting that the level and status required to use it were lower than the White Tiger Katana. It had some powerful bonuses on it.

Just what the hell was Motoyasu II? Some kind of forging god?

I didn't like it. Not one bit! Were we going to have to suck up to that perv to get him to make the best weapons now?

Rishia's own weapon was semitransparent and couldn't activate copy, so there was no way to use her new one. The gear that the old guy and his master had provided would fetch a pretty penny if we sold it though. Not too shabby, if we considered it our reward for the invasion of Q'ten Lo.

Chapter Four: Fitoria's Request

It was around the time the sun had begun to set.

"Right. We are heading out tonight to take care of Fitoria's request," I announced. I had to admit I was a bit anxious about this one. Who would be best to take along? Fitoria had said that Filo and I should be able to handle it without too much trouble. If that was the case, did I really need to worry too much about the party I picked? Still, I had my concerns.

"Master Naofumi! I want to go with you," Atla piped up.

"Raph!" offered Raph-chan. She was a lock, of course. As for Atla, it wasn't going to be all that dangerous, so it was probably fine to take her along too—even if that meant having to take her brother along as part of the set.

"Then let's count Atla and Fohl in . . ." I started.

"Fohl actually isn't here at the moment," Raphtalia corrected me.

"Indeed, my brother headed out after breakfast with the Hengen Muso Style master," Atla confirmed.

"What? Where could he possibly have gone that's more important to him than being close to his sister?" I asked, somewhat meanly.

"Well, it seems my overwhelming victory against Atla using

the Raph species last night put him at ease," Raphtalia explained. "So he headed out to learn the deeper secrets of Hengen Muso Style." What was that muscle-head thinking? Don't tell me our little chat the previous night had set him off. It sounded like maybe he was forgetting what was important in his desire to simply become stronger than his sister.

Well, whatever. If he wasn't here, so be it.

Gaelion was staying behind, no question. Filolials were going to be involved, after all. Wyndia could sit it out too. I could take some of those from the village, like Keel, but I really didn't want to think we'd be in need of such numbers.

"A shame the killer whale sisters aren't here," I commented.

"They're still out and about somewhere," Raphtalia confirmed.

"They're not going off wandering, just the two of them, are they?" I wondered. Could it be that the two of them actually got along?

I had my promise to think about, so I'd have Atla stay behind.

"Right, Atla, you can stay behind," I decided.

"No thank you. I'm going with you, no matter what," she offered defiantly. Even if I left her behind, she'd probably just follow us. Very well. For a job like this, it should be fine to take her.

"Where's S'yne got to?" I asked.

"She was tired from training with Atla earlier in the day and so went to bed already," Raphtalia revealed. Teaching the ways of life force was clearly quite a burden. S'yne had been looking very tired recently.

I didn't want to take her along just to have her collapse. The battle with the Phoenix was coming soon too, so for now I'd just have her rest up. If she did wake up, she'd just start watching over me again.

"Right. Looks like this is the team," I said. Melty had brought both Filo and Ruft along. Letting him see the rougher side of filolials would bring him totally over to the Raph side.

"Mr. Naofumi, why do you always seem to get that conspiratorial smile when looking at Ruft?" Raphtalia asked, but I chose to ignore her.

With that, the party was formed of Raphtalia, Raph-chan, Atla, Filo, Melty, Ruft, and me. A composition much like when we'd been on the run, with a few new additions for flavor.

And I was still a little worried that this party would be able to pull off whatever was needed.

"Around here, was it?" I asked. It was now night, a time period during which I really didn't want to move around much.

The moon was up in the sky, and we were in the mountainous region of Melromarc, a place with lots of mountain paths. Filo was trotting along one such path, pulling a wagon. Just a regular wagon that was used in the village. Filo's original wagon had been taken by Motoyasu after all, and the wagon we had used in Siltvelt and Q'ten Lo had been too large to bring back with us. It might have been possible to transport it back if we'd disassembled it into smaller parts and had the heroes all bring pieces, but come on. Didn't that sound like a massive pain in the ass?

"Seeing you wearing that armor, Mr. Naofumi, it feels like you're finally back to yourself," Raphtalia complimented my appearance.

"You think so?" I asked.

"It's cool." Ruft also nodded in agreement. Maybe the two of them shared similar sensibilities?

"Still, having to do favors for a filolial now . . . Do I look like some kind of handyman?" I grumbled.

"You put it off for so long, and now you're still complaining about it?" This jab from Melty. I mean, okay, it was time to take care of this.

"This is where we destroy the filolials, correct?" Atla sounded ready to let some serious power off the chain.

"We're not destroying anything, just stopping their mischief," I corrected her. Just what was it that had made her so violent?

"Raph," commented Raph-chan.

"It's probably going to be some kind of competition, a

clash between wagons maybe. I've just got you guys along as insurance," I clarified.

"Honestly, I'm more worried about the trouble the power of these weapons might cause," Raphtalia confided in me.

"Let's hope that's the only problem we have," I responded. With a party this size, I wanted to think it would be fine.

I was also afraid that S'yne's enemies, or even Witch, might be behind this.

However, it being a request from Fitoria, the chances of that seemed pretty low. Or so I hoped.

In any case, we continued along the mountain path for a while longer.

"Nothing's happening, is it?" Raphtalia eventually commented.

"I noticed," I replied. "We're just waiting for the bandits to find us, basically, so it can't be helped." This was the place, apparently. Maybe they were taking the night off?

"Do they have a hideout or something? I mean, if they're filolials, maybe a nest?" I wondered.

"No idea about that," Melty explained. Useless, honestly. It was going to be filolials, right?

Even as I thought that, something like the light of torches appeared in the distance and started coming toward us. Trotting along, they came close at a reasonable speed, heading in our direction from the distant mountains.

That was kind of them to illuminate themselves for us. We were using a lamp too, so they'd see us. That was likely what they were heading toward.

Right then. Time to see who turned up.

What? What was this?

I looked at the incoming bandits and couldn't help but furrow my brow.

The dust cleared, revealing the group that had been called mountain bandits, and had been called filolials, but now looked like some kind of wagon—or more like some insane long-hauler's pimped-out ride—glittering with Gold leaf and decorated with images of Filo.

It was floating too. Clearly floating. I hadn't seen anything like this since coming to this world.

It felt as strange as a UFO showing up in a fantasy epic.

The ones pulling this road-going travesty stopped in front of us. I made out three young girls. Feathery as they were, one was red, one blue, and one green. Meanwhile, in the driver's seat there was—

"It's been a while, father-in-law. It's me, I say, Motoyasu the street racer!"

It was the Spear Hero, flying a flag from his spear and calling himself a "street racer."

Chapter Five: The Street Racer

What? Huh? What was this moron blabbing about now?

A street racer? That wasn't even a hero anymore. And yet he had an incredible smile plastered across his face.

"W-what the hell is that?"

"My wagon!" Filo shouted.

"It's the height of poor taste! What's the big idea?" Melty jabbed.

"Hold on, Filo." I cut through the noise. "You're saying that's the wagon we used to use?!" The last time we'd encountered Motoyasu, I'd chased after him, wanting to get the wagon back, but it definitely hadn't been in this state then.

"Yeah. I can see the marks I made on it! Waaah!" she bawled. Seriously? We might not have used it all that much after buying it, with so much other stuff going on, but it had still been Filo's prized wagon. During any free time she had, I remember her always polishing it.

That same wagon was now turned into this monstrosity. I hardly had words for it.

"I can hardly see any trace of it," Raphtalia said. "Is this really the wagon that we used?"

"Raph, raph." Raph-chan moved onto Filo's crying

shoulder and attempted to console her. I understood her sympathy. I really did.

"What do you think, Filo-tan? I've tuned up the wagon you left me with all the love I could muster," Motoyasu explained.

Oh God! I hated this guy. Man, did I hate this guy! "Tuned up?" More like "messed up!"

I just wanted to punch him in the face, so hard. However, I also wanted nothing more to do with him. Fitoria! Gah! She'd set us up!

Yes, it was safe and would also be over quickly, just as had been described. But having to take on this guy? A battle over wagons like hermit crabs changed their shells! And even if we won, who'd want that wagon?

God, it was our wagon in the first place!

What about the stolen wagons that Melty had mentioned? She also failed to mention that it was Motoyasu we were dealing with! I mean, the signs had been there. I was just a moron for not noticing them!

There was no way I was playing around with the broken Motoyasu! I hated his overpowering manner at the best of times. Even if he'd realized the truth and decided to aid us, his basic nature as a perving womanizer was unchanged.

Shit, he was probably only helping because he knew I was Filo's master!

During the whole Ren episode, he'd helped out and then up

and vanished, the result of which was rolling back around with these monstrous modifications!

Without thinking, I lifted my shield. "Portal—"

"Hold on, hold on. We're leaving?!" Melty interjected.

"What other choice do we have after seeing that thing?" I proclaimed. I would have loved for someone, anyone, to provide me with some choices.

"I do understand how you feel, but . . ." Raphtalia offered.

"But this is a request from Fitoria, isn't it?" Melty reminded me.

"That's right! I owe her a piece of my mind for foisting this off onto us!" I was actually seething mad. It meant dealing with this absolute moron. I was amazed Fitoria had put up with it, although maybe she hadn't had any trouble with that.

Not to mention, Motoyasu had said that he'd rush to our aid if we needed him. And yet, after actually seeing nothing of him at all, now here he was, messing about as a street racer! Are you freaking kidding me?!

"Right, Filo! Take Motoyasu out!" I commanded. Filo would be able to handle this. I was sure of it. Not that my faith in her would have any effect on things.

"No!" she replied.

"You can't leave everything to Filo!" Melty raged, clearly preparing to lay into me. I just wanted to tell them both to shut up. I really wanted nothing to do with any of this. "That said, while I'd heard a bit about this from Filo, it's all a bit more problematic when confronted by it firsthand," Melty admitted.

"I'd heard he was broken, but this is something else," Raphtalia agreed.

"He is very strange," Atla added. "I sense a strange love from him, close to insanity. This is certainly not something to be underestimated. That depth of feeling for someone, that's something I can certainly understand—and won't be outdone for."

"What are you rambling about, Atla?" Raphtalia asked.

"That guy is weird," was Ruft's opinion.

"You've got his number, Ruft," I congratulated him. The kid definitely had a good eye.

"Why's he so weird?" Ruft asked.

"Her sister broke him, and then Filo destroyed whatever was left," I briskly explained. When I pointed at Melty, she gave a scream into the sky.

"Sister!"

"If only we could bring him back somehow, like the Sword Hero and Bow Hero," Raphtalia said.

"That's what he wants, I'm afraid," I replied.

"But tell me, Naofumi. Who's this 'father-in-law' he's talking about?" Melty inquired.

"Me, apparently," I was barely able to admit.

"But why?!" Melty asked.

"It has a nice ring to it," Ruft said.

"Ruft, listen. You must never call Mr. Naofumi 'father-in-law.' Ever." Raphtalia was quick on the uptake.

"Why not?" Ruft asked.

"The better question is, why would you want to?" Raphtalia countered.

"Because he's so reliable and teaches me so many things," Ruft explained.

"That is like a father, I'll admit. But please, for my sake, don't call him that." What was Raphtalia going on about?

Gah, anyway, explaining all of this was a pain. I just wanted to run away. This really was a mess we didn't need.

"I want to go home," Filo said.

"Yes . . . me too," Ruft agreed.

"Raph," added Raph-chan.

Filo didn't like Motoyasu much either, after all. I stroked Raph-chan in an attempt to alleviate my stress.

"Just leaving isn't going to resolve this issue, Mr. Naofumi," Raphtalia advised.

"He would be too much to subdue physically. That's how strong he is. In order to win, you would need strength such as Master Naofumi, or the Sword or Bow Hero. Even then, he would not back down," Atla announced, providing an accurate analysis. Motoyasu was surely that strong, at the moment. That was how strong cursed weapons were, after all. He likely still had it.

If we could talk him down, we wouldn't even have to fight.

From that perspective, this was a simple job. Motoyasu harbored no ill will toward us either.

"Look . . . Motoyasu, what are you playing at?" I started.

"I'm a street racer," he returned.

"That's not an answer!" I was losing my calm already. So much was missing from his reply I almost didn't know where to go next.

"Why have you become a street racer?" I ventured.

"These girls said they wanted to do it, and so I'm letting them be free," he explained.

"I see. I think you're the one suffering from excess freedom," I sniped.

Filolials wanted wagons. They had a hermit-crab-like habit of stealing them from each other, and yet he spoke of freedom? I didn't understand it at all.

Seriously, the moment the word "filolial" had been mentioned, I should have seen this coming. I was distracted by other words, like "Fitoria" and "mountain bandits." Or to put it more accurately, I'd driven all thoughts of Motoyasu from my head altogether.

"Can someone tell me, why does he call you father-in-law!?" Melty asked, still stuck on that.

"Because I'm the one who raised Filo, apparently," I explained. So "owner" meant "father," did it? Filo might be under my command, but she certainly wasn't my child.

Even if I was her parent, Motoyasu was older than me. So why did I have to suffer being called "father-in-law" by someone older than I was?

"Now, dear Filo-tan, allow me to introduce our darling children!" Motoyasu proclaimed.

"These are your kids? Together?!" When she dumped him in the mountains, had she given him a pity lay and literally laid eggs before making a run for it?

"No! He's lying, Master. I'd never do such a thing!" Filo was quick to defend herself.

"She most certainly would not," Melty backed her up. "Stop making up such lies!" Motoyasu, however, just gleefully started in on a story none of us wanted to hear.

"The red one is Crimmy. Her name comes from 'crimson.' Next is the blue one. Her name is Marine, which comes from 'aquamarine.' Finally, we have Green. Her name comes from 'green!' Yeah, you guessed it!"

"We're not his kids, but nice to meet you!" All three of them gave a slightly out-of-sorts bow.

So they weren't his kids after all!

Oh, these rascals! There had been three women in Motoyasu's party before, including Witch. Even after his mental break, he still wanted to be surrounded by women, although, at least this time they all seemed to like him.

In any case, these were his followers now. He looked totally broken and yet was still exactly the same.

"But I must say, there are a lot of pigs around you, father-in-law," Motoyasu commented.

"Just you listen to me! Hold on. What do you mean, pigs?" Melty raged.

"Pigs? What are you talking about?" I also asked.

"Exactly what it sounds like. Pigs. Do you have a fondness for swine?" he inquired with a straight face. Right, right, hold on. Back in the inn once, Motoyasu had gone on about women being pigs. He'd called Raphtalia a raccoon-pig too, or something like that.

Could it be?

"Hey, Motoyasu. What do you see here?" I ask, pointing at Melty.

"A blue piglet. All that oinking must get annoying, right? Ugh, I really dislike it," he replied.

"You're kidding! 'Pig'? He's talking about me?! I'm going to rip his head off!" Melty was incensed.

"Give it up. This is all your sister's fault," I said.

"My freaking sister!" Melty exclaimed. I mean, I could understand not being able to put up with being called a pig.

Still, it was as I expected. Motoyasu had been taken completely by the curse series and now saw all women as pigs. The fact he didn't respond to anything Melty had asked him meant he couldn't even hear what they were saying. Dammit, I just wished he'd stop saying bizarre stuff to confuse us!

Where, then, did he obtain his three filolials? If I had to make a guess . . . Yes, just before encountering Motoyasu again, the slave trader had been acting a bit odd. He'd definitely been avoiding meeting my eyes. Damn slave trader! I'd make him pay for this!

"Well then, father-in-law. Time for us to race, I say!" Motoyasu proclaimed.

"Why?!" I shouted.

"There's a goal in the pass up ahead that will act as our destination," Motoyasu continued, oblivious. "The one who reaches it first will get to steal away an angel from the other racer. Are we agreed?"

"No, we're not. You don't get to decide that!" I raged.

"Motty, are we going yet?" the red one asked.

"Soon, soon, I say," Motoyasu replied. Motty? Is that what they called him?!

Those three colors too—red, blue, and green. They reminded me of the starters from a monster-raising game. All he needed was a yellow one and he'd have the full set . . . Ah, and Filo was golden in her human form, which I guessed counted as yellow.

"Let the race begin, I say!" Motoyasu enthused.

"H-hey! Listen to me for a moment!" Before my words

even reached him though, Motoyasu was heading back the way he came. Those three young girls trotting along and sounding so happy was like something scraping at the surface of my eyes.

If this was happening in my world, he'd already be in jail.

Still, at least he was consistent. I remembered him racing before. Back then he'd been riding a knight's dragon. Hadn't Witch made him do it?

In any case, this looked like the rematch. Was Filo really going to have to race Motoyasu?

"W-what should we do?" Melty asked.

"Ignore him and leave?" I asked hopefully.

"Which would mean we lose the race, wouldn't it? What about the request?" Melty pressed me.

"I don't know. I don't care either. Just talking to him was enough. Time to claim the reward," I stubbornly insisted. That Fitoria! Making Filo and Melty a little stronger wasn't going to make us even for all this. I was going to have to ask for a bigger reward. We didn't have the strength to handle this.

A tactical retreat was in order to come back with Ren and Itsuki.

"Huh? What's the meaning of all this?" Filo asked.

"The thing is, Filo, if you lose to that Spear Hero, you will become his," Melty gently explained.

"That's the short of it. Thanks for everything, Filo," Atla cut in.

"Atla, that really wasn't called for . . ." Raphtalia chided.

"This is all a bit scary," Ruft ventured, watching the others squabble while he clung onto Raph-chan. There was no need to be so scared.

"What?!" she exclaimed. It sounded like Filo had finally realized what the details were of this proposed race. "No way!"

"Uwah!" Melty yelped.

Filo, suddenly desperate not to lose, took off on her running rampage. The next moment, Melty's screams echoed out and it seemed that Filo had accepted the race.

However, considering how far behind we now were, we were also losing. Badly.

What course was this race even taking? Motoyasu had all the advantages. These mountains were his home turf, right?

I brought up the map . . . As we rattled along though, it was so hard to read! Anyway, when I spread the map out . . . there was just a twisting mountain path, which looked completely unsuited to any kind of "race." Much of the path was created along the contours of the mountains, creating what we would call a "trail" in my world.

Filo looked like she wanted to do this, so I decided to give her some support. It wasn't like he'd said we couldn't use magic.

Still, would Zweite Aura be enough to catch up? Ah crap. Without Sadeena, I couldn't use Descent of the Thunder God. Was there anyone in my current party who could stand in?

Melty was water-based, so maybe she could use similar magic. Raphtalia and Raph-chan were totally different, so I'd have no luck with them. But hold on. When I most recently tried to cast Aura, I'd sensed the same kind of feeling as when I'd done it with Ost.

I took a deep breath and started to incant the magic. I felt like I was finally capable of pulling off the stuff that Ost had taught me. I reviewed everything I knew, turning it over in my mind. Way of the Dragon Vein involved incanting by receiving power from the media that provided it. In this case, that was external life force. Along with that, I also drew out some SP—the power of my shield.

The magic, meanwhile, was internal magic. I stocked that in a separate vessel. I drew out the life force and then, following the lead of the power, called up the puzzle pieces. At the same time, I imagined the magic incantation.

Three puzzle pieces that I had to connect appeared close to me.

This was the feeling! More, more, I wanted more magical knowledge.

"Mr. Naofumi? I sense a powerful flow of energy from you at the moment. Could it be . . ." Raphtalia had noticed that something was going on, at least.

"I sense warm power flowing out from you, Master Naofumi! Something incredible is about to happen!" Atla enthused.

"I don't care about that! Can someone stop all this shaking!" Melty yelled.

"W-w-waaah!" That sounded like Ruft.

"Raph!" Raph-chan responded. I opened my eyes a little and looked at the two of them. Ruft had clearly tumbled out of the wagon, and the now large-sized Raph-chan had safely grabbed him.

"I, the Shield Hero, order heaven and order earth. Cut free the bonds of truth, reconnect them, and spout forth pus. Power of the Dragon Vein, I, the one formed of magic and the power of the hero, the source of your power, the Shield Hero, now orders you. Reconsider the state of all things once more and provide my intended target with everything."

I reflected all of my past experience with the spell. I was starting to understand the differences between using Way of the Dragon Vein and regular magic.

While they were rooted in a very similar place, the level of difficulty was completely different because magic that involved inscribing the magic lettering onto your own power to trigger it placed its focus on ease of activation. Learning more advanced forms of magic meant having to register it to yourself first. While it was simple to use, on the flipside of that, it could take a long time to read magic intended to interrupt that of an enemy.

On the other hand, the Way of the Dragon Vein involved conducting power from close by, and so you needed to calculate the forms for yourself. That was why you couldn't just use the same form. You weren't incanting the same elements each time, and so the pieces you were combining the magic from kept changing.

A good analogy, perhaps, was the difference between languages and mathematics.

If you were incanting magic to unleash a blazing fire, for a regular spell you just had to simply read the word for "blazing fire." But if you wanted a small fire or a complete conflagration, those were different words. So you had to learn those too.

However, when using Way of the Dragon Vein, you just had to produce a formula with a product that equaled fire. The calculation could be "fire" + "oil," or they could be "conflagration" plus "water."

Maybe that was why blocking it was pretty easy too. All you needed to do was guess ahead in the magic they were trying to read and force the answer first.

That also explained why it was useful in cooperative magic, because it meant you could still complete the spell even if you didn't solve all the puzzles alone.

However, I had also just discovered that you couldn't mix these two together and incant them at the same time. While magic and the Way of the Dragon Vein were in principle incredibly close to each other, they were as incompatible as water and oil and couldn't be mixed together.

However, SP and life force . . . EP was capable of mixing these two oil-and-water types of magic.

In other words, this was magic that only a hero could use.

Right. I completed the power and activated it.

"Liberation Aura!" Ost, my friend! I'd finally reached the point of using this magic for myself! Your efforts were not in vain!

That said, Ost might not have been too pleased to see me using it on Filo in order to defeat Motoyasu.

"Go! Filo!" I shouted, designating her the recipient of the Liberation Aura. With this, I could now use this power without having to pay any significant cost!

"Here I go!" Filo started to run at multiple times her previous speed!

"Filo! Use the center of gravity of the wagon to take the curves while maintaining this speed," I ordered her.

"Sure thing!" she replied. That suggestion from me was all it took for Filo to start drifting the wagon!

Just how was she doing that? I was extremely worried that the axles were going to break.

That said, Motoyasu was doing the same thing. He was tearing along ahead of us and was so far away that flight was still probably the only way to catch him. Motoyasu was also cornering while drifting his wagon.

It looked like Filo was actually faster, but her opponents

knew the course well, and with our delay in starting, it was still unlikely we'd be able to catch them.

"Right! Left! The right fork is faster there!" I gave instructions, map in one hand. It wasn't easy to do since we were still bouncing along. Our wagon was made of wood too and had quite a few people aboard it.

If we needed more speed, maybe I shouldn't have brought so many people with me.

"Hey, Filo," I began.

"What?" she replied, even as she ran. In the back of the clattering wagon, everyone else was just clinging on for dear life, desperate not to be thrown out.

"You think maybe we could leave the cart and chase them without it?" I suggested.

"No way!" she quickly shot back.

"Why not?" I inquired.

"This is my race! I can't leave the cart behind during my race!" she explained.

"Hmmm." What was this, some kind of instinctive battle between filolials?

When I gave it some more thought, maybe we should lose to Motoyasu on purpose, and then Filo would become his . . . but since she had sworn loyalty to me, that wouldn't work. So instead I should somehow get an exemption from that rule. Then I could dangle Filo like a carrot in front of a horse and lead him along into whatever I wanted!

"Master, you're thinking something naughty, aren't you!" Filo shouted. What, did Filo have eyes in the back of her head?

"Naofumi, for the sake of all that's holy, will you stop making that face when you're brewing up some kind of scheme?!" Melty added. Gah, it looked like they were all on to me.

"Mr. Naofumi! Filo, you too. Just try to stay calm!" Raphtalia's voice was more panicked than either of us; I was the picture of composure.

Now we were coming up to a rope bridge made of vines.

"H-hold on, Naofumi! That looks like a rope bridge!" Melty had spotted it too.

"Yeah. I reckon Filo can handle it," I replied, still calm. Liberation had given her an unholy boost in speed; it was quite incredible. She had her skills too. Nothing to worry about.

Even if she did screw up and we fell, we could just use a portal to fly back to safety. The wagon . . . would have to fend for itself.

"Raaaaaagh!" Filo headed out onto the bridge without a moment's hesitation. We immediately started to hear the popping sounds of vines breaking along the bottom of the bridge. Melty let out a scream that almost popped my eardrums. Even more amazing was that Raphtalia screamed as well—my name—long and loud.

At their screams, Atla darted her head around and took hold of my sleeve.

"E-everything is okay, isn't it, Master Naofumi?" she tentatively asked.

"Yeah," I replied with confidence.

"G-good. What's gotten into those two?" she inquired.

"I don't rightly know. Maybe they should have more trust in Filo?" I prompted. But they just kept screaming. Indeed, perhaps now also enraged by my comment, Melty grabbed me and started shaking even as she screamed.

"This is impossible! We'll fall! We have to get out of here!" she managed.

"Raaaaaagh!" Filo plowed onward. With a definite snapping noise, the thickest vine supporting the bridge gave way.

"It's broken!" Raphtalia screamed. Honestly, I thought she'd hold up better in a crisis than this.

Filo accelerated away even faster, and for a moment I thought she was leaving the cart behind. Then she grabbed a vine supporting the bridge at high speed and kicked out at the wagon catching up behind her, knocking it over to the other side.

"Guwaaah!" Everyone inside the cart was slammed into the wall, suffering various bumps and bruises as a result.

"Yaah!" Having released the vine, Filo gave a cry as she used her mighty legs to propel herself after the wagon, catching up and then setting off once again.

"Uwah. I don't think one life will be enough for this race,"

Raphtalia bemoaned.

"What a coincidence. I was thinking the same thing," I confided in her.

"If you think that, pay more attention to the course!" she raged.

"If we hadn't just done that, we wouldn't have a hope of winning!" I shot back. In actual fact, it had proven to be quite the shortcut. We were really catching up now.

Bumped along by the clattering wagon, I checked the map again. I only had the light of the torches to go by, but Motoyasu looked to still be plenty far ahead. Just how much of a lead had he got on us?

I guess there was a reason he called himself "street racer." Shit, maybe he was even using his own secret shortcuts.

"We've got a nightmare five-curve hairpin coming up. Watch out for that," I warned. Just the image on the map was terrifying; one wrong step and we'd be taking a new shortcut straight down the mountain.

I certainly had no recollection of arriving in a race game world.

"I'm on it!" Filo proceeded to use jumps to leap over each of the curves of each hairpin. The wagon sounded like it didn't agree with that decision. In fact, it felt like a blender that was about to break apart, with Raphtalia and the others getting blended inside.

"Waah, aaah!" Ruft was having the hardest time of it, and Raph-chan had grown large in order to hold onto and try to stabilize him.

"Aaagh . . . Raph!" Raphtalia shouted as she herself risked tipping over the side.

"Raph?" Luckily, the oversized Raph-chan used her tail to grab Raphtalia. The thing that caught my attention most, however, was what Raphtalia had just said. Could it be that, in moments of crisis, she also made a "raph" sound?

Nah, probably not. She'd likely just been calling to Raph-chan for aid.

Raph-chan also looked over at Melty, bouncing around in the wagon, perhaps thinking about helping her. But she was bouncing so hard there was probably little she could do. I decided to try and hold her in place using two Float Shields, but—

"Owww!" Ah, I hit her with one of them. Well, so long as she held onto it!

"This is quite thrilling," Atla exclaimed. For some reason, she wasn't being shaken around at all, riding the bumps as though she was carved out of the wood of the wagon.

Being in the driver's seat, I had a much better time of things.

Maybe it was thanks to her magic and life force. But no, that should mean Raphtalia would be okay too.

I would have liked to help them all, but if I let go of the

reins, I risked getting thrown out myself. If that happened, with my high defenses I'd probably survive . . . but we'd also probably lose the race. Raph-chan was helping Raphtalia, so it looked like she'd be okay for now.

"I never dreamed that Raph-chan would be saving me," Raphtalia commented.

"Raph," Raph-chan offered, hugging Ruft to her tummy and giving Raphtalia a peace sign.

"Uhh . . . I'm gonna die. I'm seriously gonna die," Melty moaned, clinging to the Float Shields and offering up some uncharacteristic childlike whining. I wanted to say: *You were the one who started this! Put up with it!*

She should be grateful to the world in which she was born and the blessings of Fitoria that she could take a beating like this without dying, honestly.

"If you don't like it, you'll just have to send Filo to Motoyasu," I reminded her.

"No!" Melty adamantly replied.

"Choosing to prioritize friendship? See, you'll make a great queen," I remarked.

"Hearing that doesn't make me happy at all. In this situation, not at all!" she sullenly replied. The back of the wagon was starting to look like nothing more than a pile of corpses though. It might have been better to bring Wyndia and Gaelion along after all.

I could at least let these guys out . . .

"Wouldn't it be better if you guys got out?" I suggested.

"How are we meant to do that?!" Melty retorted.

"Use magic!" Seemed simple enough to me.

"I can't use magic under these conditions!" Melty shouted back.

"Sure you can. I know. Shoot some water magic and use the reaction to push you out. How about that?" Seemed like a valid idea to me.

"You've got to be kidding!" she replied.

"Not at all. I'm being totally serious here," I told her. That seemed like a pretty basic escape method that Melty could possibly use.

"That look in your eye . . . you really are serious! I really have to do this? To save the world?" Melty was incredulous.

"I mean, if you're asking if you really have to do it, I've got nothing for you," I admitted. I was simply postulating one way she might escape the wagon without dying.

"Mr. Naofumi! That's quite enough messing—" Raphtalia started. Whatever.

We really were catching up anyway, but the goal was also drawing closer. We were going to lose at this rate.

Ah! From beyond the cliff, I saw the light of Motoyasu's speeding wagon. We still had to go all the way around to reach that point. If we could just jump across to there, we could win with ease, but it was too much to expect that.

"Filo, you can see the light on the cliff over there, right?" I asked her. "Just below that is the goal. At the moment, we're going to lose!"

"Don't want to!" That was her almost petulant reply. Filo proceeded to leave the course . . . over the cliff!

"That's a cliff! A cliff! Filo, we can't fly! We're going to faaaaaaaaaaaaaall!" Melty screamed. The timing here was key. Could Filo make it?

"Yah!" With a cry, she grabbed the roof of the cart and flapped her wings. An incredible wind whipped up around us, with an accompanying incredible whooshing sound! Was Filo really going to fly? I did recall her hopping about a little when bickering with Gaelion.

Man, in Kizuna's world, she'd actually flown.

Oh? She was successfully hovering in the air.

"Waooooh!" She was doing more of a penguin than an eagle though. Was her plan just to make a gradual shortcut across like this?

It was a real gamble as to whether it would work or not. The chances of it failing seemed far higher. She was gradually losing height. Filo's body just wasn't made for flight.

Was it her weight? But Gaelion could fly and look at him. Messed up. That was other-worldly physics for you. And yet filolials couldn't fly!

Shildina had been flying around, hadn't she? And Sadeena in beast transformation too. Boy, these poor filolials really had got the short end of the stick.

I decided to help her out.

"Air Strike Shield! Second Shield!" I sent out the two shields, one after the other, right at the limit of their range. The goal was beyond the cliff ahead.

And then—

"Change Shield!" I selected the Rope Shield. It had a hook as its special effect. That was added when it awakened. The hook could be used to launch a rope from the shield and pull things in. I also had the Chimera Viper Shield, but the range on that hook was shorter.

What this all meant was that I could use the Rope Shield to make hooks appear on the distant shields and then draw the wagon toward them. Then, using the principle of a pendulum, we could swing over to the Second Shield.

"Shield Prison!" Furthermore, I created a Shield Prison below the wagon.

"Filo!" I commanded.

"Got you!" she replied. Filo kicked the wagon and we reached the distant cliff. Using the Prison as fresh footing, she started running again.

"One life . . . really is not enough for this race." Melty was rolling listlessly on the wagon bed. Honestly, I felt almost the same. I certainly wasn't going to take Filo racing again any time soon.

If there ever was another race, I'd leave Filo behind completely and just use Portal Shield.

"We're going to die! Mr. Naofumi. Seriously, this is going to get us killed! One hundred percent!" Raphtalia shouted.

"No way! We've handled fated battles with the high priest, the Spirit Tortoise, and Kyo! A mere race isn't going to take us down!" I went hard with my reply.

"Yes, it is! We're going to die. This is too dangerous!" Raphtalia was on the verge of tears. Maybe it was actually pretty dangerous. I'd been rattling along thinking of it as just playing a race game. Maybe I needed a little more self-awareness.

Below the cliff was pitch black, anyway. It wasn't like you could see anything down there.

"Don't worry. We're almost there," I reassured her.

"That was quite the thrilling attraction," Atla offered.

"This isn't some traveling circus!" Raphtalia sniped back. I guessed they wouldn't call it a "theme park" here. I'd have to ask what this "circus" entailed later.

In any case, with this massive shortcut, Motoyasu should now be far behind us. We passed through torches intended to indicate the goal and came to a stop.

"We won," I said, sounding pleased. It had seemed impossible after all the time we lost at the start, but Filo had pulled out all the stops. The downward curve of our bad luck had finally taken an uptick.

The three filolials with Motoyasu had been in human form, meaning they could also turn into filolial queens, although they hadn't had any of the cowlicks.

"Uhh . . ." Melty moaned.

"W-we survived. That was the most thrilling experience of my life," Raphtalia offered.

"Really?" I asked.

"Your mental fortifications are lacking, Raphtalia," Atla chided.

"And I'm fine with that. If you can just sit there without reacting to that, something is wrong with you on a fundamental level," Raphtalia replied. It sounded pretty convincing, coming from her.

"I won!" Filo was up on the roof of the wagon, dancing around and singing. What was it, some kind of official ceremony?

In any case, the wagon itself was pretty much scrap. It was a broken-down cart now, little more. We did pretty well to win in this thing, I reflected.

I was going to have to order a new one. It was made of wood, so it should be pretty cheap. I could see if Rat could make one at the bioplant or maybe get a ship out of Siltvelt to pick one up for us.

"I won! I won! A win for Filo! I'm the fastest! I won't lose to Gaelion!" Filo's singing was ongoing.

"Don't get too excited," I told her.

"I won't! But I won!" She wasn't stopping anytime soon. She really didn't like Gaelion either, did she?

It wasn't long before Motoyasu and his own yapping three-some tore into view.

"I . . . I lost, you say?" he lamented. Having confirmed that we arrived first, he slumped down to the ground.

Chapter Six: The Love Hunter

"The winner gets to take one filolial from the loser, correct?" I reconfirmed. It wasn't like I really needed one of them, but that was the agreement. The whole point of this thing had been to bring Motoyasu back into the fold.

Of the three of them, Green looked to be the easiest to handle.

"Right. I'll take the most peaceful looking-one of them . . . Green. Hand her over," I proclaimed.

"No waaaaaaaaaaaay! No way you're having Green!" Motoyasu lost it, grabbing all three of them protectively.

"Seriously?" He was the one who set this whole thing up, and then when he lost, he wanted to back out? Filo was more than enough. Another one? God forbid.

I just wanted a regular filolial, like the ones in the village.

Nope, not even that. Now that we had the ability to class up into the Raph species, I didn't need any more filolials at all actually.

"Heheheheh . . ." If I did class the new one up, I'd turn into a Raph-mix!

"Mr. Naofumi, stop making that face. It makes me afraid for the future." Raphtalia always said things along those lines, and I just ignored her. The moment this new filolial came under my control, it would be fated to become one of the Raph species.

"Motty!" Crimmy whined.

"Moomoo!" bellowed Marine.

"Mr. Motoyasu!" Green cried. Couldn't they even decide on what to call him?! I decided not to say anything. It was likely to just make them even noisier, and I was no stranger to having lots of different people call me lots of different things.

The three of them were all clinging to Motoyasu and crying together.

"Enough, enough. Just don't cause any more hassle for us," I said. That was it, then. Mission completed. Now, by bringing Motoyasu back in, it was finished.

"Father-in-law!" Motoyasu implored me. The guy was truly broken. Bowing low to me, groveling, he asked, "Please let me have your daughter!"

"Not this again!" I was at a loss. Seriously, what an absolute pain this guy was. After losing the race, he still comes out with this?

"Uhh . . . I'm finally starting to feel better," Raphtalia said.

"Then I'm one step ahead of you," Atla replied smugly.

"What's that supposed to mean? You can handle wagon rides well, can't you?" Raphtalia admitted.

"I did get dizzy, but I just put up with it," Atla explained.

"So you did feel sick! You just pushed through it! Because

of your history with sickness?!" Raphtalia exclaimed. They sounded like a bad comedy duo, going back and forth.

"Raph-chan, thank you," Ruft offered.

"Raph!" The boy looked like he was in good shape, Raph-chan having protected him, although maybe he looked a little pale around the gills.

"Uph . . . I feel awful." Melty didn't have to say anything for that to be clear. Meanwhile, the three around Motoyasu were saying things similar to Filo.

In the end, they were all pretty much the same.

"Boo to you! You lost, so get lost!" Filo proclaimed from on high.

"Sorry, but I can't just let you leave," I chipped in. I wanted to bring them back into the fold, or at least set up cooperation between us, and it would be a real big problem if he didn't show up when called for.

"You're not going to ask for the wagon back?" Motoyasu asked.

"I don't want it, now that it looks like that . . . Ohhh!" Filo sounded dejected, this victory not having taken the edge off the transformation her wagon had undergone. I mean, if something of mine had been stolen from me and then came back looking like that, I'd probably feel much the same way.

"Hear me, Filo-tan! Feel the depth of my feelings!" Motoyasu shouted. Without any warning, Motoyasu suddenly twirled his spear and struck a pose. This energy . . . could it be?!

"Temptation!" Motoyasu shouted. With a crackle, I felt something like a barrier expanding out from him. I remembered experiencing this before. It was a skill Motoyasu had used when he captured Ren.

Whne I thought back to that situation, Raphtalia, Atla, and I hadn't really been affected. We just had to withstand the effects of him becoming even more handsome than normal—super handsome—and start to . . . sparkle a little.

That meant Melty and Ruft were in the most danger!

"Melty! Are you okay?!" I looked over at Melty and the others.

"Ah, uhn. I'm okay . . . I did think he looked cool just for a moment, but I'm okay now. More than that, I just feel sick . . ." Melty was close to her limit.

"I wish I could say that wasn't okay, but he does have a handsome face. I can't deny that," I consoled her.

"What a sad reality we live in," Melty said. It was true. Even from a male perspective, Motoyasu had striking good looks. There was nothing wrong with that part of him.

It was his inside that was all messed up.

I was starting to think that if only he hadn't put his trust in Witch, he might have ended up as just a passionate guy with a love for the ladies and a deep trust for his allies. Maybe this was just an expression of my sympathy at how changed he had become.

Melty had resisted the effects anyway, by the skin of her teeth. Next then, Ruft . . .

"Ruft! Are you okay?!" I asked.

"R-Raph-chan . . . I love you," he said.

"Raph?" was the quizzical reply she gave. Unsteady on his feet, Ruft loosened his hold on Raph-chan and looked around, as though coming back to himself.

"Huh?" Ruft asked. So Raphtalia could withstand it but Ruft couldn't? Was it simply due to the difference in their levels and abilities? It looked like Raph-chan had released him from the status effect.

"No matter what happens, I am focused entirely on you, Master Naofumi." This from Atla, who was reading the situation and making her own contribution. The temptation skill was probably having some effect, but Motoyasu was normally so out there it felt more like a calculating move on his part.

"Glad to hear it," I blew her off. Motoyasu was the issue. What the hell was he trying to pull?!

I'd been wondering about it when we handled Ren too . . . but now he seemed more open to me, so I guessed it was worth asking.

"Tell me something. What's with that spear?" I asked.

"This is my Last Spear IV, father-in-law," he explained. IV?! Just how loopy was the poor guy? He was able to reply even with Temptation active too?

Hold on. I played it back in my mind. He didn't say "last." Of course he didn't.

Lust Spear. Okay. That made a lot more sense.

"Father-in-law, if Filo-tan so desires it, please agree to my engagement with her," he persisted.

"You're just brainwashing her with your Temptation skill, surely," I accused him.

"That's not the case at all! This is a skill that imparts the depth of my love to Filo-tan!" he insisted.

"You're having an effect on the other women too—even on the men," I pointed out. I mean, it had been a convenient skill for catching Ren when he tried to run away. It had worked on those enemies of S'yne's too, which meant it was definitely for the best that S'yne wasn't here.

Anyway, I had to wonder what he was doing using brainwashing skills. I'd made it clear how shielded I was from being brainwashed, so why try this again? Before getting broken, Motoyasu had always been babbling on about brainwashing. That much was true.

"I need only the love of Filo-tan and my other filolials, I say!" Motoyasu proclaimed.

"Yeah, good for you," I muttered. This guy just wouldn't quit. My sentiment was: whatever then, you win. I just wanted to go home.

That said, Filo was strangely silent. She'd fallen for this skill before.

"Filo?" I asked. All I got back was heavy breathing. She'd fallen for it. Love had blossomed. That was what Motoyasu had been after. It was over. I just had to give up.

"Master, I want you," she managed. So it hadn't worked on Motoyasu. That reminded me of the last time she had looked at me and breathed in much the same way.

"Raph." The still big-sized Raph-chan stepped up, Ruft on her back, and placed her paw on Filo's forehead.

"Wha-wah?" Filo came back to herself from the state of temptation.

"Raph, raph," Raph-chan soothed her.

"Huh . . . that was a little scary," Ruft said. Raph-chan lifted him over onto Filo's back, then changed back to regular size and also jumped onto Filo's back, allowing both Filo and Ruft to stroke her.

"Filo-tan, my darling! I'm here for you, I say!" Motoyasu shouted.

Ignoring the audible jealousy of his own tri-colored harem, Motoyasu threw his arms wide and waited for Filo to jump into them.

Could alluring someone using the power of his spear really be called love?

"Boo!" Filo promptly rejected him, as I expected she would. "I want to be with Master!"

"Hey, you didn't need that last part!" I chided her. Motoyasu put the tip of his flag in his mouth and tugged it downward as hard as he could, glaring at me with jealousy burning in his eyes.

"You did this!" I reminded him. "Stop looking at me like that!"

"Curse you, father-in-law! Father and child, that is a crime! I'm not jealous of that, I say!" he shouted back.

"Don't you try to take the high ground with me, you moron!" I retorted.

"What's with this lack of tension in the air?" Raphtalia wondered.

"Filo, you'd better just give up to Master Naofumi," Atla chimed in.

"What are you talking about, Atla?" Raphtalia asked her. That was the right question to ask in this situation. Just what was Atla talking about?

"I'm jealous, so jealous! So jealous over the love of Filo-tan!" Motoyasu was still having a moment.

"Shut it! Some things just should not be said out loud!" I shouted. I was at a loss. Raphtalia was right; where was the tension? The consideration for others?

"Filo-tan!" Motoyasu leapt at Filo head-on, using his best Lupin III dive. It was almost too fast to see—was this another facility of his cursed spear?!

"No! Master, Mel-chan, save me!" Filo gave her standard cries in times of distress. Had Melty ever saved her? Yeah, of course. She'd been with us when we fought the Demon Dragon.

"Filo is worn out from that race! Not to mention barely able to stand, thanks to you!" I shouted.

"Hold on! Mel-chan? Who's that?" Motoyasu had a delayed reaction to that name.

"Uh . . . what is it?" Melty managed in response, shaking her head multiple times to try and end Motoyasu's hold on her. I pointed at her, trying to make things clear to Motoyasu.

"This is Melty—Mel-chan," I told him.

"What do you want?" she croaked.

"Filo-tan! You're here with your fiancé, so why are you calling the name of someone else?" The gall of the guy! Since when did he become her fiancé? "Huh?" he continued. "Now that I look closer, I see you are the younger sister of the red pig . . . I understand why you are a blue pig then, but if Filo-tan would call you for aid, then you can't be a pig at all!" Oh? Being involved with Filo removed the status of pig?

The "red pig" had to be Witch. She had red hair, after all.

I was going to have to look into all of this a little more. Just because we knew he was cursed didn't mean we knew what to do about it. I was pretty sure I could protect everyone from him, but I needed to make sure. Best not to stimulate him unnecessarily.

"Motoyasu, I wasn't sure if I could tell you this or not, but . . . Filo already has a fiancé," I carefully explained.

"Which is me, right, father-in-law?" he replied.

"No," I said, a little bluntly.

"What?" Motoyasu's expression, which had been looking pretty happy, quickly crumbled. The fact he had believed so strongly that he was her fiancé was clearly the bigger problem here. As if I would accept that!

"Her name is Melty Melromarc. She's the next queen of this land and Filo's fiancé," I said.

"What?!" Motoyasu was aghast.

"Hold it, Naofumi. I've got a bad feeling about this," Melty said.

Motoyasu was no longer able to tell right from wrong, which meant I needed to remove Melty as a possible target for his attacks without overtly stimulating him.

"Excuse me, but what should we be doing?" Raphtalia and Atla were both pretty puzzled by this turn of events, but they'd be fine. I'd just have them recover themselves while they could.

"Incredible! Filo-tan's boundless love extends not only to you, father-in-law, but even to women! Ah, she's truly an angel of love, so say we all!" Motoyasu enthused. I decided to overlook her transformation into an "angel of love." Maybe that was the name of the videogame character he had previously mentioned being his type.

"But hold on . . . You're talking about the sister of the red pig?" Motoyasu realized.

"Yes, but she's completely different from the worthless Witch! A most capable young woman and next in line for the throne. I'm sure that Melty can be trusted with Filo. Do you think you can defeat her?" I asked.

"Naofumi! Stop this at once! It's going to end up with me skewered on that spear!" Melty bemoaned.

"Just leave it to me," I reassured her. "I've got an idea."

"Nothing you could have said would make me worry more!" she fired back. Ignoring her worries, I turned back to face Motoyasu.

"Motoyasu, don't you dare think about ending Melty," I threatened. "If you do, Filo's rage will know no bounds! She will hate you forever!"

"That's right! I'll never forgive you if you do anything to Mel-chan!" Filo added.

"Filo, please don't upset the Spear Hero any more than this!" Melty pleaded.

"T-this can't be . . ." Motoyasu muttered. I was really hoping that would mark the end to his rampage. "I'm so jealous! So jealous, I say! So jealous of Filo-tan loving you!" Motoyasu proceeded to grab onto Filo like a child and throw what could really only be called a tantrum.

What was he doing at his age?

"Hey! Get off!" Filo shouted.

"Yeah, get off her! At least let Raph-chan and Ruft go!" I said, making my priorities clear.

"What about Filo?" Melty asked.

"Motoyasu won't hurt Filo," I explained.

"Raph?" Raph-chan questioned.

"Should I be getting away with Raph-chan?" Ruft asked.

"Raph, raph," Raph-chan seemed to explain, tapping Filo on the back. If she moved away now, Filo might end up under the effects of Temptation.

"Master! Mel-chan!" Filo herself called for aid again. The accessory for protecting against status effects wasn't ready yet. I really needed to get on that . . . and then I had a thought.

"Whenever she gets into trouble, Filo only ever calls for Melty or me, right?" I said.

"What are you talking about? Naofumi, hurry up and save her!" Melty moaned.

"If we take Motoyasu down by force, Filo, Raph-chan, and Ruft could be put in danger. As I was trying not to get him too upset, I just had that thought," I explained. Thinking on it again now, whenever Filo got into trouble, she only called for Melty or me. If she wanted aid from her friends, those she'd shared the good and the bad with until now, at least one other name should come out.

"Why doesn't she call for Raphtalia?" I asked.

"Mr. Naofumi, please don't drag me into this!" Raphtalia chided.

"Raphtalia! My big sister! Save me!" Filo shouted, almost in the same moment.

"And don't you suddenly start calling for me either, Filo!" Raphtalia retorted.

"Filo-tan, did you really just call that pig your sister?" Motoyasu asked.

"Hah! Don't talk to me!" Filo responded. Rejected by her, Motoyasu turned to look at Melty.

"Hey, fiancé! Filo-tan really did call her 'sister,' didn't she?" he questioned.

"I'm no one's fiancé!" Melty explained, exasperated. "You still believe those lies from Naofumi? How is this conversation still going?!"

"Mr. Naofumi, if I take him on using the sakura stone of destiny sword, I think maybe I can stop him," Raphtalia posited. The abilities of a pacifier could very well cause massive damage to Motoyasu. That said, we were still really just talking with him . . . right? I signaled Melty with my eyes.

Melty gave a big sigh, nodded, and explained, "About the question you just asked, yes. Raphtalia is like a big sister to Filo."

"Now you're putting this on me?!" Raphtalia fumed. It sounded like Melty had scored quite the goal! I almost wanted to make that quip but wasn't sure anyone would get it.

"I-is that so? Filo-tan's beautiful sister!" Motoyasu, without batting an eyelid, now started to praise Raphtalia, whom just a moment ago he'd been calling a pig.

Just how messed up was his head? Was it time to just stop

all this chatter, beat him senseless, and drag him back with us?

But hold on. Raphtalia proceeded to address Motoyasu, seemingly having had a good idea.

"Spear Hero, please let Filo go. Do you seek to bind her completely with your love?" she asked him.

"Ah! Whatever am I doing?" Motoyasu immediately stopped grabbing Filo and . . . What? Came back to himself?

Ah, Raphtalia! An excellent approach. Filo had been saved from Motoyasu's clutches. Finally free, she came over between Melty and me and hid—well, tried to hide—behind me.

"Thanks, sis," she managed.

"Should I bring up how you only thank me at times like this?" Raphtalia asked.

"Mel-chan! Oooh!" Half-crying, Filo moved over to lean on Melty. Motoyasu looked on, visibly grinding his teeth. Huh? An even thicker black smoke than before seemed to be pouring from his spear.

"Motoyasu, change that spear to something else!" I barked.

"What are you talking about, father-in-law? This spear appeared as a manifestation of my love for Filo-tan. I couldn't possibly change it," he exclaimed. That caused Filo to hide behind me again. She was like a terrified child, even if she was in her filolial queen form.

"No! Filo-tan!" Motoyasu suddenly gave a roar, close to a primal scream, and dashed toward us.

"Now!" Atla cried, and then she grabbed onto me. Dammit! Would everyone just get their hands off me?

"Atla! What are you doing?" Raphtalia accused, but that wasn't the problem. Motoyasu was standing in front of us, as though to protect Filo from me. Then he looked at Filo and shouted.

"No, Filo-tan! Incest is wrong, I say!"

"We aren't actually related!" I shouted in exasperation. "How many times do I have to tell you this?!" I really couldn't take any more of this situation.

"Shall we just cut him down?" Raphtalia suggested as she drew her sword from her scabbard. She also seemed to be reaching her limit.

"Might be the time," I concurred.

"Filo-tan! No!" Motoyasu shouted.

"No to you! Ah, Mel-chan!" Filo pleaded.

"Now you're coming to me?!" Melty exclaimed.

"Nuah! I will stop you slipping into the path of evil, no matter what!" Motoyasu raved. Yeah, okay. Time to cut him down and resolve this.

"Nuwaaah! Father-in-law, I'm so jealous of yoooooou! Having my fiancé Filo-tan caring for you so much, it makes me maaaaaad! That's what I think!" He'd really lost it.

"Shut it! This is exactly the kind of reason why Filo hates you!" I pointed out.

"Shall we do this?" Raphtalia asked Atla.

"Yes, we agree for once," she replied. They both prepared to fight.

So it was always going to end up this way.

"I'm so jealous . . ." he began to shout.

What now?! A black aura erupted from Motoyasu's spear. The aura turned into a thick fog-like state, making the tip of the spear even harder to see than before. The pixelated effect—it might be called—had been visible on the weapon when we saw him before, and now it looked even bigger and more pronounced.

"Wh . . . wh . . ." I turned at the voice to see Melty blushing bright red. "What the hell kind of spear are you carrying around?! Ah! It's been that shape the whole time tonight?! I didn't realize because I didn't get a good look at it!" Melty's high-pitched voice echoed out.

"Hold on . . . What do you see, Melty?" I asked her, not sure I wanted an answer.

"You can't see it, Naofumi?" she questioned back.

"From the last time we met, just the tip of his spear was pixelated—I mean, blurred." It looked like the shape had changed a bit since then too. With the pixelation, I couldn't really tell.

"Why can't you see it?" Melty asked.

"Who knows." I changed track. "Raphtalia, what shape is it?" Being unable to see it was actually making me more interested. Why was I the only one who couldn't see it?

Raphtalia just turned her face to the side without saying anything. Her face looked red too.

"That's sexual harassment! If it wasn't you, Naofumi, I'd be punishing you for this! You're just saying you can't see it to embarrass me, aren't you?!" Melty accused.

"Sexual harassment? Seriously?" Just what shape was this thing? I looked at Ruft, and he was rubbing his eyes and repeatedly looking at the spear, much like me. So maybe men couldn't see it?

The things I could think of were . . . Well, the things that would have been pixelated when broadcast on TV—grotesque stuff? No, not likely. Cutting up monsters would be covered with pixelation otherwise.

That meant we were in the territory of the Elizabeth Mikoshi, or that game with the spear called the *Male Thruster*. If I remembered correctly, it did double damage to women.

I checked the shape of Motoyasu's spear again. The shaft part was luridly decorated with a scorpion and snake. But the tip still had the pixelation on it.

"Father-in-law . . ." Amazingly he still called me that, even when he was so deeply possessed by the curse series. In fact, I was almost impressed. I'd even accept being beaten by him now.

Motoyasu . . . I didn't have a grudge against him anymore. I made a declaration. He was so pathetic I could barely bring

myself to look. *Just go*, I wanted to say. *Just leave us alone.*

"I'm taking your daughter. Using my Lust Envy Spear IV," Motoyasu exclaimed. God. This was all depressing me intently.

"Filo-tan! I will stop you and take your purity!" Motoyasu thrust his spear at Filo.

"Boo!" She wasn't interested. Then I noticed what he was pointing at. Below the waist, shall we say.

"Right, we're doing this! Raphtalia, Atla! Bring Motoyasu down!" I ordered.

"Okay!" Raphtalia affirmed.

"Understood!" So did Atla.

So we really were going to have to fight him. Immediately after starting the battle to capture Motoyasu—

"Unleash Ressentiment!" Something else flickered past me. The Temptation had been close to working on me. But the skill this time . . . Hmmm, I kind of recalled being framed by Motoyasu and Witch back then. But that was just my daily dose of grudge-induced bile. Looking at Motoyasu, who had been betrayed and brought so low, had no real effect on it.

In fact, in the next moment I saw Raphtalia's face and then nothing happened. So just what kind of skill had it been?

"Ooh . . . my head feels all funny," Melty moaned, leaning on Filo for support.

"Raphtalia . . . brother . . . how jealous I am of you receiving Master Naofumi's love. Unforgiveable!" Atla started to mutter to herself.

"Ah . . ." Even Raphtalia was holding her chest, suffering.

"Are you okay?!" I asked, mainly directing my comments at Raphtalia.

"I'm f-fine . . . but this isn't easy to bear. It's worse than the Temptation skill," Raphtalia managed.

"What's going on?" I still wasn't really feeling it.

"I think it's something that makes people feel jealousy," Raphtalia managed around her own moaning. Even though she had decent protection against this kind of status effect, she was taking this much damage? What about Filo, Raph-chan, and Ruft then?

"Raph." So Raph-chan seemed fine.

"Mel-chan! Are you okay?" Filo asked. She was more worried about Melty.

"I'm fine," Melty replied. "Don't worry about me, Filo."

"Shield Hero, is there anything I can do?" Ruft bravely asked.

"Nope. Just stay close to Raph-chan and Filo," I told him. Thanks to Raph-chan, it looked like he was holding things together.

Still, if Motoyasu could create a field to cause double status effects, we needed to take him down right away! Everyone had been jealous once or twice in their lives, surely. But this was a mental attack, as I had feared. Why had he unleashed it though?

"My heart . . . grows stronger!" he bellowed. Right. He was

using the power of jealousy to enhance himself. "Now! Fly to my intended! My charging heart of love!" Motoyasu lifted his spear high above his head.

"Haaaaaah!" Amid the entire crazy situation, Atla—perhaps losing her mind entirely—suddenly attacked Raphtalia.

"Watch out!" I warned her. Raphtalia smoothly avoided Atla's incoming strike.

"What do you think you're playing at, Atla?" Raphtalia asked.

"You hoard all of Master Naofumi's affections for yourself . . . No matter how hard I try, I can't become Master Naofumi's shield . . . because you exist, Raphtalia!" On unsteady feet, Atla charged forward, as though in all the world she was only aware of Raphtalia. Motoyasu had really done a number on her feelings of jealousy! Dammit, not the best timing for her to go crazy!

"Raph!" Raph-chan clearly wanted to help, but if she left Filo, that would likely mean Filo would start rampaging. She was totally pinned in place.

This was turning into a real nightmare!

"Raphtalia! Atla! Waaah . . . spear guy, move!" With that, Filo kicked Motoyasu in the chest.

"Guwah . . . I'm so happy to be kicked by you, Filo-tan. It feels as though my heart might burst from your foot pressed against it!" Motoyasu expressed nothing but pleasure at getting his ass kicked, an enrapt expression on his face. I'd clearly heard some nasty sounds when the blow landed too—damn, she still had Liberation Aura on too!

It really showed just how crazy Motoyasu was about Filo.

The situation was certainly not improving anyway.

"Die!" This from among the combined squawking of the three under Motoyasu's control, who had been silent until this moment but now launched an attack on Filo.

"W-what are you doing, my lovelies?" Motoyasu stepped forward to protect Filo. The three of them moved to attack Filo regardless, one ripping off a kick, another using magic, and the third swinging a battleax in human form.

The one kicking was Crimmy, the one incanting magic was Marine, and the human form one with the ax was Green. All of them had a crazy look in their eyes.

"I hate her! She holds all of Motty's love and yet allures other men instead! I hate her so much!" Crimmy cried.

"Moomoo belongs to us!" Marine screamed. At least she was willing to share.

"Yes. I won't accept this interloper!" Green agreed.

"S-stop this! Girls, please!" Motoyasu tried to stop the very thing he had unleashed.

"We want to gobble you up! That bitch is in our way!" they all proclaimed together. Then Motoyasu started fighting the three of them to protect Filo.

While they couldn't match Filo's speed, all three of them were definitely faster than before. Lust was firing them, girded by jealousy—a nasty combination.

Faced with three of them, even Motoyasu was forced almost completely onto the defensive in order to keep Filo safe. They were his precious daughters after all. His was as likely to harm them as he was to harm Filo.

"Atla! Come back to yourself!" Raphtalia had her own problems.

"Raphtalia . . . when I wore the miko outfit from my own race . . . Master Naofumi didn't look at me once," Atla lamented.

"You can't hold me responsible for how other people react!" Raphtalia opined.

"N-Naofumi! What do we do?!" Melty shouted.

"That's what I'd like to know!" I fired back. Look at this mess! Not only was Raphtalia fighting the enraged Atla, but Motoyasu had ended up having to fight his own three filolials, who he had also powered up, while Filo looked on, protecting Raph-chan and Ruft.

How the hell had it come to all of this in such a short space of time?

"Ah! Uh! My angels! Stop this! Nuwaaah! I will protect you, Filo, father-in-law!" Damn, Motoyasu was so loud.

"Motty is mine—"

"No, Moomoo is mine—"

"You're wrong. Mr. Motoyasu is mine—"

The three of them at least agreed on the final part. "That bitch can't have him!" Have at it then!

They all looked like Filo, but without the cowlick. Crimmy mainly used her claws but sometimes spat fire. Could filolials do that? Maybe it was a type of magic.

Marine seemed based mainly in magic, but sometimes she plucked out feathers and threw them like a Feather Shot attack.

Green, meanwhile, had stayed in human form the entire time. Looking just like a human with wings, she swung her battleax around and unleashed magic. She was the one who looked most like a demi-human as she fought. A pretty brassy combat style too, despite how docile she had looked.

All three of them fought very differently from Filo. Was that just down to filolial individuality? I didn't really want to know.

"Gah . . . Atla is attacking with a speed I've never seen before!" Raphtalia interjected from her side of the battle.

"Do you want a hand? Some support magic?" I offered.

"No, Mr. Naofumi. Please stop the Spear Hero as quickly as you can! If he puts that spear away, it might stop all this!" Raphtalia struggled to get that much out, taking Atla's strikes on her blade even as we conversed.

"Haaaaaah!" Atla was totally out of it.

What to do then? Motoyasu and his three opponents

looked like they could go at this all night if someone didn't step in. Stopping Atla's rampage meant first stopping Motoyasu.

It made me want to think about how we reached this situation in the first place.

It was all Motoyasu's fault, of course. Filo also had some of the responsibility for breaking Motoyasu so completely. Somehow I needed to persuade Motoyasu and get him to change that spear, stopping its effects.

I wasn't sure if he would even listen or not, but I had to give it a try.

"Filo," I said.

"What?" she replied. She didn't look happy about this situation.

"Repeat what I'm about to say to Motoyasu!" I ordered her.

"No! Don't want to!" Seriously? Couldn't she see what was going on? Filo was the only one who could bring this situation under control.

We might have been able to stop Motoyasu by force, but it wasn't a sure thing as to whether that would work on him. I needed to shake him mentally.

"If we don't do this, who knows what Motoyasu might do!" I pleaded with her. It was true that his spear was already spitting out more cursed smoke. I really wanted to stop this as quickly, and as peacefully, as possible.

"He's right. Please, Filo, do what Naofumi asks," Melty said, agreeing with me and prompting Filo to resolve the situation.

"Uh . . ." Filo still wasn't sure.

"Raph!"

"Being a hero is real hard work, isn't it?" Ruft noted.

"I guess so," I agreed. Raph-chan and Ruft were a little out of the loop perhaps, but they were still able to read the situation.

The problem was Filo.

"Look, Filo." I changed my approach. "At this rate, we've no idea when Motoyasu may blow up completely. If that happens, I can't guarantee what might happen to you. Do you want to get stabbed by Motoyasu's spear?"

"Stabbed by his spear . . . An interesting choice of words, Naofumi," Melty jibed.

"But I'm not wrong, am I?" I fired back, at which Melty gave an exasperated shake of her head. She must have some idea of what Motoyasu was after.

"No!" Filo shouted.

"Then I need you to do this for me. Raphtalia is really struggling with Atla too." I was watching that battle out of the corner of my eye, Raphtalia desperately fending off Atla's attacks, as I continued to persuade Filo.

What the hell was going on here, seriously? I'd thought this to be a simple request, and look at what it turned into.

Fitoria! You'll pay dearly for this! She'll never hear the last of it.

Putting this one off was absolutely the right thing to have done!

"Stop this, I say!" Motoyasu had been trying to talk his retinue down for the entire time. As if it wasn't all his fault! His own three seemed to be in love with him and so jealous of Filo.

Not that he'd listen even if we said that. So I'd have Filo resolve this.

"Hey! Spear guy, listen!" At Filo's shout, Motoyasu turned around.

"Of course! What is it, sweet Filo?" he asked.

"Right, well," Filo started. "I like platonic relationships. I'm not going to think about anything more until the world is truly at peace." What else? What else was there? "I like people to be loyal, and kind to everyone, and never cheat, and always abide by the conditions of a bet. Also, they need to keep promises, not just pay lip service to them—" I had Filo run down an exhaustive list of all my problems with Motoyasu. Hopefully this would change him . . . The part about Filo's tastes was a total lie.

Filo liked Melty, surely. That was who she was always hanging around with. She'd almost been affected by Motoyasu's Temptation skill, saved only by Raph-chan, but if that hadn't happened, Filo would have gone for Melty. Surely.

"Naofumi, you'll have to explain the meaning of that look later," Melty commented.

"No idea what you mean," I replied.

Filo, meanwhile, hadn't finished her explanation. I remembered something else I wanted her to say.

"Ah! Finally, you have to listen to what people tell you, especially my master. You need to listen to his orders at all times. Oh, and until the world is really at peace, just leave me alone!" That last part hadn't come from me. Filo could be cunning at times, couldn't she?

"I-is that all true, Filo?" Motoyasu's reaction suggested he had bought it. Good! Now, Filo just needed to get him to change the spear.

"So I need you to—" Filo looked at me, eyes wavering. She'd forgotten what I told her! After remembering stuff I didn't even need her to say! "Ah, right, right. I'll really hate you if you don't change that spear to something else! Please, never use that spear again!"

"N-no! Don't hate me! I'll never change to this spear again, I say!" Motoyasu quickly changed his spear at Filo's suggestion.

Ugh, what a dope. So easily manipulated. I couldn't believe he went along with it so easily.

In the moment he changed the spear, everyone in his retinue collapsed as though their batteries had been plucked out.

"Uh . . ." Atla stopped moving too.

"Now!" Grabbing that tiny opening, Raphtalia whacked Atla's solar plexus with the hilt of her sword and knocked her out.

"Raph," Raph-chan said.

"Yeah," Ruft agreed. After checking that Filo and Ruft hadn't been affected by Motoyasu's skill, Raph-chan climbed down from Filo's back along with Ruft. Then Filo turned into her human form.

Having seen all that, I turned back to look at Motoyasu.

"Now then . . ." I proceeded to give Filo the next thing to say.

"Right then . . . I like heroes who fight for the sake of the world. But I don't like people so caught up on me all the time that they can't work with others! Please, do what my master tells you!" she pleaded.

"Very well, I say!" Motoyasu had changed his spear, but his silly verbal tics remained. Was that an effect of the curse series? Like when I'd lost my sense of taste, were his visual and hearing senses being impaired?

If Filo had saved him though, surely they should be fixed too, no?

"Father-in-law, I now solemnly swear that I, Motoyasu Kitamura, shall contribute to your cause as a love hunter, seeking to bring true peace to this world and to win the heart of Filo." Yeah, he was still talking garbage. "I will officially come and stay in your territory, father-in-law, if you can just give me some time to get my belongings ready."

"I'd really rather you didn't come at all, but I guess it's better than having you wandering around," I managed.

"Mr. Naofumi, you need to be careful what you say." I couldn't help but nod in agreement with Raphtalia's caution.

"Very well. Just be quick about it," I told him.

"As soon as my preparations are ready, I shall descend upon you! My angels, we are leaving! Portal Spear!" Motoyasu shouted.

"S-sure thing!" Everyone in his retinue picked themselves up, and in the next instant, all four of them were gone.

"He left the wagon behind," I muttered. It was impossible to miss the thing, the teeth-jarringly decorated sparkly monstrosity making its presence painfully felt.

"Yes! The spear guy is gone! But my wagon . . ." Filo lamented.

"This really is in the worst possible taste," Melty commented, moving over to the wagon and checking it out. I was in complete agreement. I'd had an Internet friend with a car that was pretty outlandish, but I'd never dreamed that the wagon I purchased for Filo would end up stolen and turned into this.

"My wagon . . ." Filo was getting some serious consolation from Melty. I shared an unspoken look with her, knowing what had to be done, and then I spoke with a sigh.

"Right. I'll buy you another one, so cheer up, okay?" I told her. That looked like the only way to cheer Filo up.

"Yay!" She immediately did so.

"That's great, isn't it?!" Ruft offered, whose own eyes had been as round as saucers when looking at the golden monster.

"Yeah!" Filo agreed.

"What an incredible wagon . . . It reminds me of one I had decorated with filolials that I received in tribute once," Ruft admitted.

"There was a wagon like that," I recalled.

"Yes, we saw it in the castle storeroom, didn't we?" Raphtalia corroborated.

"Really?" Melty asked. "What did you think of it, Raphtalia?"

"A better design than this one. That's for sure," she replied.

"I bet," Melty said. I'd never considered someone could make something so offensive to the eyes, honestly. Motoyasu wasn't just a moron; he was terrifying to the extreme.

"In any case, that completes the request. Back to the village! Shall we portal it?" I asked.

"You want to leave this here?" Melty cut in.

"Yeah, that's what I was thinking," I replied.

"Hold on. If we do leave it here, what if someone else starts using it? Or some wild filolials come along and take it away?" Raphtalia made some good points, I had to admit.

I checked with Filo.

"Uhh . . . I don't want to leave this thing here!" she responded.

"We could destroy it?" I just wanted this over with. "What do you think?"

"At least discuss it with that blacksmith you favor so much. He might be able to cheaply restore it to normal?" Melty suggested. Filo had a clear look of disgust on her face, this being something that Motoyasu had been touching. But as it had also originally been hers. She seemed to be having difficulty making a decision.

"In any case . . . looks like we should just cover it with a cloth and take it back with us. I really just want to get back. Filo, can you and Melty handle getting it back?" I asked.

"Hold on! No way! Just think what it'll be like for us transporting this eyesore?" Melty complained. I mean, I could say the same thing, but . . . fair enough.

"It's not like our wagon can really be called a wagon anymore. That's true," I conceded. "I guess we can make use of it." And so that was what we decided to do—make use of the wagon that Motoyasu horribly modified.

Right away though, I noticed something strange. All kinds of work had been performed on the undercarriage so it hardly vibrated at all.

"It looks ugly, but he's done a lot of work to make it easy to ride in," Raphtalia conceded.

"Do you think he used his hero knowledge to do this?" Melty pondered.

"Considering how nice this all is, he may have put his money where his mouth is and got some merchant to hook him up," I contemplated.

"I wonder . . . Anyway, if only it didn't look like this, Filo could really make good use of it," Melty commented.

"Uhh . . ." Filo didn't sound convinced. She made an extremely displeased face as she pulled the wagon along and we made our way back to the village.

Chapter Seven: Filolial Terror

I took a look around the village. Good. Motoyasu hadn't arrived yet. I didn't know when that would be but thought it'd be best to set up a separate facility for him to use.

Motoyasu had talked about making preparations of some kind. I was still wondering what that might entail.

"Yaaaaawn . . . I'm wiped out," Raphtalia moaned.

"You said it," I agreed. "After all that, it's almost time for the sun to come up." After we arrived in the village, Filo's cowlick started to twitch.

"Yes? Okay. Got it. Master!" Filo said.

"What now?" I was so tired.

"As reward for this, Fitoria has taught me some magic called 'Sanctuary.' It lets me create a zone that dragons don't like being inside," Filo reported.

"What's that good for?" I asked.

"Hmmm . . . I'm not really sure, but she said she can make your village filolial territory and make it so that monsters can't attack," Filo explained.

"Raph?" Raph-chan and Filo both tilted their heads. It was Fitoria we were talking about, so there had to be something behind this.

"No thanks. If we're talking monsters, this village is Raph-chan's territory," I replied.

"Mr. Naofumi, where did that come from?" Raphtalia, with the slumbering Atla on her back, posed this question with her eyes narrowed in a worried expression.

"It sounds like the filolials and dragons are about to start fighting over whose territory this village is, so I'm nipping it in the bud. If they are going to be a problem, Raph-chan can have the title and be done with it," I declared.

"Raph!" Raph-chan sounded more than ready for the responsibility. Raphtalia looked completely at a loss for a moment and then gave a deep sigh.

"I guess you and Raph-chan have already created the Raph species, haven't you?" she conceded.

"Yeah, I guess we have," I agreed, somewhat smugly.

"That's nothing to boast about," Raphtalia shot back. "Anyway, I'm going to go and get Atla into her bed."

"Sure thing," I said. Raphtalia, with Atla still on her back, headed off toward Fohl and Atla's house.

"First things first, let's get this monstrosity into the village storehouse. Then I'll get the old guy to take a look and try to restore it," I decided. We all climbed into the wagon.

"I'm totally wiped out," Melty commented. She looked it. I wouldn't make it much longer without some sleep myself.

"Raph," Raph-chan said.

"Is this the kind of work filolials and heroes do?" Ruft asked. I held my head for a moment, thinking. He wasn't wrong, but I wasn't sure how to answer him.

"A-anyway, Motoyasu will be here soon, so we're going to get pretty busy. We'll need to get a house ready for him, just like Ren and Itsuki." I diverted the topic of conversation. I could sort that out using the shield, for sure.

"Huh?!" Filo spotted something.

"Huh? Filo?!" Melty barely had time to speak, and then Filo—who had been pulling the wagon with Melty on her back—leapt away from it like a frightened rabbit and bolted away.

"Where are you going, Filo?!" Melty managed to ask.

"Master! You take it from here!" Filo shouted back and then dashed off in a cloud of dust. What was going on there?

"Raph." Raph-chan picked up the slack right away, turned large, and started to pull the wagon in place of Filo. We soon reached the warehouse.

Ruft and I climbed down from the wagon and watched as Raph-chan moved it inside. It was early morning and everyone else in the village was still sleeping.

Maybe Ren was awake, doing some practice swings for his early-morning training. That would be about it. In any case, this was early morning, with only a very few people awake . . . the kind of time I normally fed the monsters and cleaned the monster stable.

"Hey, Naofumi!" Ren, rather than perform his morning training swings, came over to me.

"What's up?" I asked.

"Not sure. I heard someone talking in the new monster stable that you set up. I was going to check it out. Then I saw you so I wondered if you knew who it was," he explained.

"Talking?" I said.

"Yeah. I'm not totally sure, but it sounded like . . . Motoyasu? Have you managed to persuade him to join us?" Ren guessed. I didn't reply right away. It had only been a few hours. He really had gotten ready that quickly and come right over? Was that possible?

So Filo had run off with Melty because she sensed Motoyasu's presence. That sounded right. Well, if he was here, I was going to have to admonish him about leaving his nasty, trashy wagon behind.

"What should we do?" Ren gave a worried point at the spare monster stable, from which a different sound could be heard from the Raph species and other monsters.

"I'll go and check it out," I reassured him.

"Will you be okay?" Ruft asked, also worried. He even grabbed my clothing from between a gap in my armor.

"Should be fine," I managed. Motoyasu should be listening to me now. I needed to find out what he was doing in the monster stable.

"I'm scared. It's like there's something in there," Ruft said as we approached.

"That's a coincidence. Me too," I replied. Creeping timidly closer, I placed my hands on the massive doors.

There was definitely a commotion coming from inside.

I'd only placed one in here, if I remembered correctly—Filo's underling. I'd been planning to increase that number eventually. Still, now there were far too many voices for just the three filolials that we'd seen Motoyasu with.

I tried to check the inside through one of the windows, but it was still too dark inside.

Just what was going on? My whole body had broken out in a nasty cold sweat. Some primal part of me was saying that this door should not be opened.

Kicking this problem down the road wasn't going to solve it though.

I summoned up my courage and opened the door.

"What the hell?!" The inside was pitch-black. No, it wasn't. There were so many filolials that it just looked that way.

"Ah, the fragrance of filolials! Let me breathe deeply!" Right in front of my eyes, Motoyasu was hugging a filolial and smelling its plumage. In front of him was a veritable horde of filolials. All of them turned to look at the sound of our entrance. I suddenly felt so many eyes on me.

"Who's that?" multiple voices asked.

"Ah, it must be that 'master' Moto was talking about," someone replied.

"Yeah, I bet it is. He's glaring a bit, but he looks kinda friendly," another commented.

"Oh, I bet he is. That boy next to him . . . he smells nice too," a third voice said.

"I know, right? Like, just looking at him fills me with energy. I wonder if he'd play with us?" a fourth filolial pondered.

"I'd much rather be with him than Motopy! He makes me want to be my best self," a fifth espoused. Hold on. Motoyasu had more than three of them? Had he raised all of these filolials?!

I felt goosebumps across my entire body.

But there was no time for that!

"Waaaaaaaaaah!"

"Master! Play with us!" They spoke almost with one voice. *Bang!* I slammed the doors shut again.

"Run for it!" I told Ruft.

"You said it!" the kid quickly agreed. Then, together, we both screamed as though our throats were being ripped out.

"Someone! Help us!"

A few seconds later, the doors opened and the horde of filolials charged straight for us. There had been a faction of filolials that even Fitoria had been concerned about. She'd given us prior warning about them. Maybe this was my fault for not realizing this might happen. Seriously though, she could have explained properly!

"Gaaaaaaah!" Some filolials grabbed Ruft and he let out a scream. He was likely having flashbacks about that time I'd tricked him into thinking Filo was about to eat him. Ah, good times.

"W-what's going on?!" Ren had clearly noticed the situation and gave a shout. *Slowpoke! Hurry up and save us*, I was thinking.

"Motoyasu! Aaaah! What the hell are you doing?! Gaaah!" My own screams rang out. The rampaging filolial crushed me, and that was when I passed out.

After that, apparently, S'yne, Raph-chan, and the Raph species all heard the commotion, came out to fight the filolials, and succeeded in rescuing both the unconscious Ruft and me.

When I eventually awoke, it appeared I'd been clinging to the large Raph-chan, totally out of it from the shock of the filolial attack.

"Raph." That was the sound that awoke me, and I looked up to see Raph-chan's fluffy fur. She was stroking me with a gentle look in her eyes.

"Uh . . . where am I?" I asked.

"Your room, Mr. Naofumi," Raphtalia replied, looking at me with worry in her eyes. I checked my surroundings. Much like me, Ruft was also trembling as Raph-chan was stroking him.

Finally, there was a gift from S'yne in the room—a large Raph-chan doll.

"My memory is a bit fuzzy," I began. It felt like I'd had an experience too terrible to remember.

"I can imagine. After what I just saw, I'm not surprised you lost consciousness. The rest of us had to watch the filolials and Raph species fighting over the two of you. Clearly it's my fault for leaving your side even for a moment to go and put Atla to bed," Raphtalia lamented.

"Aah . . . so scary. Filolials are so scary!" Ruft sounded as though he might never recover from the shock. I looked at him and felt much the same.

"Why did it come to this? Why does the Spear Hero always distress you so much, Mr. Naofumi?" Raphtalia wondered.

"I'd like to know that myself," I concurred.

"He may not have meant any evil by it this time, but it all seems so messed up," she continued.

"It was the same as before. Motoyasu doesn't mean to do harm. I understand that, but still . . ." When Witch tricked him, his only mistake had been to trust her. He'd had no evil intent of his own. This time was the exact same thing.

"Still, in light of what we have coming up, we need to discuss things with the Spear Hero," Raphtalia concluded.

"Not that I want anything to do with him," I finished with a sigh. With that thought, I turned and looked at Raph-chan again. Ah, my healing oasis!

"Raph?" she quizzed me. Raphtalia even laid off of her normal warnings after everything I'd been through. In any case, it was carved again into my soul just how terrifying filolials could be.

Chapter Eight: The Third Hero Conference

It was a few days later in the evening and I'd come with Raphtalia and Filo to bathe in the hot springs on the Cal Mira islands. Raphtalia said that she couldn't relax in Q'ten Lo. Itsuki and Rishia had returned too. So I'd brought them along as well.

After taking a bath, I checked the state of my own curse.

"The curse has lifted," I said.

"Great," Ren replied, who had bathed with me.

"I'm making good progress myself," Itsuki commented. He'd be fine in combat at least. But he still didn't talk much and was often just completely zoned out.

"I hear you, father-in-law!" Motoyasu arrived in the changing room. He had his retinue—just the main three, thank God—along with him.

"What do you want, Motoyasu?" I asked.

"Shall I wash your back for you?" he replied.

"No need. We're just getting out anyway," I told him, blowing off his suggestion. I just wanted to avoid him as much as possible.

"So, Ren, have you read the inscriptions yet?" I asked.

"About that. We need to have a serious discussion about the future and collate all of our information. After we get out of here, how about holding a hero conference?" he suggested. Not something we could discuss in the bath, was it?

"Hmmm . . . okay," I agreed. "Motoyasu, you hurry up with your bathing too."

"Understood, I say, father-in-law. I might mention that I have read the inscriptions too," he added.

"What? You can read the language in this world now, Motoyasu?" I asked. As far as I knew, Motoyasu had been unable to read it.

"Yes, father-in-law. Your commands are absolute, I say! So I spent many days working hard, learning the language from the chart you left in Filo's wagon," he explained. Ah, right. I had made something like that a long time ago. He'd learned the language from that? That wasn't really why I'd left it behind, but . . . putting him right would just give me a headache, I was sure. Best to just leave well enough alone.

"Everything I do, I do for Filo," he stated proudly.

"Yeah, whatever," I replied. It was the best I could manage. So he'd learned it so quickly because it was the language of Filo's world. What wonders a fool with conviction might achieve. He had the drive, I'd give him that. "You just hurry up and join us," I told him.

"Understood, I say!" he responded.

"Yahoo!" cried his three followers. Obeying my orders, they dashed off toward the hot springs. I decided not to bring up those three. Ren and Itsuki looked like they wanted to avoid the topic too.

"Now, I would like to bring to order the Third Hero Conference," Ren declared, raising his hand. It had been a little while as we'd finished our bathing and we had gathered in the same room that we'd used for discussions back when we visited the islands before.

The others from the village, including Atla and Filo, were taking a break. Raphtalia was watching them in another room. I hoped Atla would maintain control of herself. I really needed Fohl to get back quickly.

"As we don't have a moderator, I'll handle the proceedings," Ren stated.

"Sure," I agreed. Ren had been pretty full of energy recently—burning with the desire to fulfill his duty and fight the waves.

I was just prioritizing making it out alive. I didn't expect to get quite as serious as him about everything. I guess being so self-absorbed was just like Ren. Still, he was headed in a much better direction than he had been in the past.

"So? What do you want to talk about?" I prodded.

"We're going to be taking on the Phoenix soon, right? I thought all the heroes should have a bit of a chat and discuss things like power-up methods and the progress we've been making," Ren explained.

"Sure, I guess. But I explained all that already, didn't I?" I asked. I had already explained to everyone, including Motoyasu, the things we had discovered in Q'ten Lo, such as sharing of power-up methods, all of which had been proven to work.

"That's not all. We need to discuss any new weapons and skills we have obtained," Ren went on.

"Hmmm. You might be right," I acquiesced. No harm could come from it.

"First, just to confirm, you have already achieved the power-up, correct?" Ren asked.

"Yes," Itsuki confirmed.

"Me too!" Motoyasu added. Then they actually used energy boost.

"I can also use a bit of life force now," Itsuki added vaguely. He then used a little of it, showing how it differed from energy boost.

"Like this, I say!" Motoyasu seemed to have a better handle on it than Itsuki. He'd been the last one to come to the village but could already use it. What was going on with him?

"Your orders are absolute, father-in-law. You told me to master life force, so of course that's what I have done," Motoyasu explained intently, flexing his fist as he did so. "All I do, I do for you, father-in-law."

"We're getting off topic again, but if you've got good enough control of life force, that only leaves learning the Way of the Dragon Vein—Liberation-class magic," I concluded.

"We're all still working on that. It is going well though, thanks to you, Naofumi. We'll get it soon," Ren said. Our evening training recently had all been me teaching them magic.

The battle with the Phoenix was getting close.

It was still fresh in my memory how Motoyasu had really been opposed to Gaelion placing the blessing of the Way of the Dragon Vein on him. His attitude had been that the enemy of the filolials was also his enemy, and he would rather die than receive any blessings from them.

For the sake of our future operations, I ordered him to put up with it and he was blessed in the end.

"Indeed. I'm sure it will help in our future battles," Ren said.

"I concur!" Motoyasu agreed. Everything was proceeding unbelievably smoothly, to be honest. I could barely hide my surprise.

"So are we finished?" I attempted to wrap things up. Much easier than expected! But then Ren shook his head.

"Not yet," he stopped me.

"What? Still something to talk about?" I asked. In response, Ren changed his sword and showed it to me.

It was a strange-looking weapon, like a bunch of strings connected together. Honestly, it looked pretty weak.

"What's that thing?" I asked him.

"It's a sword called the Comradery Blade. It's got a skill that it can teach you called ally growth adjustment (small)," he explained.

"What are the conditions for it?" I asked. I wanted to know.

"No idea. It was unlocked by the time I noticed it," Ren replied apologetically.

"Hmmm." That wasn't much help, but ally growth adjustment (small) sounded like the same type of skill as the slave growth adjustment I'd used. "Approaching it from a video game kind of thinking, the conditions are probably something like trusting your allies with all your heart." I went on. That sounded like the easiest starting point. Ren nodded in agreement.

"Yeah, that's probably it," he said. With a bitter expression, he then muttered, "Which means I didn't trust my allies before. If I'd obtained this sword sooner, they might not have had to die."

"Maybe not. But that doesn't mean the experience was meaningless," I said.

"A very Naofumi-like take on the situation. Anyway, if I have further discoveries like this, I'll share them with you," Ren said.

"Hey, I know. Ren, try putting some of Eclair's hair into it," I suggested. "If you've achieved the Comradery Blade already, that might score you the Comradery Blade II or something like that."

"I'm not sure what Eclair would say about that . . ." He hesitated. Yeah, she probably would have a complaint or two. But hold on . . . What if Ren made a familiar using Eclair's hair? Yeah, that was something to think about.

"Father-in-law. I'll try putting feathers from everyone into my spear too," Motoyasu said.

"I've already completed the filolial line," I replied.

"I'd expect no less, father-in-law! How did you collect them? Please, share your wisdom with me!" he said.

"Shut up, Motoyasu." I shot him down. "Work it out for yourself." Maybe I should tell him, just to piss Fitoria off. But no, I should keep the information to hold over her in the future. If she gave us another weird request, I could threaten to unleash Motoyasu on her. That could be his reward.

"That reminds me, I've learned a new skill—well, a powerful skill that you all already know about actually," Motoyasu recalled.

"Oh yeah? Like what?" I asked, maybe foolishly. Motoyasu proceeded to change his spear.

Hold on. It looked like the very spear that Sadeena had been boasting about nabbing from her childhood home. What had it been called? The Water Dragon's Harpoon?

"Filo-tan's big sister lent it to me to copy, father-in-law," Motoyasu explained. What? Had Sadeena been back to the village and given Motoyasu a weapon already? Had she heard from Raphtalia?

"So what skill did you learn?" I kept things moving along.

"Brionac, I say!" he revealed with a flourish. That was the skill that the high priest of the Church of the Three Heroes had tried to unleash using copies of the four holy weapons, right? That had been a copy. Was this the real deal?

"I've also discovered that applying things like life force and energy boost at the same time can greatly reduce the charge time," Motoyasu revealed.

"Wow," I managed.

"That's amazing, Motoyasu." Ren was a little more forthcoming with his praise. Itsuki was just kind of staring vacantly on.

In any case, it meant Motoyasu had acquired a pretty powerful skill.

"What about you, Ren?" I asked. "You've got the weapon that Motoyasu II is reforging for you in Q'ten Lo, right?"

"What kind of love hunter is this fellow who bears my name?" Motoyasu asked.

"You just stay quiet," I told him bluntly. It would be more trouble than it was worth to try and explain. He wasn't a "love hunter," anyway. He was an old perv.

"It's still being purified. He said it should only take a little longer," Ren reported.

"Okay, good," I replied.

"However, it's not like the Spirit Tortoise Sword or Spirit

Tortoise Katana that I'm currently using. It's a much more powerful weapon. I'm not even sure whether I'll be able to handle it at the moment," Ren explained. It had a pretty powerful curse on it. We just had to hope we could get our hands on it quickly. "The old guy's master said he'd need to make some adjustments to let me use it, so I'll just wait a little longer."

"Understood. If you can master it, it's going to make things a lot easier going forward. We'll just have to look forward to that day and wait," I said. Once the purification was finished, would the stone that formed the core have to be fed to Gaelion? There weren't many other ways to use it outside of enhancing Gaelion and letting a sword-wielder other than Ren use it. Did we even have anyone who used a longsword?

Eclair used a dagger. Raphtalia, a katana. Maybe Shildina would be able to use it? It seemed that the healing of the hole in her soul perhaps had caused her oracle powers to decline somewhat. It was now impossible for her to become anyone else at least, but she could likely still copy their skills.

"Thinking about the Phoenix battle, it seems most practical if I defend while chanting support magic," I suggested. These would be called "buffs" in a video game. Because I was the one who could use Liberation Aura—which provided a boost to all stats—it was most efficient for me to be the one who cast support magic.

Of course, dropping beast transformation support would

be even more efficient, but that was never a sure thing.

"I can use rucolu fruit to recover magic," I continued.

"Ah, the rucolu fruit. They always seem to come up when anyone in this world is talking about you, don't they, Naofumi?" Ren jibed.

"They do taste really nice," I replied, a little defensively. I also remembered how they knocked Motoyasu right out. It seemed anyone other than me eating them was a pretty bad idea. "If you guys could also recover using them, you wouldn't have to waste time drinking magic potions and stuff like that," I pondered. When a battle drew out, the need arose to replenish things like magic and SP. With its high healing potential, the rucolu fruit was a real effective item when it came to cost-performance.

"Sure, but they also make us collapse if we eat them," Ren countered.

"You might be able to build up some resistance if you level up a bit," I replied.

"No way. Just smelling the stuff makes my head spin," Ren stated stubbornly. Even Motoyasu had a dry smile on his face concerning this topic.

"I've been thinking about this for a while, Naofumi. Now I finally see the truth of it. You have the special ability to nullify intoxication," Itsuki said, not making a lick of sense. Hold on. What did he just say?

"Special ability? Is that some kind of system I don't know about?" I asked. There were skills that increased resistances to status effects. Maybe that was what he meant. If so, however, I could report that I unfortunately had learned no such skill.

"No, I mean it's an ability you had prior to coming to this world," Itsuki explained.

"What's that supposed to mean?" I replied. What was he talking about?

For a moment there, anyway, I had flashbacks to when I first chatted with Ren and the others like this. It had been like fanboys discussing some online game. Back then, Ren had said that normal MMOs were outdated, causing confusion among the rest of us. Now I felt something similar from Itsuki and his comments.

Ren seemed to be feeling something similar too, because he was looking at Itsuki with his eyebrows drawn together.

"Hey, Ren, do you have any idea what Itsuki is talking about?" I asked him.

"No, sorry. There's all sorts of possibilities, so I can't really say," he replied.

"Hmmm," I pondered. Ren was like me, quite capable of extrapolating information, but seeing as Itsuki probably couldn't lie at the moment anyway, just asking him outright seemed like the best approach. He responded quite openly to questions at the moment. He'd surely regale us with stories of these "abilities."

"Tell us, Itsuki, what are these abilities you are talking about? Do you mean the power of the legendary weapons?" I asked.

"No. The legendary weapons may very well have such abilities, but I'm clearly talking about something completely different," he explained.

"Hmmm. I don't recall anything like that." Even Motoyasu didn't seem to have a clue. So this was clearly knowledge unique to Itsuki's world.

"Itsuki, tell us more. Back in your world, just what are these 'abilities'?" I pressed him.

"What do you mean, 'what'? Why don't you understand them, Naofumi? Did you live so far out in the sticks that ability management hadn't even reached you yet?" Itsuki asked casually with no expression on his face. It looked like these "abilities" were just an everyday part of life for him. Even his curse-infested thinking wasn't puzzled about concepts like "do you breathe air?"

Perhaps this was very much the kind of response that you would get if you asked someone else how to breathe.

"Right, so tell us all about them from the beginning," I asked.

"Very well. These abilities were discovered in my world about twenty-five years ago through research into individuals who were causing all sorts of disasters and incidents. It is the name given to certain powers possessed by each individual. They are also called things like 'psi' and 'supernatural powers,'" Itsuki revealed. Right, so hold on. So in Itsuki's world—

"Ren, do you understand all this? Hey, you've got VRM-MOs in your world, right? So you've probably got something like this too?" I asked him.

"You think we're all mind wizards or something? Are you joking?" he replied. Hmmm, as the resident of what to me was basically a sci-fi novel, I would have thought Ren could understand.

So this meant Itsuki's world was a near-future setting with crazy mind powers? I would probably have been pretty into the idea of crazy psychic battles before I came to this world.

The issue now was, in this world with these newly revealed abilities, what kind of standing Itsuki had held and what kind of abilities he brought to the table.

"Okay. So in the world you come from, how are these abilities handled?" I asked.

"First, every prefecture has at least one school where those with abilities are taught. I mean, there are generally a lot more than just one," he continued.

"Okay," I prompted.

"Abilities are divided into ranks, with S at the top, then A through F. Classes at these schools are divided up into those ranks," Itsuki explained further.

"So everyone in your world can use abilities?" I asked.

"No, not at all. In fact, there are many more people who can't," he replied.

"What about you personally?" I pressed on to the heart of the matter.

"I have an ability called 'Accuracy,' and I'm E class." Accuracy, huh? I guess that finally explained, after all this time, why Itsuki generally never missed when he fired an arrow.

"What is this accuracy ability, then?" I asked for clarification. "Just so we're clear."

"It's a skill that lets me use ranged weapons with far greater precision than a normal person. I could even be a pretty mean sniper, if I wanted to," he explained. That also explained why during the suspected kidnapping incident he had fired toward me even though Melty had also been there. No one would have taken that shot if they weren't completely confident in the result.

So he wasn't just a moron who loved justice. This definitely changed how I felt about his actions back then. Indeed, although his comments had seemed completely natural, they might also have alluded to this new truth we had just learned.

Still, "Accuracy?" From what I'd heard about it so far, it seemed like a pretty potent ability. If there was S down to F, then why was it closer to the bottom of the pile?

"That sounds like a quality ability, so why's it ranked so low?" I probed.

"I'm E class because I'm not compatible with the higher ability 'Ultra Accuracy,'" he explained.

"It has an 'ultra' on it, so I presume that's pretty good," I said.

"Anything you fire never misses," he replied.

"Wow." That sounded broken.

"Even if you turned away from the target, the arrow would surely fly around to it," Itsuki added. Homing capabilities?! Ultra-broken, for sure! "Lots of baseball players have that ability. Of course, its use is carefully controlled."

"In other words, Itsuki, you have a low-ranking ability, so at your little school for the gifted, you were seen as low-ranking?" I laid it all out.

"Naofumi, that's not a nice way to put it," Ren cut in.

"That's right though," Itsuki answered honestly. If I'd been trying to be mean, he hadn't picked up on it. "So I played games to get away from my horrible reality. When my ability was detected at elementary school, making it seem like I was special, I let it go to my head. Once I actually reached junior high and started the special school, I learnt that there's always a bigger fish. It almost wiped me out. Nothing changed in high school."

So while most people were just normal, Itsuki had been born with special powers, and that had given him confidence during his younger years. Once he went to a school for people with similar gifts though, he had been slammed with the reality that his own ability actually wasn't all that great and had started to play games as a result.

Sure, comics and games with a main character with such abilities normally featured someone who was, well, actually powerful. But when it came to actual abilities in real life, there was good and bad ones. Not having one at all might be less hellish than getting stuck with a crappy one.

His focus on justice then had come from the heroes of comics, cartoons, and games who worked with the abilities they had been given to defeat evil.

"I understand now. Do you think I have an ability that prevents me from getting motion sickness or drunk?" I asked.

"Yes. I am estimating it as the ability 'Nullify Sickness.' There's a lower version called 'Resist Sickness,' which would be an F rank ability," Itsuki revealed.

"What about mine then?" Couldn't hurt to ask.

"Its prospects are a C or D rank, but it's a conditional S rank when fighting supervillains with gravity-based powers," Itsuki explained.

"Hmmm. And what do you mean by 'prospects'?" When we fought Kyo, I'd been unable to move when he used that gravity attack on me, so it didn't sound quite right to me.

"Think about it. Not getting motion sickness means you are resilient to the effects of gravity, with exceptional semicircular canals. A vital skill for astronauts, for one. Some people were advocating for the name to be changed to 'Nullify Gravitational Load,' but research was still being conducted," Itsuki revealed.

It sounded like this skill could do quite a lot of stuff!

But no, come on. I was just lucky enough to not get motion sickness . . . At least, that was what I'd been thinking. But maybe I was starting to feel otherwise. I could scoff down the same rucolu fruit that had made Motoyasu pass out, and I felt nothing when riding Filo even at top speed. The others might have gotten used to that, but they still said it was hard. So it had to be pretty rough.

Nullify gravity though? I'd definitely been pressed down by the gravity attack that Kyo unleashed, so that side of this was more suspicious.

"Of course, there are various branches of the ability, so I can't say for sure. But maybe in your case the emphasis is just placed on not getting sick, rather than the gravity side of things," Itsuki clarified. So the same kind of ability, but with subtle differences. Like not getting sick at all, or just not getting motion sickness, maybe. "I also think," he went on, "that you might have double abilities."

"You mean two of them?" I asked.

"Yes," he confirmed.

"Like what?" I asked.

Itsuki's world from my perspective was the near future where everyone was getting supernatural abilities. If you considered then that the reason Itsuki had always quietly mocked Ren, Motoyasu, and me was because he'd thought we didn't have said abilities, that might also explain quite a lot.

Still, Ren had a world with VR and Itsuki had superpowers. What about Motoyasu? Maybe it was a world where choices appeared at critical points during conversations with pretty girls, or something like that.

Whatever. I didn't care about Motoyasu. He was a mess. He wouldn't give me a proper answer even if I pressed him for one.

"I think your other ability may well be called 'Animal Friends.' It means animals just take a natural liking to you. You'd be a great veterinarian," Itsuki went on.

"Indeed. From what I've seen of you recently, Naofumi, I could agree with that. Look at the filolials and the Raph species," Ren added.

"Uhh . . ." My trauma of being trampled came back to me again.

Still, Ethnobalt had been pretty friendly with me. Demi-humans and therianthropes were the same. I was starting to see something in Itsuki's explanation.

Animals had always taken a liking to me, since I was small. When I would walk in the mountains, wild birds would land on my shoulder. I'd encountered a bear once and escaped by playing dead.

However, it did lick my face. I'd learned afterward that

there were better ways to deal with bears.

A big dog in the neighborhood had let me ride it too. It had sat in front of me, offering its back. I'd sat on it just as a joke, and it had run off with me aboard.

I'd even swung a stick around, playing as the Ainu chick from that fighting game.

"Yeah, maybe in your world, Itsuki," I conceded. I was starting to see what had warped the poor guy too. "Let's put aside the abilities I may have and talk about the magic you've learnt for the upcoming battle."

"Okay," Ren said.

"Very well," Itsuki said.

"I'll show off the magic I've learned, I say!" Motoyasu said. I understood this might bring out the tendency to brag.

I was also interested in what each of them had learned from the inscriptions on the Cal Mira islands. If they had learned Aura, for example, someone other than me could also help out with support.

"Ren, I'll start with you," I said. "What did you learn here on the Cal Mira islands?"

"Zweite Magic Enchant," Ren replied.

"Magic Enchant, you say. What's the effect?" I asked.

"Magic for swords. It allows further magic to then be applied to your sword, after which you can cut down enemies for as long as the magic lasts," Ren explained.

"It's not a combo skill?" I checked. Those allowed a hero's skill and ally's magic to be combined together to create a special skill.

"No, it's different from that. You can get a pure power increase from it, and it's not applied with the aid of an ally," he said.

"Which means what?" I asked.

"Even enemy magic can be applied to the sword. It can even nullify weak magic attacks and use them to attack," he answered.

"Interesting," I commented. Pretty convenient magic. You could deal with incoming enemy attacks and look for an opening to counter.

"The only issue," Ren went on, "is that I could only learn up to Zweite. I tried to get Drifa, but I couldn't do it."

"Fair enough." I moved on. "Motoyasu, what about you?"

"I learned Zweite Absorb, father-in-law," he proclaimed.

"Sounds good. What does it do?" I asked. From the name, it sounded like it could absorb magic.

"It can nullify and absorb Zweite-class magic. However, I can't move while I'm casting it," Motoyasu explained. That was definitely an issue, considering what he brought to the table in terms of combat strength. I guess the point was to cast it first and preemptively stop opponents from using magic at all.

"What's its range like?" I inquired.

"Looks like a diameter of around five meters, from what I saw," Motoyasu said.

"I see," I pondered. Sounded like a pretty strange piece of magic, but not without some potential. Looked like the inscription was dealing with support-type magic.

They had both said just up to Zweite, but if they used the Liberation method, they might be able to get up to the next level. There were lots of applications for that, so with some adjustments maybe they could use Drifa too.

I could only use that for healing and support, but what about Ren and the others?

"What are your magic aptitudes?" I asked.

"Yeah, we never talked about that," Ren realized. "You are healing and support, right, Naofumi?"

"That's right," I confirmed.

"I'm water and support," he replied. "Although there's some water magic that can heal, so it isn't quite so cut and dried."

"Father-in-law, I'm fire and healing," Motoyasu chimed in. "Although I can also use fire for some support."

"And I'm wind and earth. Just like you guys though, I can use some healing and support too," Itsuki said. So Ren was water and support, Motoyasu fire and healing, and Itsuki wind and earth. A pretty good split. And they also had access to some healing and support within those categories.

"I can't use healing and magic as effectively as you,

Naofumi," Ren clarified.

"My fire healing is strong, I say!" Motoyasu boasted.

"That goes without saying," I shot back. Motoyasu could use healing magic too.

Anyway, this meant, as expected, I didn't have any attack abilities. The old woman at the magic shop had said something about that. The basic nature of a person has some influence when casting magic, and even a simple healing spell is affected by that nature.

That meant a little fire would get mixed in with Motoyasu's healing.

And then, if someone cast magic that didn't suit their nature, such as Motoyasu using support, the effects would be dramatically reduced.

That reminded me. There was an attack spell classified under healing. What had it been called? Decay?

I'd tried casting it myself, but it had failed.

The magic shop lady had said it was rare to find someone quite so completely unsuited to attack magic.

"The spells from the inscriptions seem pretty special," I commented. Aura boosted all stats. Magic Enchant gave magic to weapons, including enemy magic. Absorb nullified magic.

"Itsuki, what about you?" I knew I was forgetting someone.

"Zweite Down. The exact opposite of yours, Naofumi. It reduces all stats," he replied.

"Hmmm." So I made allies stronger, and Itsuki made enemies weaker. That could be powerful, if used well.

Ren could absorb enemy magic and turn it to attack. Motoyasu could absorb and nullify it. So as long as we used them effectively, these could all be quite strong, although it wasn't clear whether S'yne's foes and the forces from the other world could even nullify magic.

"In that case, until the Phoenix battle, we're going to work on getting you all to learn the Liberation class."

"Understood, I say!" Motoyasu gave an energetic reply. Did he understand what that meant? Was he just agreeing for the sake of it? "I'm next, then," he continued.

"Huh?" I said. What did he have to talk about?

"It's time for me to tell you about the work I was doing prior to coming to your village," Motoyasu said.

"You were raising filolials and being a street racer, right?" I retorted. Just remembering all that made me angry. After all the trouble we dealt with helping Raphtalia, and look what this moron was off doing!

"That's part of it, but I was also quietly protecting your village, father-in-law!" Motoyasu revealed with a flourish.

"Huh?" Again, I had no idea what he was talking about.

"There were quite a few suspicious-looking characters heading for your village, father-in-law. But I totally cleaned them away. Don't worry," Motoyasu explained.

"Hold on. What are you talking about?" I said. He was cleaning up people heading for the village?

"Y-you think this is okay, Naofumi? It sounds like Motoyasu has been up to no good?" Ren asked.

"We need to hear more, to find that out. Motoyasu, spill it," I told him. Depending on how things had gone, it might turn out he'd killed some of our allies.

"First, guys like those who attacked us when we fought Ren attacked me numerous times. I defeated them. Of course, I use the soul weapons, just like you instructed. That let me defeat them with ease," Motoyasu said. Had S'yne's enemies been close to the village? If Motoyasu had been defeating them without anyone else knowing, no wonder we hadn't experienced any attacks!

Of course, we didn't know how many had come.

"There were others approaching the village with murderous intent too. I also defeated demi-humans and therianthropes. They were using some very strange weapons. After a while, those ones stopped coming," Motoyasu continued. I had nothing to say to that. He'd been defeating the assassins from Q'ten Lo too? That sounded suspicious, but if I asked for proof, he'd probably bring me a skull or something. It was best to stay quiet.

Motoyasu wouldn't lie about something like this. Not at the moment.

"There were also people in robes of some kind lurking

around. I took them out too," he said. Remnants of the Church of the Three Heroes perhaps?

So without anyone else knowing, had he been protecting the village all this time?

"I see," I said.

"What do you think?" Motoyasu asked.

"Ah well, I think you've done pretty well. But I'm still not giving you Filo," I said.

"I'll do my best until you approve of me as her fiancé, father-in-law!" Motoyasu stated.

"Hey, Naofumi," Ren said. "I mean . . . is Motoyasu all there?"

"He's a totally different person," Itsuki added. They were both looking at me with concern in their eyes. As if these two could talk!

"I want to think he's fine," I managed.

"He's basically Motoyasu, but something's broken about him. It's scary. I hope the curse is broken soon," Ren said.

"Me too. Just what kind of curse is it?" Itsuki wondered.

"Good question. Motoyasu, what is the cost of your curse?" I asked. He'd unleashed quite the variety of curse skills. He had to be paying something.

"Cost? What do you mean?" he asked back.

"You used Temptation and Ressentiment on us, right?" I reminded him.

"I don't recall paying anything," he returned. His face made it clear he really had no idea. No stat reduction? Nothing like that?

Hold on. Maybe the cost was his current disposition, although Witch certainly had done a number on him.

"O-okay then. Just do your best to be ready to fight the Phoenix," I said.

"Understood!" he replied. I'd have to check thoroughly and make a decision later.

"That covers the effects of our magic." I moved on. "We're going to be taking on the Phoenix as our next enemy, but what about after that?" The four heroes other than me all had a certain degree of understanding, although we'd all kind of come to think that the others couldn't be relied on too.

"After the Phoenix, it's Kirin and then Dragon," Ren said.

"That's the way!" Motoyasu was clearly up for it.

"Do you think enemies from another world are going to attack again, like with the Spirit Tortoise?" Ren asked.

"No sign of it at the moment. We've got eyes out for that kind of thing happening, not just in Melromarc, but everywhere. Anything relating to the four benevolent animals in particular, we've really got locked down. If something was happening, word should have come to the village, but nothing has happened yet," I told them. Even if something like that did happen, someone like Ost would surely show up to ask for our help. If possible, I'd like to resolve the situation just by talking, but those like Ost coming from the side of the four benevolent animals also wanted to protect the world and wanted to complete their duty of blocking the heroes. It would be a pointless spilling of blood, but if that was the only way they knew to live, then we could only consider it the role of the heroes to give them a worthy battle.

"There's a very strong possibility that those with a connection to S'yne back in the village are going to get involved somehow, so we need to keep security tight," I said. Who knows what kind of shit they might try to pull and how it might aggravate the Phoenix? There was no harm in being prepared for anything.

"Understood," Ren replied.

"The Phoenix is apparently sealed in the west. If we can send one of the heroes ahead, that'll save the rest of us some movement time," I posited. I'd heard about the location from the queen and others from this country. If someone could get a portal there before the deadline, everyone else in the village would be able to keep training.

"I'll go and get a portal position!" Motoyasu thrust his arm into the air. Keeping him in the village was going to generate so much noise anyway, and he'd probably do nothing but play with his filolials, so best to just let him go.

"It sounds like there may be notes there on how to defeat

it, but I also want to prepare thoroughly before the battle. Right. Anyone got anything else to add?" I was keen to get this over with.

"Actually, about that . . ." Ren started.

"Yeah?" I asked. He looked away from my gaze. Maybe it was something difficult to say. He certainly didn't seem very good at making requests of people.

From his standing, I guess I could understand that.

"I want you to lead the operation, Naofumi," he finally said.

"I'm likely to stand at the head of the party and give orders from there," I replied. When fighting the Spirit Tortoise, I'd been right there on the front lines, after all.

Of course, actual operational orders would be aided by the queen and other leaders of each nation. But with my experience of raising my own force, I'd likely handle most of the heavy lifting.

"Well, that's not exactly what I mean. I want you to give us orders too. You said it before, right? You've got experience with a guild," Ren recalled.

"I guess I might have mentioned that," I confirmed. Upon defeating the high priest and learning that power-up methods could be shared, we'd had a hero conference then too.

"When we first met, Naofumi, I did think you looked a bit like someone I know," Ren admitted.

"A friend of yours? That guy you mentioned a few times?"

I vaguely recalled something. Ren gave a distant stare for a moment, as though he was about to slip into a flashback, and then looked at me again.

"That's right," he finally continued. "He was like a mixture of you from the past and you now. He just wanted to look after everyone, and people were just naturally drawn to him." Me from the past, huh? Back then I had the confidence to talk to anyone. Rather than worry about maybe being tricked or abused, I'd just wanted everyone to get along and have fun.

"He ran a big guild. I know you did too. But that's why I want to leave this to you," Ren explained.

"Still, I can't beat out experts in this stuff. Large-scale battles and raids running on a fixed set of rules, however complex, isn't much help here," I cautioned.

It was one of the major aspects of an Internet game. It was a way to proclaim your strength within the server you played on, including access to dungeons that only the higher-ranking guilds could enter and rare items that only they could obtain. Among the vast array of these events, guilds and teams allowed for the kind of experience you could never obtain while playing solo.

That said, it was a little hasty to compare the waves to that. It was impossible to tell what was going to happen during them, demanding everyone be ready for anything at all times.

"What scale of guild did you run in that game? I was just

thinking you never told us the details," Ren asked.

"Of multiple servers, there was one . . . I was part of the leadership of perhaps the third-largest allied guild, but we weren't big enough to appear in world tournaments," I explained, realizing I'd never told them this. I'd held quite a lot of authority within the alliance, but not the most. My character hadn't been the highest level, and I'd really just put my emphasis on making money and building connections with people. Part of the reason for that had been because expensive gear and healing items had been very important in the game.

"So you've got a lot more experience than us, clearly," Ren said.

"I mean, I guess so. But it's rarely helped out. Maybe when ordering people about to get away from the waves," I replied. During the first wave, it had been all I could do to protect the villagers, and things had been no different in the second wave or the third. During the fight with the Spirit Tortoise, the queen and the coalition army actually gave the orders. All I did was hold the Spirit Tortoise in place alongside Ost.

I mean, okay, maybe I had the most experience with this kind of stuff among the four holy heroes. Ren had only helped some others who also played solo get their game into shape. Motoyasu had run a smaller guild. Itsuki just played console games, right? They might have been strategy games, but I wouldn't put money on it after seeing him fighting the waves.

All he could probably do was help form a plan to fight the Phoenix during the next wave. We'd start by checking the site and looking for information, then research ways to defeat it.

"What's this *Quest for the Phoenix* game like, then?" I asked.

"In the game story, after the damage from the Spirit Tortoise, each country starts seriously investigating what's going on. But they still fail to seal the Phoenix away, and it ends up reviving," Ren told me.

"I see," I replied. Back with the Spirit Tortoise they acted like they could just defeat everything with game knowledge. I guess this showed how the relationships between the four of us had progressed.

"After this . . . before the battle, we're going to have the heroes all make accessories," I told them.

"You mentioned being able to add powerful effects to skills and attacks, right?" Ren recalled.

"You don't have any game wisdom to share?" I prodded. Ren tilted his head and thought for a moment, then replied.

"There are accessories that can increase certain skills or abilities when equipped, so . . . I guess I do." Yeah, good point. I'd experienced some things like that myself. Games had things like that quite often, although it could hardly be called much of a new discovery.

"Anyway, equipping accessories can enhance skills or provide unique ones. Accessories are developed by discussing them with me, a therianthrope called Imiya in the village, and the alchemist Rat. You guys can help us start looking into all that," I said.

"If that's what you want," Ren said. His strangely detached reply was a bit like Itsuki, which I didn't need more of, but it was better than him launching into another rampage.

Anyway, the plan was the re-creation of the scabbard that Raphtalia had used in Kizuna's world—to get as close to that as possible. The accessory dealer had also reported that work was advancing on the mass production of a prototype of an accessory that allowed drop items to be obtained from monsters, just like a hero, via use of a dragon hourglass. There were lots of orders for those already.

We'd use those as funds for our forces, creating a foundation to further enhance our strength.

All the heroes were now aware of the item creation, and so this looked to have been a pretty productive gathering. Nothing like the train wrecks of the past.

"The only other thing to do is raise our levels as much as possible," I concluded. Ren raised his hand and commented on that.

"I personally feel that Q'ten Lo is the best for efficient experience gains."

"Hmmm," I pondered. He had a point. Experience acquisition in Q'ten Lo, which was the homeland of Raphtalia's parents, had been mysteriously efficient.

"About that . . ." Itsuki also raised his hand, almost looking apologetic. "Rishia said that, since you grew those sakura-like trees in the village, the monsters lurking nearby have also seen an increase in experience."

"What?" First I was hearing of this. Some kind of secondary effect? No, but the sakura lumina trees came originally from Q'ten Lo. Maybe they had the effect of boosting experience.

"Searching for better hunting grounds . . . Sadeena did mention that the sea regions do give good experience," Ren said, his voice shaking a little. He couldn't swim, although apparently he'd made some progress with that.

Getting Sadeena and Shildina to show us the best oceanic spots might make a good hunting trip too. In terms of underwater gear, we did have that Pekkul Costume . . . but there was only one left after all that other stuff went down.

"All we have to do is keep on training until the day of the battle. That's our role here," I said. All sorts of stuff had happened since I was summoned to this other world, but that simple truth remained unbreakable. There weren't many days left until the Phoenix would revive, but that didn't change what we had to do.

"We also need to select the allies to fight with us against the Phoenix. Do you have any picks in mind, Naofumi?" Ren asked.

"Anyone who wants to try it, I'm going to let them—aside from the ones who clearly wouldn't stand a chance, of course," I replied.

"I see. You've got some pretty tough allies on your side, what with Raphtalia, Rishia, and Sadeena, to name but a few," Ren commented. Indeed, those were some of the strongest in the village. Raphtalia in particular was a key combatant, taking the fight to our foes in my place.

"You're going to take Atla too, then?" Ren asked.

"Huh?" What was this? Ren asking about Atla by name? "Why her in particular? I mean, sure, she's strong," I asked. She trained with me and Raphtalia, as well as fighting some pretty blazing battles with Raphtalia every night.

"If I'm honest, I think Atla is the one from the village who's made the most progress," Ren admitted.

"I agree," Itsuki offered with a nod.

"I thought it would be going too far to attack her at full strength with a powerful hero weapon, so I hold back against her. But on a technical level she overtook me real quick. That's how good she is. She's a genius, really," Ren explained. He was right. Atla was developing quickly. She'd started off with some skills, and different from the richly experienced Sadeena, but Atla had the ability to learn stuff just by seeing it—even though she couldn't see.

There had been more times recently when, even backed

by the Raph species, Raphtalia hadn't been able to contain her. That had to be due to the defensive life force that S'yne had taught her.

Atla and I, with help from S'yne, had both learned defensive life force. Having Raphtalia focusing on the mastery of the techniques she acquired in Q'ten Lo was keeping her behind in terms of other progress.

The techniques had names, and I took a moment to recall them.

First there was Gather.

This was a technique that could use the power of life force to bend the trajectory of magical attacks, such as fire magic, and draw them to the user. Useful when bearing the brunt of a magical onslaught. The range had a diameter of about ten feet. Of course, that could be extended further with further deployment of life force.

Next was Wall.

This allowed an invisible wall to be created in the air for a few seconds, impeding the movements of opponents. It was a bit like using Air Strike Shield. It could stop normal attacks and magic attacks too. The strengths of this technique were its versatility and being able to cover a pretty wide area if you wanted. The weaknesses were the actual defensive power it offered and the length of time it lasted.

Finally there was Bead.

This was a counterattack. It allowed magical attacks to be collected together using life force, concentrated, and then thrown at the enemy. Of course, there was some magic that simply couldn't be thrown back, and so it wasn't all-powerful. It operated much on the same principles as reflecting magic with my shield.

And Atla could use all of these.

Of course, these techniques had been created around me and my specialization in defense, and Atla was adapting them to her own purposes.

"I can't read her movements, and she's fast," Ren continued, oblivious to my musings. "Just when I think an attack has gone in, she immediately redirects it and takes no damage at all."

"At the same time, she comes at you with defense-ignoring attacks like they are nothing. She's very difficult to handle," Itsuki added.

"But you manage it somehow, right?" I asked. She wasn't that strong yet, surely.

"Yeah, sure. But if we fought one on one, I'm sure I'd have to get pretty serious," Ren admitted.

"It would be hard to stop her without hurting her badly," Itsuki agreed. Fully enhanced heroes would have to fight her seriously or lose? Just how strong was she becoming?

Of course, we didn't want to kill anyone in the village by

mistake, so we had to hold back quite a bit. That wasn't easy either.

"It sounds like Fohl has finished his training and is coming back . . . but I'm not sure if we can hold her back until then. She may break through Raphtalia's defensive line before he reappears," Itsuki analyzed.

"Why does she want to sleep close to me so badly?" I asked, exasperated. I'd saved her life, that much was true, but I still had my limits . . .

Things had been getting a bit easier recently, but I still had no plans to have a family. I was no Motoyasu, but was this what being attractive to the opposite sex was like?

No, no, with Atla, it was more a racial thing, combined with feelings of affection due to me saving her life. I mean, consider her age. Because I was acting like a parent to Raphtalia, I treated Atla in much the same way.

"Fohl and Atla are both so strong. I think the Phoenix battle is going to be pretty easy," Ren said.

"Well, for one thing, I don't think Atla will be joining us," I replied.

"Why not?" Ren asked, puzzled.

"I made a promise to Fohl that I wouldn't involve her in any more dangerous battles. So I'll respect the wishes of anyone in the village who wants to fight, but I'm taking Atla out," I explained. I was not a monster. Not a complete one. There was also a reason why I always kept Atla with Fohl. When it came to a Phoenix-class battle, there was no telling what might happen. Fohl had some mercenary experience and was working for me for the money. But Atla was just a slave I'd purchased as part of a package deal.

I'd thought she'd probably be okay if Fohl was along too, but he'd never go for that now. She'd made it alive through numerous dangerous battles. That much was true. But in many cases she'd also really just got caught up in them rather than choosing to be there.

Seeing as we knew beforehand just how dangerous this was going to be, Fohl would surely ask me to leave her behind.

It was just as I'd explained all of this that I heard the click of the door behind me.

I turned around to see Atla standing there, gripping the doorknob, trembling as she turned her face toward me. Shit, bad timing.

"What's up, Atla?" I asked, playing it low-key.

"Master Naofumi . . . you're not going to allow me to join you in an important battle?" she said. The shock was clear on her face—she had suddenly been benched after coming along so many times already.

"That's the short of it. I made a promise to your brother," I confirmed.

"Master Naofumi, I made a declaration that I would

become your shield. That means I must always be close to you in battle!" she stated, indicating a burning desire to come along. I understood how she felt, I really did, but it was going to be just too dangerous. I understood how Fohl felt too.

"It's a little too late for that now, I'm afraid. I've already made the promise. I never break a promise, ever. And I made this promise—it's a real thing." Even if Atla wanted it, Fohl would never allow it.

"My brother . . . made you promise . . ." Atla walked away, unsteady on her feet. I didn't like the way she was moving.

"Naofumi, do you think she'll be okay?" Ren asked.

"Can't say I'm not concerned, but going after her now would be playing right into her hands . . ." I muttered. Atla could come on too strongly even for me sometimes. She said things like "A god can't be wrong!" which made her a bit of a liability if I pushed her too far.

I could understand why Fohl just wanted her somewhere safe, although I was also impressed by her desire to protect me. As the Shield Hero, it was nice to have someone standing up for me for once . . . but I also didn't want her to actually become a shield either.

"Mr. Naofumi?" Raphtalia knocked on the door and then poked her head around it. "Atla just walked past me, looking more dejected than I've ever seen her before. What happened in here?"

"Well, I made a promise with Fohl about not letting Atla join us in the Phoenix battle. I was just talking about that . . ."

"I see. She heard you," Raphtalia said, looking back behind her. "I'll be taking part, just so you know."

"Yeah, I know. I'm counting on it," I said. However, I did also have feelings of wanting her to stay behind too. That was why I could understand Fohl's request.

"Whatever happens, I will fight for you, father-in-law!" Motoyasu shouted eagerly, but it was easy enough to ignore him.

"There's going to be trouble when Fohl comes back," Ren commented.

"Oh, Fohl . . . time for you to show your mettle," was Raphtalia's take. That wasn't going to be an easy conversation. Would Fohl really be able to stop Atla?

With that, the conversation between the heroes came to an end and we started our preparations to take on the Phoenix.

Chapter Nine: Siblings' Squabble

It was two days later.

Fohl returned to the village, having finished receiving his instruction from the old lady. She had apparently been very pleased with the rapid progress being made by those under the heroes.

There was the Shield Hero power-up method. But maybe this was partly thanks to me.

"Brother! I want to fight too!" Atla pleaded.

"No!" Fohl replied. This had been going on since he returned. For now, at least, it didn't look like Atla was just going to try and silence him through violence. Of course, if she tried anything so silly, she definitely wouldn't get to take part.

There was no trusting someone who'd do that.

Still, Atla was unwavering when it came to anything that might pose a threat to my life. She was absolutely devoted to me. Maybe once I'd had a bit of a fetish for having a girl follow me so blindly, but after actually meeting one, all I really felt for her was worry.

Still, I was an evildoer, one who laughed at the misfortune of others, so maybe I didn't have the right to such a reaction.

Could one as evil as me, raising slaves in order to happily

send them off to risk their lives, hope to have anything like a family? Of course not.

So I just quietly watched Fohl and Atla's exchange.

"I'm asking you so nicely and you still won't let me go?" Atla continued.

"That's right, Atla. There's no way I can take you into somewhere so dangerous," Fohl firmly replied.

"Brother, everywhere is dangerous. We don't know what could happen, or when, and then we could just be dead," Atla went on.

"That's not quite right. So long as you are here, you will be safe," Fohl countered.

"Do you really think so? While Master Naofumi is away, someone may pour poison into the river. A sudden plague may kill me. People jealous of Master Naofumi's deeds may come to the village, and I'd get caught up in the commotion." Atla went straight to some pretty extreme examples.

Those things weren't going to happen . . . right? Poisoning the river? That would really be crossing the line.

Still, maybe I'd talk with Rat about planting some bioplants to keep the river clean.

"Can you at least be a little realistic?" Fohl chided.

"I'm just telling you that 'safety' is an illusion. I want to protect Master Naofumi from that sadness! Everything I just said, those things that could happen, they apply to Master

Naofumi too. If I'm not there, a stray arrow may hit him," Atla continued. Huh? So now I was involved too?

She really was twisting things to her own convenience.

This was another world. It would take more than a stray arrow to kill the Shield Hero.

"I don't want to sit around just being protected! Please, let me fight too!" Atla still wasn't done.

"And I'm telling you that isn't going to happen!" Fohl remained steadfast.

"I'm not weak anymore!" Atla countered.

"That arrogance is what puts you in danger!" Fohl shot back. Seriously. Were they ever going to stop?

That said though, if I got involved, the result wouldn't lead to anything better. There was nothing I could do. Even if I tried to use her age as a reason, there were other young girls just like Atla who would be fighting.

I guess it was a little late to point out how terribly twisted I was.

"We can't reach an agreement, can we, Atla?" Fohl finally conceded.

"No, we can't." At least Atla was in agreement about this.

"Then, as those of the bloodline of the hakuko, you know what we have to do," Fohl said. He raised his fist at Atla and unleashed a wave of murderous intent.

What the hell was about to kick off?

"I do," Atla replied. "For the sake of showing my resolve, I'll now display my strength to you, brother."

"If you lose to me, you'll keep my promise. This is the very reason I went and trained," Fohl revealed.

"I will be true to my word. If I can't even defeat you, brother, I've no place to claim I can defend Master Naofumi," Atla replied. Another bit of a jump from her.

Anyway, I'd heard a lot of chatter about fights between Fohl and Atla. Fohl would generally win if he had Raphtalia's help, apparently. I looked over at her now.

"Without your help, can Fohl beat Atla?" I asked.

"Maybe once every three times, although since Q'ten Lo, I think that's bumped up to two in three," she informed me. Not a sterling record, but not bad.

Ren and Itsuki had said Atla was developing faster, but when pure guts were thrown into the equation, Fohl's chances likely increased. He'd been a fighter since before he met us too, so it could come down to the one with the most experience.

"Come then, brother. We fight," Atla declared.

"Indeed," Fohl replied. The siblings pointed their fists at each other and prepared for battle.

The two of them had quite different fighting styles.

Fohl normally used his fists to punch his foes, while Atla mainly used thrusts with her fingers extended. Rather than punching, it was more like she was stabbing at weak spots.

This fight would decide whether Atla was going to take part in the battle with the Phoenix. The wind blew through, and a single bioplant leaf danced past.

The moment it fell to the ground, the fight started.

With a shout, Fohl moved—and fast—right up in front of Atla, then struck down with his fist and a grunt. Atla used her own hands to redirect the blow, avoiding it by a hair's breadth.

Fohl's fist stuck into the ground.

A thud rang out, and cracks spiderwebbed out from the impact.

"Now!" Atla shouted. From behind Fohl, her own attack came down.

"No way!" Fohl was practically standing on his hands, his fist still stuck in the ground, and he twisted his body to deliver a kick to Atla.

With an annoyed sound, she blocked the kick with one hand, then twisted her body around his leg to absorb the impact before landing again. She attempted another strike, but Fohl leapt up from his inverted position, recovered himself, and then launched a flying kick at Atla.

All of this took only five seconds. These hakuko really didn't mess about when it came to martial arts.

The two of them dropped back and calmed their breathing.

"Just as I thought. You're clearly becoming stronger and stronger, Atla. As your brother, that makes me very proud," Fohl stated.

"That condescending tone is exactly why you will lose, brother," Atla fired back, not taking the compliment.

"Three months. In just three months, I can't believe the progress we have both made. Truly remarkable," Fohl commented.

"I agree. Three months seems short, but it's long enough for a person to change," Atla replied.

"You've changed, Atla. I can't believe how you used to worry about being a burden, just by being alive," Fohl recalled.

"I haven't changed at all," Atla countered. "Just my being alive continues to cause trouble for so many people. That's why I want to lighten the burden I create. I'm including you in that, brother. I want to protect you too," Atla confessed.

Having both caught their breath, they continued the conversation while continuing the fight.

"I don't want to wait somewhere safe for the danger to pass. If I can use my strength to protect Master Naofumi, you, and the others in this village, I'll happily step up. If that's what Master Naofumi is trying to do, then I can at least keep him safe while he does it," Atla said.

"Why do you always have to bring him into it?!" Fohl raged.

"Don't you see it, brother? Don't you understand what lies there in the deepest part of Master Naofumi?" Atla asked. To that, Fohl had no reply.

The fight continued, neither able to land a decisive blow.

Both of them moved so fast that everyone watching could barely keep up.

"Oh my, look at them go!" Sadeena offered.

"Amazing. This is how people from other worlds can fight?" Shildina commented too, each sister voicing her opinion almost at the same time. Hah! The pair of them were a little better. Just the night before, Sadeena had done something to piss Shildina off, and the two of them had basically re-created their scrap in Q'ten Lo.

"Shildina!" came a child's voice.

"Ruft . . . whatever is the matter?" Shildina asked the boy, who was standing at her side. Ruft had been gradually increasing his level, as an aside here. He was getting a little taller too, perhaps. The change wasn't as pronounced as with Raphtalia.

"That's quite an impressive battle. Shildina. Do you think I could ever become that strong?" Ruft asked.

"I don't think you'd be suited to fighting exactly like that," Shildina replied.

"Me either," Sadeena chimed in. "I wouldn't recommend anything but close-quarters fighting for you, little Ruft."

"Tell me, Shield Hero, why are those two fighting?" Now Ruft turned his attention to me.

"We're going to be fighting a monster called the 'Phoenix' before too much longer, and they're trying to decide if Atla gets to come along," I explained.

"T-that sounds dangerous! Will I have to fight it too?" he asked timidly.

"In your case, Ruft, I'd stop you myself even if you wanted to. You're still too low a level, and, well . . . other stuff," I covered. I wanted to keep Ruft as insurance, in case Raphtalia decided she didn't want to take over as Heavenly Emperor of Q'ten Lo. After he'd grown up a bit, no one would think he was the same kid, even if we took him back. He'd pass him off as a distant relation who just looked like him—something like that.

"I see . . . but I can kind of understand how they feel. It's plain on both of their faces that they want to fight for someone," Ruft observed.

"Hmmm." I agreed with the kid. They had good intentions, surely.

Ren and Itsuki were following the battle with their eyes, each gripping their own weapons hard. Perhaps they were considering what action would be best to take. I might have done the same, if I was more objective about the whole thing.

Motoyasu had gone to set up the portal location, so he wasn't around. He probably wouldn't be that bothered about this anyway.

"Atla, you've made your resolve firm to me. But I still can't accept you going into danger. It's time for me to end this!" Fohl declared. Then he thrust his arms in front of himself and started to focus his awareness.

With a suitable roar, Fohl transformed into his therian-thrope form.

That alone was enough to give his abilities a real boost. This hadn't been a real battle until this point.

"We'll see about that. You are going to have to accept it! I'll fight you at full strength too!" Then both of them triggered Hengen Muso Style Muso Activation.

It was like the very air was vibrating.

Everyone there also experienced the difference in the deadly intent emitted by these two fighters. Fohl was like a feral beast. Hot life force, almost like anger, rolled off him in waves.

Opposing him, the life force from Atla was cold, ruthless almost, like something other than human.

So we had burning heat, seeking to bend his opponent to her knees—and chilling cold, looking for any chance for the kill.

The spectators held their collective breath as the two combatants powerfully clashed again.

"Hengen Muso Style Fist Technique! Tiger Break!" Fohl's life force swelled upward. Then he fired off a punch at Atla.

"Gah!" Each time one of Fohl's fists struck her, life force passed through Atla's body. That energy was emitted in the shape of a tiger.

It was a combination skill, an application of Point of Focus that placed its emphasis on ignoring defense. With its incredible increase in power, it would be far harder for Atla to nullify than Point of Focus.

I mean, I could probably handle it.

Point of Focus was a fundamental technique and yet also a key one, specialized for defense-ignoring and defense-rating attacks. However, all the power for that attack had been poured into ignoring defense, meaning it had no defense-rating properties.

Furthermore, it presupposed letting the life force that flowed inside flow outward. A whittling attack, basically. Like an attack that drains a spirit gauge in a fighting game.

"I'm not done yet! Tiger . . ." Fohl pressed his attack, the life force leaving Atla coming back to Fohl's hands and then increasing his power. Wow, so that was another application of this technique.

". . . Rush!" He finished his shout and launched a succession of blows at Atla. As each and every one of them landed, the very air trembled slightly with each thudding impact. Dust was thrown up from the ground, and after finishing his rain of blows, Fohl stepped away from Atla.

"How's that?!" he shouted, probably going too far. The others might have wanted to reply, but I had seen what else had happened.

"Very impressive, brother," Atla replied. She was pretty beaten up, but she was still on her feet. The same could hardly be said for Fohl, who suddenly grunted in pain. "At each point of impact, I deployed a technique that S'yne has been teaching to Master Naofumi and me," she went on to explain.

Then Atla made a Wall appear in front of her hand.

"You might want to liken it to having rammed your fists repeatedly into a very hard wall. And in each opening that you created, I took the chance to attack your arms with thrusts of my own," Atla revealed. Interesting. So she hadn't just been taking a beating.

It was a technique we had learned for defensive purposes, but against someone fighting barehanded like Fohl, it also had this application. Fohl had been wearing gloves more often recently, but he still preferred to go without. He also wasn't the type to fight his sister with power-enhancing gloves on.

Even so, Atla was weaving between those high-speed attacks to strike back at her brother's arms. Just how crazy was she?

"Impressive, Atla. You've really given me a beating," Fohl admitted.

"Not as bad as the one you've given me," Atla spluttered, coughing up a little blood. So she hadn't been able to stop all of those attacks.

"Now it's my turn. You can see this, can't you, brother?" There was a bead composed of life force above Atla's palm. It swelled up to reveal a tiger trapped inside.

"That's my life force?" Fohl asked.

"Correct. The life force that you unleashed at me. I couldn't get all of it, but I managed to trap some of it, like this. Now, you know what happens next, I presume?" she taunted. In an instant, Atla rushed up to Fohl and rammed the bead into his abdomen. From the look of the technique, she was doing more than just reflecting back the life force she had collected. It was very similar to the Point of Focus that Eclair and Rishia often used. It was like adding an attack to the counterattack move Bead. Why, if one was going to give it a name . . .

"It's only temporary for now, but maybe we could call it Bead of Focus," Atla suggested.

However, in that same instant, Fohl launched a fist imbued with concentrated life force right at Atla.

"Hengen Muso Style Fist Technique! Tiger Blow!" The ground erupted upward as they clashed, throwing dust and dirt into the air. Two shadows burst out from amid the cloud, spinning through the air as they went flying away.

Then, moaning, the two of them lay on the ground.

That was how powerful the attacks had been. One, or even both of them, might well be unable to continue the fight.

I checked their status.

Neither one of them was dead, but the health of both had been seriously depleted. Atla looked to be at a slight disadvantage.

"Managing this with just basic techniques—" S'yne started, who was also watching nearby.

"She is saying that it is quite impressive to have reached this level using just basic techniques," her familiar explained.

"You said it. That's basically a whole new move now," I agreed. She gathered and collected together the life force sent into her body, concentrated it, then returned it to the opponent and made it explode. I wasn't at that level yet.

With a groan, Atla unsteadily stood back up. Fohl staggered back up to his own feet too. He almost fell back over but managed to stand firm. Atla fared worse and appeared ready to tumble forward.

"Atla, I've beaten you," Fohl said.

"N-not yet you haven't," Atla retorted, stamping the ground with a *thud*.

"Look at yourself. You can barely stand!" Fohl replied.

"Brother . . . when faced with a battle you can't afford to lose, would you just give up and collapse?" Atla asked.

"No, I guess not," he admitted.

"Then there's only one thing to do. The same thing you would do, brother," Atla stated.

"Very well. Then I'll end this," Fohl replied, turning his fist on the tottering Atla again. Fohl was looking pretty unsteady himself, of course.

If this was going to "end it," did that mean one of them

would die? That was what it was starting to feel like. We didn't need anyone dying before the wave even started.

Huh? Ren started saying something to me.

"Naofumi, watch this. What happens next is the reason we think Atla is stronger than Fohl."

"What's going to happen?" I rarely got to see Atla fighting at full strength, after all. So I didn't know what was going on, but Ren and the others seemed to know.

Atla started breathing heavily. Life force started to gather around her. What was this? It looked like her wounds were healing a little, even.

"She can recover her stamina in the middle of battle. So the longer the break goes on for, the more of a disadvantage her opponents are placed at," Ren explained. Just what was the extent of her powers? When had she learned this technique?

Well, Fohl was also catching his breath in a similar way, recovering his health.

There was still much to learn from the Hengen Muso Style.

With her own shout, Atla thrust her fist at Fohl and charged forward. Fohl swung his own fist in reply. With a *thud*, both attacks landed.

With that, both of them stopped moving.

Having fallen quiet, I moved in closer to the pair to see what was happening.

Both of them had passed out standing up! They were

completely out of it. Quite the party trick, but I guess I should've expected it from these two muscle-heads.

"As the source of your power, I, the Shield Hero, order you! Let the true way be revealed once more, and heal these before me. All Zweite Heal!" I intoned healing magic with an area effect and healed the two of them.

Fohl was the first one to recover consciousness.

"Ah! I was . . ." he started.

"It's a draw. You both passed out together," I reported.

"I see . . ." he replied. Fohl lifted Atla into his arms, as she still hadn't come around yet.

"So? Are you going to make her stay behind?" I inquired. Fohl didn't answer the question but started off toward their house. It didn't look like his silence was due to any feelings of dislike toward me, because his face looked like he was smiling.

Whatever could have made him so happy?

Then Fohl did say something.

"You have my gratitude for having made Atla this strong."

I watched them leave, her still in his arms.

"He thanked you, didn't he?" Raphtalia said. Then she stood, watching Fohl's receding back with a distant look in her eyes. "Honestly thanked you, Mr. Naofumi, for having raised up his precious Atla to be this strong."

I hadn't done anything I thought I deserved thanks for.

Still, I could understand. In the same way, I was proud of

the progress Raphtalia had made. If there was someone who had helped her achieve that, I might feel the same way toward them.

"Hmm." That said, Atla was becoming too powerful to ignore. She was already plenty strong, but she still had plenty more potential too. I should probably start counting her as second only to the heroes in terms of strength.

"Little Shildina, we can't let those two make us look too bad," Sadeena commented.

"Indeed. We have to show sweet Naofumi what we can do too," Shildina replied. These killer whale sisters always had something to say!

"I already know all too well how strong you pair are, so no need to show me anything," I told them firmly.

"One thing, sweet Naofumi," Shildina said, a bit of a troubled look on her face.

"What now?" I asked.

"Oh, it's nothing much. I just need you to tell the village filolials something," she replied. Ruft and I both jerked in response to those words. The trauma . . . The trauma rose in me again.

"Tell them what?" I ventured. I really wanted to keep my distance from them.

"I need them to stop pestering me about how to use magic to fly. Can you ask them to stop?" she implored. Ah, right.

Shildina could use magic to fly—well, swim—through the air. I could understand why the filolials, flightless birds that would use wind magic, might want to try and copy that particular trick.

They'd been giving it a try but hadn't been able to get it to work.

Filolials were great at vocal mimicry, but it seemed flying using magic was a bit more difficult for them.

"That's hard magic that only little Shildina can use. I'm even jealous of that myself," Sadeena piped up.

"Ah, as if you can't fly a little yourself," Shildina shot back, glaring at her sister.

"Not like you can. I just use a magnetic field through an application of my lightning. I can barely hold it for thirty seconds," Sadeena stated. But in beast transformation support she could become a killer whale and fly all she liked . . . No, best not to say that. Some of the sparks flickering between them might transfer over to me.

"I'd tell them that I can't fly for extended periods myself, but they still pester me so, climbing onto my back and asking me to fly with them. I don't have much choice, so I launch them around a bit." Shildina started to shake a little, and I placed a comforting hand on her shoulder, well aware of her suffering. So she could at least launch them. But with those numbers, every day, day after day, that wasn't going to be easy.

This was like a gathering of a support group for sufferers

of filolial attacks. Man, I wanted to get those creatures out of my village.

"We'll have to put the Raph species to work," I said.

"Okay . . ." Shildina replied.

"It started with Ruft, and now I'm seeing that you also seem to be getting along mysteriously well with Shildina, Mr. Naofumi . . . and hey, don't bring the Raph species into this either!" Raphtalia had noticed how I was smoothly inducing Shildina to make use of them.

"So, Raphtalia, you're going to persuade those filolials, are you? Make them understand that only Shildina can use that technique?" I rounded on her, just a little.

"Well . . . she really is the only one who can use it?" Raphtalia confirmed. Hah, see, she didn't want to do it either.

"The only way is to incant magic using your voice and your awareness at the same time. If you can't do that, you've got no chance," Shildina confirmed.

"Okay . . . I'll give it a try, although I can't promise anything," Raphtalia said. The flightless filolials just wanted to fly.

As for Shildina's flight, I very much suspected that she used it to get a look of the lay of the land, due to her terrible sense of direction while on the ground.

The day passed in that fashion.

The next day, I was researching accessories, apart from Raphtalia.

"Master Naofumi!" Atla appeared, accompanied by Fohl and looking very happy.

"What's up?" I asked.

"I've been allowed to take part in the expedition to defeat the Phoenix. Now I can go with you," she reported.

"I see," I replied. The fight had ended in a draw, but Fohl appeared to have given his permission anyway.

"That said, we'll be facing a powerful foe, so I need to become much stronger. I'm in a good mood today too. I'm going to have Raphtalia give me an even more thorough training session. I'll see you later!" With that, Atla dashed off. I thought she might try and grab onto me first, but no. She really was taking this seriously.

"You sure about this?" I asked Fohl.

"Yeah. It's better than trying to leave her in the village and having her come after us anyway and get hurt," he replied.

"You think it's that simple?" I asked. He'd certainly changed his tune.

"Yes, it is. I just have to protect Atla. Nothing has changed," Fohl stated.

"Fair enough," I concluded. Fohl had a clear soft spot for Atla. Still, the conditions might have been to win the fight, but seeing as it had been a draw, I guess leaving her behind would be difficult to enforce.

There was quite a refreshed, happy look on Fohl's face,

which kind of annoyed me. But I decided to just ignore it. He didn't say anything, but he was looking at me. There was something about him now that reminded me of how Atla felt around me.

"Stop looking at me like that. It makes me uncomfortable," I told him. Fohl stopped it right away, but from then on, I caught him looking at me in the same way often during conversation.

It was a few more days later.

Tomorrow would likely be the day that we set off for the region where the Phoenix was sealed away. Our core group would be Motoyasu, Ren, Itsuki, Rishia, Raphtalia, Filo, the filolials, Raph-chan, the Raph species, Fohl, Atla, Sadeena, Shildina, S'yne, Rat, Keel, and any others from the village slaves and monsters who wanted to come along.

Imiya and the others focused mainly on making stuff would be staying behind.

I couldn't afford to force anyone to do this, and so I cautioned them no less than three times.

"The waves aren't playtime. Even I'm not confident I can protect you all. If you don't think you can make it back alive, don't come with us!" I declared. I just had to hope that they were hearing me.

I really, really wanted to keep the damage down to the minimum—to overcome the wave with as little trouble as possible.

All the slaves nodded their agreement, but I had to question if they really understood what they were getting themselves into.

Chapter Ten: Home of the Phoenix

The queen was joining us as the head of the coalition army. She seemed to have some idea of what had gone down in Siltvelt and Q'ten Lo. I was thankful for her reconnaissance abilities.

The castle would be left in Melty's care. The town would be handled by a skilled noble, a man who had looked after Keel in Melromarc. Eclair would be handling Melty's protection. We couldn't afford to take the nation's entire fighting force with us, and she'd make an effective guard.

She'd still looked upset at not being able to fight the wave. She was pretty strong, that much was true, so I could understand that feeling. Still, she'd shaken Raphtalia by the hand and entrusted us to her.

The queen also had Trash along with her too, sitting in the wagon. He looked even older than the last time I saw him. He'd been like that since seeing Atla, apparently. He hated me, but having her—who was apparently the spitting image of his own sister—now placed under my command was probably keeping him in check. He still glared at me, but when Atla was by my side, that glare softened.

With all that going on, we arrived at where the Phoenix was sealed.

Motoyasu getting a portal for us meant the trip over was a smooth one. There was also a dragon hourglass at our destination, so Raphtalia was put to work using Return Dragon Vein to bring in some of the forces from places like Melromarc and Siltvelt.

"So this is where the Phoenix is sealed," I said to no one in particular. The country we had arrived in was, well, barely large enough to be called a country, a real tiny backwater. There were people in the castle town dressed in what looked like Chinese clothing. It was a China-like nation but with differing tastes from Siltvelt. Exactly how it was different I couldn't really express well in words.

It was like a regional thing, looking the same at a glance but having subtle differences. In terms of Japanese history, it was like the difference between the Muromachi and Edo periods.

"First let's head to the castle," said the queen, walking ahead and leading the way through the castle town. She didn't really seem to know the way, so I wasn't sure she had to go to the trouble of guiding us.

"There aren't many people here, are there?" I noted. It was almost odd. There were so few people around we almost had the streets to ourselves. The town really looked to have fallen on hard times.

I wasn't quite sure what to make of being told there was a castle here.

"After all the trouble with the Spirit Tortoise, talk of the Phoenix that slumbers here also awakening caused a bit of a panic, and most of the people fled," the queen explained.

"I mean, fair enough . . ." The Spirit Tortoise had done its fair share of damage. I could see people choosing to run from that. I guess the rumors of the damage that had been caused were enough to scare most people away.

"So? Are we going to talk with the leaders of this nation?"

"That's right. We are to have an audience with a representative," the queen stated.

"Hmmm." I wasn't convinced.

Rightly so. The chamber the queen finally led us into had only one single, young-looking kid sitting on the throne.

This was their representative? Another kid ruler, like Ruft?

But no, he wasn't quite that young. More like Melty, maybe.

"You are most welcome, the four holy heroes and the queen of Melromarc. I am the king of this nation," the boy said.

"The king? You're not the ruler I know. Whatever has happened here?" the queen asked.

"Our previous monarch cleaned out the treasure room and departed our lands, along with his minions," the new king informed us. I gave a deep and lingering sigh. Fleeing his own kingdom to avoid being caught up in the Phoenix battle—just how rotten could you get?

"Very well," the queen continued. "So you are now the representative of this land."

"That is how things currently stand," the boy agreed.

"Hey, queen," I said.

"What is it?" she asked.

"Are all the royal families in this world so extreme?" I couldn't help but ask.

"He should be of the most capable bloodline of Faubrey, so I can't fathom why he would run away when faced with crisis," she explained. Hold on. Was it the very Faubrey bloodline of Trash? The Seven Star Heroes hadn't come to see us either. They seemed pretty suspicious overall anyway. Who knew how far they could even be trusted?

"That reminds me. You ordered the Seven Star Heroes in Faubrey to come see me, right? What's happening with that?" I asked the queen.

"I've made contact with them three times, but nothing has happened yet. Then there's the incident with the one claiming to be a Seven Star Hero who you encountered in Siltvelt. Everything is still being confirmed," she explained. We needed to stay on guard, is what it sounded like.

There'd been some pretty crazy people amongst the vassal weapon holders in Kizuna's world. It was starting to look like that problem wasn't exclusive to that world.

"We welcome the four holy heroes and those of the coalition army. As requested in advance, we have also prepared the materials for you concerning the Phoenix. Please take a look at them," the king told us. Then he clapped his hands and a Shadow and a scholar came forward to show us the way.

"We'll have the coalition army remain in the castle town and its environs, if that would be acceptable," the queen said.

"Of course . . ." The boy's expression was grim. The harvest around here had been poor, I'd been told. The remaining people I had seen had looked pretty thin.

Right, of course. There was something of a global famine going on.

I had the bioplants, so it hadn't really bothered me . . . but these people looked like they could hardly get any food at all.

"Shadow," I said.

"Whatever iz it?" he asked. I beckoned him over, took some bioplant seeds from my pocket, and scattered them into his hands. "We're going to be staying here a while. Plant those somewhere to secure some food for us. You can fill your own food stores up too," I told him.

"Very well," came the reply. Then the queen also gave a deep bow at my actions, and the child-king joined her.

"Our gratitude for your mercy, Hero," he offered.

"Letting people starve is only going to blow back on us in the end," I told him. Damn. The food issues were pretty serious around here. I was starting to worry about how long the supplies we had carried in were going to last.

"Is there a familiar in this nation? Something like Ost?"

I asked. Ost had been difficult to face as an assassin, but she'd been very impressive as the Spirit Tortoise. Whomever we had to fight here, I'd like to at least say hello before the fun started.

"We haven't confirmed the presence of any such individual here . . ." the queen answered.

"Ren, Itsuki, Motoyasu, you got any game-based knowledge on this subject?" I asked the three of them.

"Not really. In the game I played, the whole world came together to fight. Anyone like that would stick out right away," Ren said.

"That's right," Itsuki confirmed.

"So say I too!" Motoyasu added. I guess Ost had been the familiar of the Spirit Tortoise, transforming herself into a human simply because the tortoise had been the first of the four benevolent animals.

Hmmm. This might even make things easier in the end.

"Let's take a look at these materials you've collected," I said.

"Of courze. Thiz way," said the Shadow. We finished our simple audience with the king and were shown through to where the Phoenix materials had been gathered.

Before that though . . .

"Raphtalia, Fohl, Atla, go and see how the coalition army is doing," I ordered them.

"They should know what to do already, right?" Raphtalia said.

"But we've got more coming in too. I need you to bring them all up to speed. If anything happens, report to me at once," I explained.

"Ah, very well. Understood," Raphtalia replied. She and the others would have no part to play in looking through the Phoenix materials.

I'd told Filo to secure a spot for her wagon and survey the surrounding terrain, so she was already gone.

Ah, having her sing for everyone might be a good way to increase morale. It sounded like she was quite a popular singer. Before meeting with us in Siltvelt, she'd been singing in each location she visited with Melty while raising her level and becoming quite famous for it. So I was told, anyway.

I'd seen anime in which singing boosted morale. Maybe it really worked.

Then I noticed S'yne, who had really been on edge, constantly looking around since we got here.

"No need to be quite so tense," I told her.

"But—"

"She says that it is just at times like this, prior to a large battle or during the fighting, that her foes are likely to appear," her familiar, the Keel doll, said for her.

"Can I go and—"

"Now she is asking if she may go and check the vicinity, just to be sure," the doll continued.

"If you feel you must. But don't overdo things beforehand and then fall asleep in the battle," I warned her. S'yne nodded in response and then headed out.

She made a good point though. We needed to keep security tight right now.

"Master Naofumi," Atla called out with her hand raised.

"What?" I asked, somewhat distracted.

"If you need anything, just let me know," she said.

"I will. S'yne said pretty much the same thing," I replied to Atla and then headed to look at the Phoenix materials.

Chapter Eleven: The Lost Hero's Diary

The collected documents explained the extent of the damage that had been suffered during the previous revival. That extent was pretty extensive, from the look of it. As expected, they had summoned a hero to aid them and ultimately succeeded in sealing the Phoenix away again.

"Ren, Motoyasu, Itsuki, do you know where the Phoenix is sealed?" I asked.

"That mountain there," Itsuki promptly replied, pointing to a mountain outside the window. It looked like something from one of those dusty old traditional Chinese landscape paintings.

"Yeah, that's the place," Ren confirmed.

"That's right. Father-in-law, that's the mountain," Motoyasu added, just to be sure.

"Okay . . . and in the game, how was the seal broken?" I asked.

"You mean the quest itself? The Phoenix revives from the sealing inscription up there," Ren informed me.

"I see," I said.

Then we turned to look at more of the materials. There was a diary left by the hero who sealed the Phoenix away. It looked to contain everything from when he was summoned to fight the Phoenix, right up until he died of old age. This was what we needed—the knowledge of those who came before us.

All we had to do was copy what the previous hero did and defeat the Phoenix that way.

Of course, if you threw in the trouble we had with Ost, it might not go quite that smoothly.

The diary described the days of fighting that took place after he was summoned to this other world and chosen as the hero of the Seven Star Gauntlets. I couldn't really tell what kind of place he had come from. There was no mention of VRM-MOs or superpowers. Maybe something closer to my world then, or Motoyasu's?

It was almost like an Internet novel written from real experience—something like that. Much of it was bragging about having defeated some annoying foe or another. There was also boasting about his forming a harem. I didn't need to hear about that. All the sexy scenes with women could be cut too. I really didn't care about him celebrating losing his virginity or all the details about how he met his first wife through to when they finally tied the knot.

She had been a princess there when he was summoned, but for us that particular princess was pretty much a taboo word. Even her name would not be named.

I needed to capture and execute her still. Just where was Witch hiding?!

Anyway, was this how things were for everyone summoned here? Myself included?

If I skipped too much, it felt like I might miss something important, so I read it carefully. I really needed to find some useful information quickly. Still, I had to start wondering what he was thinking, leaving this as his legacy for future generations. The only conclusion I could come to was that it was just for himself, an unfiltered outpouring of his feelings. It was written in Japanese, so no one in this world could read it. That meant he probably never intended for other people to understand this. Otherwise, he would have likely dramatized it up a bit.

I read on and simply had to believe he didn't intend to leave this behind. It would be too painful of a legacy otherwise.

Ren looked a bit puzzled by it too.

Motoyasu . . . was having Green read it. He was messing around with the feathers of all three of them. Could she even read Japanese? She did look like the smartest of the three, but still . . .

Itsuki had an indifferent look on his face. I presumed he'd speak up if he spotted anything.

I really needed this terrible piece of literature to hurry up and get to the Phoenix battle. With that in mind, I kept reading . . . and ended up reading it all.

For some reason, most unnaturally, the key sections about the battle with the Phoenix and anything else relating to the four benevolent animals or the waves were completely missing.

I'd also been hoping to learn something about methods to class up or the power-up method.

"Hey. The very part we want is missing!" I said.

"These are all the materials we have," came the response.

Really? The book was pretty beat up and barely legible. Maybe someone had intentionally removed the parts we wanted. That was what I almost wanted to think, seeing as how just the most important parts were missing.

"There was conflict in this region and much was lost to fire," the scholar revealed.

"Fire that was pretty choosy about the pages it burnt," I snarked.

"I'm so very sorry . . ." the scholar apologized, checking over the pages again.

"Naofumi, if there was ever someone here like that Makina in Q'ten Lo, that might account for the missing information," Itsuki said.

"Yeah, good point," I agreed with him. Were there people like that everywhere in this world? People who plotted to destroy books and historical materials?

"There's one more thing, right here—a written copy," the scholar said, handing over a sheaf of papers. They didn't even have the decency to bind it into a book. It was full of holes too.

Still, we managed to find—barely—some information on the Phoenix.

The goal of the Phoenix . . . as its source . . . prevent . . .
It cannot be sealed during the terminal wave.
To defeat it . . . simultaneously . . . both . . .
Its attack patterns—

That was as much as we could read from the crappy copy. Halfway through, the Japanese basically fell apart and became unreadable. We only managed to make this much out with all the heroes working together.

Cutting off just before talking about attack patterns—were you kidding? I almost demanded that the one responsible for "caring" for these texts be brought before me.

"We discovered its purpose from the Spirit Tortoise and in Kizuna's world. It's to prevent the fusing of the worlds due to the wave," Ren recapped succinctly.

"I'm not sure what good that does us," I said.

"I mean, if we'd fought it without meeting Ost, Kizuna, or the others, I doubt we'd ever have worked it out ourselves," he said.

That didn't get us any closer to working out its attack patterns though.

"Next, we have a mural that the hero from the past left behind. Please follow me and we can take a look at that," the scholar revealed.

"Sure," I said. Hoping for something as enlightening as the one in the town of the Spirit Tortoise, we headed toward the temple——which, as expected, had been transformed into something of a tourist trap.

Chapter Twelve: The Final Seven Star Weapon

"What are so many of the coalition army soldiers doing lining up over there?" I asked. As we proceeded toward the temple with the mural, I noticed a long line in front of what might be called the front gate. It was a building a little distance away.

There were even merchants walking along the line and selling their wares. I was impressed by their guts. They missed no chance for a sale, even with the revival of the Phoenix looming ever closer.

"We will need you to see that later as well, Hero," the scholar said.

"Hmmm." No need to ask for details now then.

The key thing at the moment was finding a way to deal with the Phoenix. There was a good possibility that something only I could understand was going to be written in the mural. After all, to the people of this world, it might just look like a fancy pattern, but in our world, it could be writing.

And so we entered the temple.

It had, as I had expected, been converted into a tourist destination, due to its links to the legendary hero. We proceeded through the stone temple. It had a pretty overstated atmosphere. The sound of our footsteps rang out loudly.

Then a priest-looking guy came out to meet us. His clothing looked like that of a clergyman. What was this Chinese-Western mixture?!

He illuminated the dark temple with a candle. There were statues of the Phoenix dotted around the interior. With the darkness as well, it honestly kind of put me on edge.

"So? Where's this mural left by the hero?" I asked. The walls were covered with what looked like Mayan wall paintings and other stuff that looked like text I couldn't read. None of the styles were uniform or even seemed to make sense.

It was really starting to feel like some shady guide had tricked us into coming to some cheap tourist trap.

"This way, please," the monk said and led us to a large mural right at the back of the temple.

It was so dark, though, that I couldn't make out the whole thing.

"It's dark, isn't it? First Glowfire." The queen illuminated the dark chamber with some magic. What appeared from the gloom was indeed a large mural depicting information on the Phoenix. I couldn't be sure that the hero had really left this, but it seemed to start with the image of a large bird turning its surroundings into a sea of fire.

So its attacks were fire bombardments caused by flapping its wings and slashing with those nasty claws.

The Phoenix looked like a bird based on a peacock, but

with scales. Its tail and wings almost looked aquatic . . . It wasn't just all red either . . . and then, when I started to look at the coloring, there was a bit of a bombshell—the mural actually showed two birds flying around, one of five different colors and then the other showing the opposing five colors.

However, perhaps due to the length of time since it was created, the mural was also in pretty bad shape.

Still, as I took in the information, I started to see how it might attack.

To start with, one of them used magic and wing flaps to launch a bombardment from high above, while the other flew at low altitude while blowing fire and attacking with its claws. That seemed to be the basic tactic.

Of course, I was just getting all this from a painting that primarily existed to tell a story.

"It looks like a pretty tough battle," I said. The creatures burned by its flames seemed to be roaming around like burning zombies. Was that a thing?

Yeah, maybe it was. The Spirit Tortoise had done something similar.

Furthermore, the feathers that came free when it flapped its wings seemed not only to attack but also become familiars. Now that sounded like a real pain to deal with.

However, when comparing its size to the houses also depicted there, it didn't seem as large as the Spirit Tortoise. Still, it was surprisingly big though. Each one was maybe going to be a little bigger than father Gaelion had been prior to his rebirth.

And there were two of them. "Phoenixes" was actually more like it.

"Ren, does this all match with the attacks of the Phoenix in that game?" I inquired.

"Yeah, pretty much. It didn't have that breath," he said.

"They've got some attacks I haven't seen before too. Sending people flying by flapping its wings and summoning tornadoes both look new to me," Itsuki filled in.

"Father-in-law, there's one I've not seen before either," Motoyasu said. "That's summoning familiars." So there was quite a gap between the game and this reality.

Still, and I thought this every time, it was odd how Ren and the others seemed to always be missing key pieces of information almost intentionally. With incomplete information, anyone could get this stuff wrong. If I'd been in the same position, I might well have made the same mistake with the Spirit Tortoise.

The Phoenix had one especially surprising attack.

There was an image of one bird being defeated and the other swelling up. The images continued to show the swollen bird exploding apart, scorching everything with a massive explosion. This attack had caused the hero to retreat the first time he saw it.

The whole scene was up there on the wall.

It almost looked like he defeated it with one dying and the other blowing up. But when I looked more carefully at the pictures, the exploding one was shown splitting into two while blowing up.

This image seemed to suggest that if one of them was defeated, the other would self-destruct while regenerating into two new ones.

When fighting the Spirit Tortoise, Kyo had been involved. So we hadn't been able to defeat it even when the correct conditions were reached. It looked like this time defeating just one of them meant the other bird would launch a powerful counterattack and also then regenerate the defeated one.

There was even a scattering of stars drawn around the regenerated Phoenix. Perhaps it was visual language from our world to show it as being new.

Beyond that, the wall was cracked, making it hard to see everything, but it was possible to deduce that defeating both of them at once was the way to end the battle.

"Looks like we have to take them both down at the same time. If that fails, the remaining Phoenix launches a powerful self-destruct attack and then regenerates into two more birds." I spelled it out for everyone.

"As I thought, it's different from the game. In the game they share HP, and if one is defeated, the other goes down too," Ren recalled.

"A self-destruct attack, with an option for regeneration. That sounds nasty." Itsuki was as emotionless as ever, his voice a wooden monotone. He sounded like he completely lacked any kind of enthusiasm for this endeavor. From what he said though, it did sound like a serious analysis.

"Not to mention," I picked up his thought, "if one of them is always high up, attacks are likely to hit the lower one more often." That would be really dangerous, taking the whole regeneration thing into account.

"In that case, Itsuki and I will attack the high-altitude one, while father-in-law and Ren deal with the low-altitude one. How about that, I say?" Motoyasu suggested. Itsuki and Motoyasu could target enemies at a distance and I was purely defensive. Ren, meanwhile, was a close-combat fighter, so it wasn't a bad plan.

"I think that'll be how this turns out. Taking your weapons into account, Itsuki and Rishia should attack the high one, along with Motoyasu," I said.

"Okay," Itsuki replied.

"What about the coalition army?" the queen asked. It would be nice if we could defeat this just using the heroes, but that really wasn't looking too hopeful.

If the coalition army was going to take part, we should use them. That meant only one thing, pretty much.

"We need anyone who can attack at long range. If it's a

weapon, then I guess it'd be bows. And then anyone skilled at magic should attack the high target. Everyone else, attack the low one. Your majesty, I'll let you handle the planning and formations for that," I said. Still, we had all four heroes as optimized as could be. I really wanted to finish this one as easily as possible.

If there were still any unknown elements, they could cause issues, of course. Still, we had a good idea about its attack patterns now and should be enough to form a suitable plan of action.

Of course, all these records from the past might not be completely accurate, so we'd have to keep our wits about us too.

"Very well. What should we do about training?" the queen asked.

"Good question. Let's have our fliers play the two birds and sort out formations that way," I suggested.

"Understood. In that case, let's perform a coalition army joint training session for the Phoenix battle with the coalition army at once. I hope the heroes will also participate," she said.

"Sure," Ren confirmed.

"Leave it to me, I say!" Motoyasu enthused.

"I'll do my best," Itsuki said. I mean, that was why we were here. The goal was to keep our losses down as close to zero as possible.

That was the main thing.

"Now then, let's go and take a look at the other building we passed on the way," our guide suggested. Having finished looking at the Phoenix mural, the queen and the heads of this nation led the way back outside.

"Just what is that place?" I asked.

"The last of the Seven Star Weapons is housed there. It currently hasn't selected an owner," came the reply.

"Hmmm." Very interesting. "What's with the massive line of people though?"

"Surely you can work that out, Hero?" That might have sounded condescending, but it was delivered with the utmost respect. He was right too. I could pretty much work it out.

It had been the same kind of thing when Raphtalia was chosen.

The Seven Star Weapons were legendary gear that people from this world could also hold and use. Of course, anyone summoned from another world could apparently use them too. The people were lining up to try and prove that they were the Seven Star Hero, capable of wielding the sealed weapon.

There had to be a way to make some money off such a popular attraction.

One piece of silver to try your luck . . . This world had a whole hero-worshiping thing going on though, so that would probably just piss people off.

We passed alongside the line and entered the building they were queuing up for.

The item everyone was waiting to get a hold of was there in the center of the temple: one of the Seven Star Weapons embedded in a stone tablet on the wall.

The guy at the front of the line touched it and tried to take it for himself. A lot of grunting was involved. He was a coalition army soldier. His face turned bright red with the effort involved.

"That's it. Next," said a monk watching over the proceedings. The reddened challenger's shoulders slumped, and he shuffled off back the way he came.

Would they really be so happy to be chosen?

Having been chosen as the Shield Hero myself, I knew the pain such a fate could inflict. Maybe I was just being arrogant and selfish, standing there thinking that these normies were the lucky ones.

These thoughts going through my head, I checked the Seven Star Weapon.

They were gauntlets.

Based on appearance alone, they were really simply gauntlets. Almost like gloves. Like the Small Shield, they were really simple. In the center of each one, as expected, there were gemstones.

The hero weapons generally had such stones. They looked like fairly basic starting gauntlets.

"So this is the final Seven Star Weapon?" I asked.

"That is correct," our guide confirmed. Of course, the Seven Star Hero who sealed the Phoenix away last time used the gauntlets, so it makes sense they would be found here. That suggested there might be another Seven Star Weapon in the town where the Spirit Tortoise had been sealed. Might be worth checking out.

"Tell me, queen. What're these gauntlets doing here? Why doesn't Faubrey do something with them?" I asked her.

"This country was once very prosperous—according to the legend of the Gauntlet Hero," she explained.

"What about the Spirit Tortoise?" I asked.

"That one was sealed by a hero from another country," she answered.

"Okay then," I said. It sounded like the Phoenix was a relatively new legend. In any case, digging down into all this would just be a pain, so I decided not to bother. "And now they're waiting here for a new owner?"

"Correct. Most of the visitors to this country are here to see the gauntlets and hopefully claim them," she told me.

"Well, then . . ." I'd have my slaves try it too. It'd be funny if Atla obtained them. I couldn't deny she had the potential for it. Then I asked, "How long is this line going to be here?"

"During the daytime, it's here for as long as this place is open to the public," came the reply. Wow. Okay, this thing sure was popular.

"It's the times we live in. There are many adventurers who want to prove themselves too," the queen explained.

"Okay, I know this is asking a lot, but tonight do you think we could have my guys give it a try as well?" I ventured.

"I'll see what I can do. Please enjoy a little free time until the mock battle." Then she took her retainers and headed off back to the castle. As a result, that night my slaves were given first try at obtaining the weapon. It had been worth speaking up about, no doubt.

I brought my slaves from the village with me to the temple housing the Seven Star Gauntlets.

"Wow. These are the Seven Star Gauntlets?!" Keel looked at the gauntlets embedded in the tablet, sounding a little too excited.

"There was a big line of people in the daytime," Raphtalia commented. So she'd seen them too. The desire to become a hero was something shared in all worlds, from the look of it. Everyone loved the tales of a legendary sword stuck into a stone and stuff like that.

Of course, I loved them too.

Raphtalia herself had just happened to be there at the time and ended up becoming the holder of the katana vassal weapon. So you never knew what might happen.

"I feel the same kind of power that comes from your

shield, Master Naofumi." Atla was also there, alongside Fohl, both facing toward the Seven Star Weapon.

Those were the big two. I reckoned either one had a pretty good chance.

"I see. Sounds like it's the real thing," I commented. If this was just a sculpture carved into the stone, a lot of people had wasted their time queuing up and then wasted their time being dejected at not getting chosen.

Of course, there might also be those happy it was proven to be a fake. Of course it was if it didn't select them! It just depended on the person.

"In any case, you guys get to give it a try now at night, when this place is normally closed up. Everyone is going to get a turn," I told them. My proclamation was met with general agreement. At least they could do that much.

I wasn't really expecting anything. A few of these people seemed likely to be chosen.

"What about me?" Filo asked.

"If you want to fight with gauntlets, you can give it a try," I told her. She also fought in her human form and had recently taken to throwing her morning star around. She might just have what it takes.

However, she'd probably do better with claws than gauntlets. We were meant to find that one in Siltvelt, but that hadn't worked out.

"I'll give it a try!" she said. The other slaves also started to line up. Ren, Itsuki, and Rishia were already off resting in their lodgings. Motoyasu was here, of course, because of Filo.

"Come on, form an orderly line!" Sadeena ordered. She really was like a substitute parent to the slaves. Shildina was helping out too. They'd proven to be pretty close sisters, in the end.

They both fought with harpoons. What would happen if the gauntlets chose them? Might bring a bit of a gladiator vibe, but I wasn't really buying it.

"My turn!" Filo stepped up. As I had suspected, the gauntlets didn't respond at all. She tugged and pulled on them for all she was worth anyway.

"Gah! They won't come out!" she complained. I had to stop her after she transformed and started grabbing them with her legs. We didn't need the whole wall coming down.

Luckily, even that had no effect.

"Considering the danger we face at the moment, you didn't think about summoning a hero?" I asked the queen, just off the cuff, wondering why the gauntlets didn't have an owner yet. She'd told me before that all four of the holy heroes had been summoned due to the crisis faced by the world. That suggested that the Seven Star Heroes should also be chosen.

Indeed, currently they all had owners, so I was told, apart from the gauntlets. In that case, summoning a hero from another world to use them might be a good idea.

Of course, it wouldn't be the best situation if someone like the guy from the diary showed up, but it could also be a lot worse than him. Someone like Kyo from Kizuna's world might show up. He'd been born over there, of course.

"We tried the ritual numerous times but have seen no results," the queen revealed.

"Hmm." Fair enough. So it was a Seven Star Weapon that still didn't respond to a summons.

Thinking about it, these weapons had laxer conditions than the four holy ones. The four holy weapons were restricted to people from other worlds, while both people of this world and from others could use the Seven Star Weapons.

"It's an extension of fighting barehanded, right? I started out beating on monsters with my bare hands, so I understand a little of that," I said.

"Indeed you did," Raphtalia remembered. That had been back when I first got her as a slave, mainly to relieve stress.

"The gauntlets are much like your shield, Hero Iwatani. It's a Seven Star Weapon that mainly places its focus on defense," the queen explained.

"I see," I replied. Among my own shields, there were small ones much like these gauntlets. Maybe there was even some overlap in the categories. That could be useful. One strength of overlapping weapons was sharing them among allies.

Katanas, for example, fell into the sword category, so it was easy for Ren and Raphtalia to share weapons.

"What about the Seven Star Heroes? Have they made contact?" I asked.

"We are having trouble getting in touch with them. Faubrey is searching for them in earnest, I assure you," the queen informed me.

"There may be fakes out there too, pretending to be heroes. Need to be careful of them," I warned. We'd met and dealt with just one such fake in Siltvelt. I do think we should meet with them and talk, but all due care should also be taken.

I did want to ask about what kind of weapons they had and about power-up methods and stuff too.

Maybe if Trash would finally confess to having the Staff—unlikely, considering who he was. Depending on the situation, it might be better to get a new Staff Hero selected.

I mulled these things over as I watched the slaves. It was finally Atla's turn. She touched the gauntlet and tried to pull it free . . . but nothing happened at all.

"I couldn't do it," she said, quickly giving up and coming over to me. She could have tried a bit harder. "I searched it out using life force, and I found it isn't compatible with me," she reported.

"You understand that much?" I asked.

"Just a vague feeling," she confirmed.

"Wow." I was impressed.

Next was Fohl. He had a pretty determined look on his face.

"Oh? Brother, good luck! I'm sure you can do it!" Atla suddenly cheered him on.

"Sure thing!" With a shout, Fohl eagerly grabbed the weapon and pulled with all his might.

"What was that all about?" I asked Atla. It was rare for her to say anything like that to her brother. If there was a reason, I wanted to hear it.

"I felt something different in the life force, from when I tried. I was sure for a moment that my brother would do it . . . but he's disappointed me again."

"Atla?!" Fohl despaired. That was mean. Building him up just to tear him down again. Oh, Fohl, your sister was just toying with you.

These thoughts running through my head, I silently watched the rest of them try, but none of them could take it.

Chapter Thirteen: The Night Before
the Phoenix Battle

After that, I had a meeting alone with the queen in the castle.

I needed to report everything that had happened recently to her, hear reports from her side of things, and decide on the materials and other supplies we needed from Melromarc in order to prepare for the Phoenix battle—lots of things to do.

"We have the Phoenix battle in the next few days and more fighting ahead. How have things been in your lands, Hero Iwatani?" the queen eventually asked.

"I'm gathering quite a merry band," I replied.

The main thing I needed to be careful of was that they didn't think they could just do anything they wanted because they were allies of the heroes. I told the queen how Itsuki's companions had done all sorts of shady things while they were traveling with him. Just like Witch, they were now wanted criminals, but they'd vanished completely—for the moment.

Then there were the guys who seemed to have been the Church of the Three Heroes. The ones who Motoyasu took care of. If anyone could tell me, I really wanted to know why I had so many enemies.

I'd recently been thinking of spending some money to hire

a shadow human from Zeltoble, to be honest.

"I've also heard that Melty is helping to rebuild a town within your territory, the one that Count Seaetto used to manage. It sounds like a good experience for her," the queen commented.

"I'd say Melty is a big reason everything runs so smoothly. She'll make a fine queen," I replied.

"For you to praise her so highly, Hero Iwatani, my daughter must be working really hard," the queen said.

"Yeah, I guess so," I responded. She'd helped a lot with Motoyasu too. In the chaotic stable filled with the willful filolials that Motoyasu raised in the wild, Melty had stepped in and helped to start training them.

Maybe it was Motoyasu's influence, but Filo's Underling Filolial #1 had also started to look like a queen. I still hadn't seen her talking though. According to Melty and Filo, aside from the three who formed Motoyasu's direct retinue, all of the other filolials had been brought together by Underling Filolial #1 . . . whose name was Chick . . . apparently.

I guess she had some skills after all.

In order to fight the Phoenix, we'd also brought along the filolial army that Motoyasu raised. They were in competition with the Raph species, basically. Gaelion was going to talk with the dragons that the dragon knights rode and fought alongside them.

Command of the demi-human therianthropes was going well, with Raphtalia, me, Fohl, and Atla acting as representatives. Werner from Siltvelt was handling business too, by all accounts.

Then there was the Q'ten Lo contingent. Hearing that the new Heavenly Emperor Raphtalia was going to be fighting, some volunteers had expressed a desire to fight alongside her, and they'd already been added to our forces.

The queen was responsible for leading the humans.

Otherwise, the command structure was pretty solid.

There were many soldiers among the Melromarc forces who had experienced the fight with the Spirit Tortoise, so they should be able to keep up.

"Don't you dare touch Atla!" I heard Fohl's voice from the castle gardens. Huh? What now? He had been on standby in the garden . . . waiting for me, basically.

Atla and Fohl weren't suited to this kind of meeting, so I'd planned on filling them in later. It sounded like something had happened first though.

I took a look out the window to see Fohl having to forcibly carry Atla away from Trash.

Trash gently extended his arm forward, seeming to cut the air. Then he muttered something to Fohl before turning his back and moving away.

Atla shook her head, while Fohl narrowed his eyes, thinking about something.

The queen came to stand beside the window with me and watched Trash with something indescribable in her eyes.

"I hope . . . he finds himself again—his former strength— as soon as possible," she said. I'd expected as much. Somewhere deep inside she was still hoping that Trash would make it back to his old, intellectual self.

"If you ask me, I think it'd be more practical to take the Seven Star Weapon from Trash and give it to someone else," I said.

"I am sorry about this . . . but if Trash could just return to himself, I assure you that he would be able to do ten times the things anyone else could with the Staff. Even if you order it, Hero Iwatani, I cannot have the Staff taken from him," the queen affirmed.

Trash was apparently the Seven Star Staff Hero. I'd never seen him holding the staff and honestly wondered if the original king was dead and this was just a doppelganger.

Just where was he hiding the Seven Star Staff?

"Hmmm. But we don't have much leeway. If an enemy appears that we can't handle, and he won't share the hero weapon power-ups, then we'll just have to find someone else to wield it, even if it means executing him," I warned her.

"I understand," she replied. The queen was looking off into the distance but nodded at my words. I must have been imagining things, but for a moment those eyes looked just like

Raphtalia's when she was expecting something from me.

Having finished my discussions with the queen, I headed down to talk with Fohl in the garden.

"Master Naofumi!" Atla shouted. She was with him too, so . . .

"Atla, I'm taking a trip back to the village. Can you go and call Raphtalia and the others for me?" I asked her after lightly ruffling her hair to stop her from refusing.

"Very well! I'll do whatever you order me to, Master Naofumi!" With that, Atla rushed off happily. It felt like I'd started to understand how to get her to do what I wanted, recently.

"Fohl, wait a moment," I said. Her brother had been about to go after Atla, so I stopped him.

"Huh? What is it?" he replied.

"I saw you and Atla talking with Trash. What was that about?" I questioned.

"Is there any reason I have to tell you that?" he came back, a bit aggressively.

"Can't you tell that he's planning something? You know what he did to your people, right?" I fired back. Fohl quickly backed down. He had surely been told the stories when first meeting the queen. With seemingly no response to that, he started to tell me what happened.

"He started asking Atla all sorts of probing questions. Even started asking me the same thing. Things about our mother, stuff like that," he revealed.

"Did you tell him anything?" I asked.

"No, I turned him down . . . but—" Fohl's reply was cut short for a moment, as though there was something else he couldn't quite say. "He looked even older than before and seemed so listless."

"I'm not surprised," I commented. According to what I'd been told, Trash's younger sister had been a lot like Atla, which meant he probably empathized with Fohl.

"After seeing us together, he stared off into the distance and told me that I have to protect my sister, no matter the cost, or that I'd regret it. I mean, talk about stating the obvious," Fohl continued.

"I see." It might be obvious, sure, but Trash was definitely placing himself in Fohl's shoes.

I'd seen this story before.

I didn't want to know the details, but apparently Trash was a pretty capable fellow, back in his youth. Everyone in Siltvelt—his enemies at the time—had said the same thing. So it had the ring of truth to it, although I didn't exactly see where it was coming from.

Meanwhile, Atla was probably physically much stronger than Trash's sister had been and had a personality that was a bit like hers. But also, she was a bit different. Hmmm, maybe I could taunt him a little with that next time I saw him.

But I really wasn't seeing much of him recently.

Heh. I've not forgotten my grudge against you, Trash!

Atla came back with Raphtalia and the others, so we returned to the village.

"Well then. It's pretty late. How about we all get some sleep?" I suggested.

"What is the meaning of this?" Fohl suddenly came up and interjected. I'd finished the meeting with everyone from the village about the Phoenix battle and was about to return to my own room in the village when Atla and Fohl approached me.

"The meaning of what, exactly?" I asked.

"Is something the matter?" Raphtalia also asked him. It turned out that there was an issue with Atla's placement in battle.

"Why is Atla also on the front lines?" Fohl asked.

"I want to be with you at all times, Master Naofumi," she said.

"Fohl, wouldn't you rather be with Atla too?" I pointed out. I'd placed her there in order to keep Fohl focused on the fighting and because of Atla's own clear combat abilities. But maybe Fohl would prefer she was away from the front, even if it meant not being as close to him.

I guess Atla's problem was that I'd be standing at the very front, and she didn't like being any further back than that.

"Atla, if that's your issue, then you'd need to be placed at the very front," Fohl pointed out.

"I'm fine with that," she replied.

"No! You need to be further back, where it's safer!" he objected.

"Brother. That'd mean I hardly get to participate. Would you be fine with things if you were placed in a rear support unit?" she asked. Fohl made a noise, clearly having no reply.

"Come on, don't get beaten that easily," I chided him.

"Master Naofumi, I've told you before, haven't I? I want to become a shield to protect you," Atla stated.

"I mean . . ." Was she looking to steal my job or something? Not to mention that would only rile up Fohl even further.

"I'll let you stay a little behind me then, but it would be meaningless for you to stand any further forward than that. Even Raphtalia understands that much, right?" I asked, looking for some backup.

"That's right." Raphtalia nodded at my words. There would be a time to push forward, and I needed to make that decision. She talked about protecting me, but look at what we were going to be fighting. I needed her to be a little more prudent.

"Very well," she said, giving a bit of a stubborn nod. "Even so, I still want to protect you, Master Naofumi."

"I've been wondering this for a while now. Why are you so fixated on protecting Mr. Naofumi, Atla?" Raphtalia asked.

"I've been wondering the same thing," Fohl concurred. "Why do you want to protect this guy, of all people?"

"Raphtalia, brother, don't you understand?" she asked, lifting her eyebrows as though annoyed by the very question. "I don't want to rely on Master Naofumi's kindness forever. Just seeing him step in front of us, get hurt in place of one of us, makes my heart ache in my chest," she explained.

I felt like pointing out she was denying the entire point of me in combat, but on some level her words also reached me. It wasn't a bad feeling; I could say that much. Even if it ran contrary to the abilities of the Shield Hero.

"Do you think I'm joking? The person I want to stand alongside isn't the hero, but just the man, Master Naofumi." Not the hero, she said. I wasn't sure what she meant, but I guessed that was Atla's take on things.

"What are you talking about?!" Raphtalia was less receptive to the idea.

"Great question! Atla, you can do far better than this guy!" Fohl put the boot in. Hold on though. It did sound a bit like a profession of love. I hadn't realized that was what was going on here. She'd said similar things before, but I'd really just let them slide.

"Master Naofumi," she said to me directly.

"What?" I tried not to be too blunt.

"I'm drawn to your fundamental kindness. Please try not to

risk your very life just to protect the rest of us," Atla pleaded. All I could do was defend, and here she was asking this of me.

"Haha, yes, yes. Well, thank you. I do understand what you're trying to say, but I'm a crafty one, I'm afraid. You see, I'm just getting you guys to do what I can't do myself," I explained.

"So tell me, Master Naofumi, if you could fight the enemies for yourself, where would you be on the battlefield?" Atla asked. Hmmm. If I could fight normally, what would I be doing?

An interesting question . . . but I'd still be standing at the front.

I wasn't sure I'd place any trust in these slaves. When I'd first been framed, if I had any attack power myself, I probably would have raised my level alone without buying a single one of them.

"Master Naofumi, I ask this one thing of you. Don't take it for granted that you have to get hurt. Your true nature, Master Naofumi, is how much you give to others . . . and as you continue to give so much of yourself, who will heal you? Who will give back to you?" Atla asked, turning to look at Raphtalia.

"I agree with what you clearly want for Mr. Naofumi, Atla. But you're forgetting something. Mr. Naofumi himself also has a say in all this," Raphtalia told her. At those words, Atla bit her lip in annoyance.

I wasn't sure what was making her do that.

"Master Naofumi . . . if someone were to lose their life

in the coming battle, I don't want you to ever blame yourself, thinking you were unable to protect them," Atla told me. Her intent was so infused in those words I couldn't have ignored them even if I'd wanted to.

Atla was making clear both the feelings of the protector and the feelings of the protected.

"Those who do nothing but receive from others become something less, something corrupted. They just sink further into corruption. That feeling of slipping away, without even understanding that it's happening . . . I never want to feel that again," Atla said.

"I understand," I managed. She wasn't wrong. Many people had died in the previous fighting and the time before that, and before that. I'd tried to save as many as I could but wouldn't deny my failings.

That said though, corruption could happen in other ways. For example, like Atla was doing now, affirming everything that I did. Praising everything someone did as incredible, so incredible, caused the same issue in a different way. It made them think they could do anything they like. I thought Kyo was maybe one who had become corrupted by such an environment. He had apparently started out as a genius, but look at how he'd ended up.

"Brother. I'm no longer someone who just receives, who just takes from you. I'm going to be like you and Master

Naofumi and defend everyone," Atla stated.

"Atla, what do you mean?" Fohl asked.

"Brother, I know what you're thinking. So long as I'm safe, it doesn't matter what happens to anyone else, right?" Atla said. Fohl gave a surprised gasp. I mean, there was certainly a feeling that Fohl didn't really care about anyone other than Atla. "I don't want to see any more of that from you, brother, although . . . I'm not sure it's my place to say that. Well, goodnight." With a slightly sad expression on her face, Atla left.

"I'm only thinking of Atla? So the real reason I get so irritated by her fixation with this guy . . ." Fohl trailed off in thought.

"What?" I waved my hand at the stunned Fohl. He snapped back to himself with a pretty pissed off expression and then left, just like his sister.

I was never going to understand either of them.

"Dependence on Mr. Naofumi . . ." Raphtalia seemed to be deep in thought about something too. Was this really an issue that required so much thought?

Chapter Fourteen: Fighting the Phoenix

"This is the place?" I asked. Before the revival of the Phoenix, I'd brought my allies to the midpoint on the mountain where the birds were sealed, based on the information obtained from Ren and the others. Our intent was to investigate a certain object in the shrine here . . . the sealed Phoenix itself.

The shrine was very well-maintained.

"This is the shrine with the seal," I confirmed.

"Yeah, this is the place," Ren replied. Both he and Itsuki pointed at something inside . . . a statue. It was like one of those Buddhist thousand-armed Kannon statues I'd seen in temples in Japan seated on a carved flower.

"That statue can be moved around. Using the mechanism at the base will open a path forward," Itsuki explained.

"Although you need to complete a quest and get permission from those in the shrine first," Ren added.

"Fair enough. I'd say we've already done that part," I quipped. Prior to when we set out, someone who apparently tended to this shrine had indeed given us his permission. We were dealing with the kind of secrets that were passed down from monk to monk now.

Ren and Itsuki started to manhandle the carved petals,

tugging them up and down. It was like some kind of puzzle box.

Eventually there was a clicking sound. Ren and Itsuki gave the statue a push and it finally moved.

Motoyasu? Oh, I'd ordered him to just play with his filolials.

"This is the way," Itsuki said.

"Waaaah!" Ignoring Rishia's fear, Ren and Itsuki proceeded to lead us down the stairs that had appeared beneath the moved statue.

At the bottom of them we found a stone monument. It was bright red from heat.

"So this is the seal of the Phoenix," I stated.

"It's incredible. A lot like the one that sealed the Tyrant Dragon Rex, don't you think?" Raphtalia said. I agreed with her.

"I sense an incredible vitality here. We cannot underestimate this foe, brother," Atla contributed.

"Indeed," Fohl confirmed. Even though it was still sleeping, Atla and Fohl were clearly already feeling pressure from the presence of our upcoming adversary.

"Don't do anything to set it off," I cautioned. Taking all due care not to do anything that might break it, we examined the seal carefully and determined that it was going to break in accordance with the time displayed by the sand timer.

"Think we could get it to revive sooner if we wanted,

Ren?" I asked. We needed as much time to prepare as we could get, so I certainly wasn't going to do anything so stupid.

However, Ren was staring at the stone in shock, my words falling on deaf ears. The same for Itsuki. There was no expression on his face, but his hands were shaking.

"What's up?" I asked, maybe not wanting to know.

"This is impossible, surely. Why's it already broken?!" Ren exclaimed.

"Huh?" I asked, tilting my head. In response, Ren and Itsuki both pointed slowly at a pile of rubble next to the stone seal. Having had it pointed out to me, I looked more closely. It appeared to have been a statue of the Phoenix.

Then, taking a look at the pieces, it appeared to have been busted up pretty recently.

"This isn't going to weaken the seal, is it?" I asked. It would be a real problem if the time until the seal broke had been shortened, or anything like that.

"That's fine. Or it should be. That's also not the problem though," Ren replied. What else could it be, then? I had a nasty feeling twisting in my gut.

According to Ren and the others, no one like Kyo was present, who had taken control of the Spirit Tortoise. So that wasn't a real possibility. But if it was something Ren and Itsuki did know about, and wasn't related to the breaking of the seal, then I could think a few things. None were good.

"The problem is when the seal breaks and the statue nearby has been destroyed!" Ren exclaimed, pointing again at the broken Phoenix statue.

"The kind of problem I'm thinking of . . . would be in game terms—it'd mean a harder boss fight," I guessed. I really didn't want this to be true, but I asked them the most likely thing that came to mind.

The bosses that fought in special quests during certain video games could sometimes be enhanced depending on the approach taken in fighting them. Depending on the game, there might be rare items that could only be obtained from those kinds of enhanced bosses, but of course, it also made defeating the boss more difficult.

If such an element was in play here, who the hell would ever risk it? If the results were the same between normal and hard, wouldn't you play on normal?

I certainly didn't want to have to try my hand at a boss on steroids just for the chance of rare items when getting killed would mean I was actually dead.

Ren and Itsuki both nodded at my guess.

"That's right. If you come to the place where the Phoenix is sealed with the flag triggered for having defeated it once and one of the statues is destroyed, you can challenge the hard-mode Phoenix. It drops some powerful gear, so it's endgame content," Ren explained.

"Same kind of thing for me," Itsuki added. "There was an event to fight a stronger version of the Phoenix." Man, this was giving me a headache. I'd hoped to fight the normal Phoenix, win, and get past this problem. But now we had to fight a more powerful version for no good reason?

This wasn't like the story quests in an Internet game. It was a battle with a boss far harder than the story version.

"Maybe it broke due to the passage of time, or maybe . . . In any case, this isn't a game. This is reality, so I'm really hoping I'm wrong." Ren said. There was weight to his words.

"Think we could piece it back together? Like a jigsaw puzzle?" I offered, a little optimistically. Both Ren and Itsuki remained silent, perhaps unsure of exactly how to answer.

Yeah, that probably wasn't a thing. Whatever technique had been used to create the seal, it wouldn't be so easy to just glue it back together.

"Anyway, I'm just glad we didn't end up having to suddenly fight this enhanced Phoenix without any warning. That take-away is enough from this. Maybe we'll try to weaken it again by repairing the statue . . ." As I spoke, I happened to notice something. On the wall of the room, there was a picture very much like that from the scrolls about the Phoenix that we saw stored in the castle.

This one, though, looked more . . . sinister than the pictures back in the town, perhaps. It looked like it had a blazing circle of light behind it.

It even showed the Phoenix statue being destroyed. *Thanks for the tip, hah!*

"...and also look into whether the statue crumbled naturally or someone broke it while also preparing to fight the enhanced Phoenix!" I regained my train of thought and finished.

"Okay!" Ren agreed.

"Understood," Itsuki said with understandably less enthusiasm.

"This is all turning into quite the big deal," Raphtalia said. I could only agree with her. At least the seal had been protected. That was something, but still . . .

This hidden content was utter bullshit!

"Whatever comes, we just have to deal with it!" Atla added. I mean, she wasn't wrong.

The temple monks later explained that one day they had gone to check on the sealing stone and the statue had already been destroyed. We brought in a specialist in these things and their investigation revealed that it had been broken quite recently. However, in this instance, "recently" was quite a broad term. It could have been anything between a few days to a few months, making the whole analysis pretty unreliable.

Was it the work of man or just a natural disaster? It was a pain in my ass either way.

And so the days passed until the appointed time for the battle with the Phoenix.

The day of the Phoenix battle.

I expanded the blue timer icon located in one corner of my vision.

00:12

It was twelve minutes until it happened, then.

This wasn't my first time in this kind of situation, but my heart was pounding nonetheless. I knew I just had to fight as normal . . . even better than normal, but still I couldn't get used to this feeling.

The surrounding area had all been evacuated of residents, meaning only the heroes, their respective retinues, and the coalition army now remained here.

This wasn't a sudden occurrence, like it had been with the Spirit Tortoise. The evacuation had been completed without any particular problems. I'd also made sure they weren't going to let anyone in who might get in the way.

The queen and the coalition army leaders were taking command at the back. The heroes, including me, were on the front lines. S'yne was on high alert too. She apparently hadn't seen anything suspicious yet.

I just had to pray that nothing untoward was going to happen.

"We've done all we can to prepare to fight the Phoenix.

Everyone fight as hard as you can in order to return from this alive," I commanded from the head of the army. My simple order was met with cheers of agreement from the slaves and the coalition army as one.

This had been a long time coming. Reflecting back on everything that had happened, I looked up at the place where the Phoenix was sealed.

We should be tackling the waves, really, and yet here we were, spending so much time on this.

We'd chosen a barren area just down the mountain on the path to the town, thinking it would be easiest to fight it there.

We'd also looked at all sorts of other ways to fight it, like maybe using the gravity field from the Spirit Tortoise gear to drag the high-altitude one down. All sorts of ideas had been kicked about.

The issue with that one was the range. It was unexpectedly short, so we'd only know if it worked on the Phoenix once we actually got to test it. The difficulty there was that I'd have to ride up to the high-altitude Phoenix and jump onto it before I could use it. I wouldn't be able to fly on Gaelion if I used the gravity field on my shield while on his back. And if I changed to it during flight, we would drop to the ground.

Ren, Motoyasu, and Itsuki had similar weapons, but we just didn't know how effective they would be. In terms of the accessories prepared for the final battle, we'd gone with a unified approach across the board to increase the power of the skill each person was most adept with.

I'd just wanted a simple increase in firepower.

Something a bit trickier might have worked too, but something simple seemed easier to handle and would also keep the loss of accessories themselves low.

"Mr. Naofumi," Raphtalia said.

"What?" I was on edge.

"Let's do our best," she affirmed.

"You said it," I agreed with a nod. Then Atla spoke up.

"Life force imbued with heat is starting to gather in the surrounding area. Master Naofumi, please be careful."

"I will," I replied. The sand timer now had less than three minutes left.

"This time, we'll settle things," Ren said.

"I'm with you," Itsuki managed.

"We shall do this, I say!" Motoyasu added. All of them gripped their weapons as they spoke.

They weren't wrong. Enhanced Phoenix or not, if we couldn't follow the plan and defeat it without too much hassle, then our future battles looked like bleak affairs indeed.

We had the power of four heroes on the field. We should be able to finish this, no problem.

    0:01

With one minute left, I focused my awareness and incanted some magic: "All Liberation Aura!"

I poured in magic and life force, converted it into the widest possible area, and gave the entire front line the increase to all the stats I had used on Filo during the race.

00:00

A sound like breaking glass, exactly like the one we heard before, rang out. A violent shockwave shook my vision, also just like before. Then a fire pillar rose from the middle of the mountain and the twin Phoenixes rose up into the air. They looked exactly like the images on the wall.

Not those from the town, of course. They looked like those from the mountain temple . . . the ones with the halo behind them.

Two powerful screeches rang out across the vicinity. And so the fight between our forces and the blazing Phoenixes began.

Just as we had expected. After having appeared, both Phoenixes flew straight toward the closest source of lives gathered together—us. It was just like with the Spirit Tortoise.

A number "8" hovered in my field of vision.

"Everyone, don't mess up the timing of the final blow, whatever you do!" I shouted.

"I know!" Ren returned, leading the attack on the low-altitude Phoenix, which was already closing in. Another screech rang out. The high-altitude Phoenix flapped its wings in our direction, causing a rain that mixed feathers with fireballs to pelt down around us.

"Shooting Star Shield!" I yelled. Adding some life force considerably increased the range and defense boost of the skill. Not to mention, the sharing of the power-up method acquired in Q'ten Lo meant that my own defense had been considerably increased. That was enough to protect the very front line, but not enough for the rest.

We'd taken all of this into account, of course.

"Just like we planned!" I ordered. I turned around to see not only the slaves, but also the coalition army agreeing with me.

It went without saying, I didn't think I could protect all of these people. But I'd done everything I could think of to make that a possibility.

I proceeded to deploy Gather toward the incoming rain of fire. It was a technique that wasn't a skill, as it was created through cooperation between Atla and me.

Like a huge funnel, it started to collect all of the blazing missiles in front of me. I could change my response based on the severity of the attack. Meanwhile, everyone else would focus their attacks on the Phoenix coming in at low altitude.

I took the incoming fire on my shield. The sensation imparted to me was like heavy rain hitting an umbrella. I had the enhanced Spirit Tortoise Shell equipped.

Spirit Tortoise Shell (awakened) 80/80 AT
<abilities locked> equip bonus: skills: S Float Shield, Reflect Shield,
special effect: gravity shield, C soul recovery, C magic snatch, C gravity shot, vitality boost, magic defense (large), lightning resistance, nullify SP drain, magic assistance, spell support, growth power
special equip effect: comet shield (Spirit Tortoise)
mastery level: 100
item enchant level 8, defense 10% up
dragon spirit defense 50, fire resistance up
status enchant magic +30

It had been enchanted with the attacks of the Phoenix in mind. It should allow me to now considerably reduce all fire-based attacks. Indeed, in regard to the current stream of burning death from above, I was neither burning nor anything close to death.

It might be an attack from the enhanced Phoenix, but it looked like I could still hack it.

That said, it also covered far too wide a range for me to

protect the entire coalition army. That, of course, had been accounted for.

Upon examining what the effects of Shooting Star Shield (Spirit Tortoise) were, I had discovered that it turned the shape of the protective shield into a tortoise's shell and caused defense to really leap upward. So both aspects had really been enhanced.

"All Zweite Resist Fire!" came the shout from the support troops at the back of the coalition army as they maintained magic to increase fire resistance at all times.

This should somewhat reduce the impact of the Phoenixes' attacks and allow us to also concentrate on attacking.

"Itsuki!" I commanded.

"I know what to do. All Liberation Down!" Itsuki incanted his magic and debuffed the Phoenixes. Now we had all our buffs and debuffs in place.

Huh?

When the feathers dropped by the high-altitude Phoenix landed on the ground, monsters started appearing from those spots. They had the name "Phoenix familiar (vassal type)" and looked like a suit of armor. Just like the mural had shown. However, they also looked a bit tougher than the ones on the wall. There were wings sprouting from their armor and their entire bodies blazed with fire. The frontline, close-combat unit dashed forward to take out Phoenix familiars that had appeared.

Right!

"Raph!" I shouted, and Raph-chan and the other members of the Raph species started to knock away any Phoenix feathers that I was unable to stop on my own. Great. That was a big help!

"Kwaa!" Gaelion and Wyndia flew toward the high-altitude Phoenix.

"We've got this, Gaelion!" Wyndia shouted.

"Kwaa!" the dragon replied.

"I hereby draw out the power of Gaelion, desirous of it taking physical form. Dragon Vein, grant me your power!" Wyndia intoned.

"Kwaa, kwaa, kwaa!" was Gaelion's addition.

"High Wing Slash!" At Wyndia's shout, Gaelion's wings started to glitter with light, and each flap of them caused blades of wind to slash forward.

Those blades jammed into the high-altitude Phoenix. It didn't like that, giving an annoyed—maybe even surprised—shriek.

I needed to focus on the Phoenix right in front of me.

"Haaah!" I grabbed the Phoenix's legs to create an opening, which Raphtalia, Fohl, and Atla made sure to exploit to the fullest.

"I've been training hard all for today! Now I'll show you my improved, stronger technique!" Raphtalia sounded pleasingly confident. Her tail started to glow, just like the past Heavenly

Emperor, and then she swept her sword down.

"Eight Trigrams Blade of Destiny Formation Two!" Her weapon sliced into the shoulder of the Phoenix.

Wow, Formation Two! It really looked much stronger than before. Now she would be even more reliable in battle!

"Tiger Break!" Fohl's fist rammed into the Phoenix's abdomen.

"Here I go!" Atla stabbed with her hand.

"Don't forget about me! Gravity Sword!" Not wanting to be left behind, Ren also unleashed a skill, leaping onto the Phoenix and stabbing it multiple times in the head.

Wow. It was like slicing butter. Ren's slashes looked to be causing some pretty serious trauma to the Phoenix.

"Okay! I'll do what I can to help out. Woof!" With that, Keel chased in nimbly behind Ren and also started stabbing away. Keel was getting pretty strong too, from the look of things. This was a far cry from the danger she'd faced when that Spirit Tortoise familiar had defeated her.

I'd known everyone was getting stronger, but it was nice to see the evidence playing out before my eyes.

The Phoenix, however, had not only an animal part, like the Spirit Tortoise, but also seemed to comprise an elemental, spectral part. Each time it was injured, fire welled up from the wound and it vanished as though healed.

"Dammit! It's got vitality in spades!" Ren complained.

Even if a wound was cut, it quickly sealed back up, preventing a deeper injury from being caused.

This was really going to be a problem . . . but at least from the look of it, we were causing damage at the same time. Just as we had simulated, the low-altitude one was using an attack-focused suicide strategy, uncaring of whether it ended up blowing up or not.

However, we'd been prepared for whatever the Phoenix might unleash. So we weren't taking much damage from both the breath and all the wing flapping. It was also very nice to seemingly not have to worry about the low-altitude one using anything as annoying as the Spirit Tortoise's SP-absorbing attack.

However, we couldn't be sure exactly what it might try to use on us. It might still have some attacks we hadn't seen yet too.

As though on command, the Phoenix gave a high-pitched shriek and the halo on its back started to glow brighter.

"Woah!" I exclaimed. Pain flowed across my skin as though it were burning. The mural hadn't shown anything like this! What was it? Some kind of special counter only used by the enhanced Phoenix? "Everyone, are you okay?" I checked.

"I'm fine!" Raphtalia confirmed.

"Me too!" Ren chimed in. It seemed that I'd taken the brunt of the attack, keeping it from affecting anyone else. Glad to hear it.

As I held onto the Phoenix to keep it from flying too high, I checked in on the high-altitude one. Motoyasu, Itsuki, Rishia, Sadeena and Shildina, and the queen were all launching their attacks toward it.

"Brionac!" Motoyasu threw a spear of light toward the Phoenix.

"Bird Hunting!" Itsuki's arrow divided into multiple shafts, all striking the Phoenix at once.

"Tornado Arrow!" Rishia's arrow created a tornado that held her target in place.

"Cooperative Magic! Image of Gale and Thunder Gods!" Sadeena shouted, while Shildina cast "Intense Collective Ritual Magic! Rain Storm!" The two sisters were leading the charge, striking with cooperative magic that combined lightning with tornadoes.

Just from a visual appraisal, it definitely looked like we were doing less damage to the high-altitude one than the one down here.

Then I had a thought. What were Filo and Motoyasu's retinue of three doing? As soon as I pondered it, however, I also remembered. They were cooperating with the filolial unit and fighting over there with them. As well as Gaelion, other dragon knights and soldiers mounted on other flying monsters—I wanted to say griffons—were all fighting the good fight up there, but we were clearly doing too much damage to the low-altitude one.

At this rate, it wasn't going to be easy to kill them both at the same time.

"Everyone, try and hold back a little, otherwise we'll defeat this one first! We need to match up the timing as much as possible!"

"I know!" Ren returned.

"Okay!" Raphtalia managed. While keeping the front lines aware of the issue, I carefully maintained Air Strike Shield and Second Shield while keeping the low-altitude Phoenix pinned down.

"Ah?! Master Naofumi, the Phoenix is healing itself!" Atla warned me.

"Shit. That's a pain," I muttered. No way Atla would get that wrong. So if we backed off, it started healing. But if we went all-out, we'd definitely end up killing this one first.

It wasn't going to be easy, but still we could handle it.

Just as I had that thought, I felt an increase in the temperature, spurring me to look at the Phoenix. In the same moment, it simply slipped out of my hand.

The Phoenix had gone and turned into pure fire.

"Everyone, get behind me! Air Strike Shield! Second Shield!" I hurriedly shouted. Was this the attack from the cracked part of the wall that we hadn't been able to clearly make out?

I placed my shield in front of me and stood ready.

With a shriek, the Phoenix came right at us—a spinning tornado of fire. It was like Filo's Spiral Strike, It was an attack charging forward while surrounded in flames.

It wasn't enough to penetrate my defenses, however.

"Everyone okay?" I asked. Perhaps because I took the charge from the low-altitude Phoenix head-on, no one behind me seemed to have taken any damage.

The rain of feathers and combat with the familiars was causing some damage to even the units not on the front line, but none of it was close to being critical.

Then I noticed something was wrong with me. My magic was being drained . . . and I had a bad feeling about what might come next.

The high-altitude Phoenix gave another piercing shriek.

"Shooting Star Shield!" I shouted.

Drawing in a breath, the high-altitude Phoenix then expelled it as a beam, almost like a red laser. The Shooting Star Shield barrier centered around me came up just in time before the beam hit.

With gasps of surprise, Gaelion and the others fighting the high-altitude Phoenix barely managed to get out of the way. Then this breath attack was unleashed upon the ground forces.

With terrible screams, part of an entire unit was blown away like toys.

Damn this fiery turkey! How many more annoying tricks

did it have concealed in its feathers?

"It drained my magic! The attack the low-altitude one just used steals away magic from the enemies fighting on the ground and then the high-altitude one unleashes that powerful breath attack!" I explained. The two birds had made one big mistake, however.

The Spirit Tortoise Shell had C magic snatch on it.

Having finished defending the attack, my shield launched a magical missile directly at the low-altitude Phoenix. But with a fizzing sound, it vanished.

It was just further proof that I couldn't counterattack for shit. It looked like gravity field didn't work on the Phoenix either.

Then I heard the moans of the injured.

"Immediately provide healing for those who've been attacked. All Zweite Heal! If you die, the enemy will take control of you! Rear units, hurry and provide aid!" At the orders I barked, the rear support units rushed forward and started to aid those who had been on the receiving end of the breath attack.

The problem was the stinking absorb attack. It just had to have one of those. The Spirit Tortoise Shell couldn't nullify MP absorption. The only thing to be happy about was—perhaps because of the Barbarian Armor having absorb resistance (medium)—my magic hadn't fallen completely to zero. We also couldn't rule out the existence of SP-absorbing attacks, which would be really nasty.

I could change to the Soul Eater Shield, which would nullify drain completely, but that would leave me with concerns about defense. It would probably still be able to handle whatever the Phoenixes dished out, but I also had the gut feeling that I'd only held out so long because of the Spirit Tortoise Shell.

There was no need to rely on the Shield of Wrath here . . . but it was still hard to know which approach to take. That had enhancements on it that really needed to be sealed away. Realizing how dangerous they were, I'd tried to change them but didn't have the required abilities or level.

The Demon Dragon really had got the last laugh, leaving that little trinket behind.

Huh? The low-altitude Phoenix was healing even more damage. Dammit . . . did using that technique also speed up its healing powers?

I looked up at the high-altitude one.

That one seemed to be taking longer to heal, but it was still a really dangerous situation.

"Finish this off before it can heal!" I ordered. There were general shouts of agreement.

"I've got this!" Raphtalia also affirmed, and then the attack started again.

Everyone unleashed their most powerful attacks, visibly beating down the Phoenix. This made the fight with the Spirit Tortoise look like even more of a joke. A lengthy joke, at that.

We wanted to be finished here in short order.

As for that one risky attack . . . if it wasn't too dangerous, I'd just stick it out with the Soul Eater Shield.

I'd given orders to focus on casting magic for fire resistance.

Right. While still keeping the Phoenix locked down, I ate a rucolu fruit to recover my magic. Then I cast All Revolution Aura again, as the first one had run out.

Was there no way to cast a decisive final blow?

Then I had an idea.

"Gaelion!" I called.

"Kwaa?" the dragon answered.

"Take Ren with you and tackle the high-altitude Phoenix," I commanded.

"Naofumi, are you sure?" Ren asked.

"We've got enough firepower down here. I need you to focus your strength on weakening the higher one. If you think you've defeated it, direct your skill down here instead," I told him.

"Sure thing," he replied. At my orders, Gaelion and Wyndia dropped back down to me. I just hoped this would make things go a little easier.

The healing was a problem, but the high-altitude one just seemed like the tougher of the two. The low-altitude one healed quickly, but it also felt like it didn't have much life.

Ren rode on Gaelion and went to fight the high-altitude

one. It felt like that one was resistant to magic but weak to physical attacks. That had to be the case as it wasn't really showing any effects from the full-scale magic of attackers like Sadeena, Shildina, and the queen.

That also suggested that the low-altitude one was weak to magic.

As though sensing my very thoughts, a Shadow appeared.

"Hero Iwatani, I have been told to azk you if maybe hitting the one you are fighting with ritual magic would maybe be more effective?" Shadow inquired.

"I was thinking the same thing! Everyone, get away from me! We're gonna have some ritual magic coming in!" I shouted.

"What about you, Master Naofumi?!" Atla asked. At her question, I looked at Fohl.

"I can take it. Once the magic is finished, start attacking again," I said.

"But—" Atla started.

"I'll be fine. Hurry up and get away," I said.

"Very well," Raphtalia backed me up. "Atla, let's go."

"You're always like this, aren't you?" Fohl muttered, obviously not pleased about something. He and Raphtalia retreated with Atla.

Having confirmed that everyone had followed my orders and fallen back, the queen and Sadeena proceeded to launch ritual magic toward both the Phoenix and me.

A typhoon made of water descended from the sky toward me.

I could withstand it, using Shooting Star Shield. The Phoenix gave a pleasing shriek, however. The typhoon was an intense one, only lasting about thirty seconds, but it looked to have done some good damage.

A shame it wasn't as strong as an attack from Ren, but it had probably done as much damage as a few successive attacks from Raphtalia or Fohl.

Just as I had suspected, the low-altitude one was weak to magic. It shrieked again, turning back into fire and charging right at me once more.

I switched to Soul Eater Shield and took it head-on. Certainly not the easiest attack to take with this approach—and this was with fire resistance magic applied. Just how powerful of an attack was it?!

Once the charge was over, I waited, shoulders heaving, for the healing magic to hit me.

I also checked whether the high-altitude one was going to unleash that powerful breath again . . . but no. It looked like if it was unable to steal any magic, it couldn't use it.

Some sparks rained down, but nothing else happened.

It didn't seem to have stopped the healing of the low-altitude Phoenix. That looked to be a separate issue.

Still, we could do this. If we pushed through, we could

finish it. We just needed to weaken the high-altitude one some more, adjust the remaining life of them both, and we could win this.

"Come on! Let's push on through and end this!" I declared. In that same moment—

From far behind us, far too far to see the source, a single shaft of light punched right through one of our targets—the weakened, almost ready-to-die high-altitude Phoenix.

Chapter Fifteen: A Forbidden Flicker

"What the—" We hadn't reached the point of striking a finishing blow yet, and the low-altitude Phoenix had just been healing itself. So who was doing something so stupid?!

I looked into the direction the light had flown from. It was far behind us, a totally different direction from where the coalition army was set up.

So what the hell was it?! Was it some kind of hidden Phoenix attack? Or maybe . . . But no, it wasn't the time to worry about that now.

The high-altitude Phoenix gave a fading shriek and then turned into a flickering fire-mist in the sky, as though burning away, leaving only feathers behind.

I confirmed the falling scattering of feathers. Okay, this was bad. Real bad.

Our forces casting magic from the rear had just completed large-scale ritual magic. Even though we now knew the low-altitude Phoenix was weak to magic, we couldn't unleash any on it right now.

Finally snapping back from our surprise, we turned our attention to the low-altitude Phoenix.

With a feeble, dull shriek, the low-altitude Phoenix completely stopped moving.

And then . . . a horrible, unsettling sound rang out.

A little at a time, the Phoenix was starting to swell up. At the same time—as though making a clear declaration that this was the self-destruct—the halo on its back turned into an enclosing sphere that started to protect the Phoenix.

Its wounds also looked to be healing incredibly quickly now, like the vitality of the pair of them was now infused into just one.

Magic and heat started to compress into the Phoenix.

"Attack Support! Everyone, throw everything you've got at it! Quickly! We need to take this down as quickly as we can!" I shouted. There was no time to try and evacuate the area. Every second I could see the Phoenix swelling larger and larger.

If we couldn't kill it before this death balloon popped, a massive-scale self-destruct attack was going to be triggered.

"I'll cast the debuff magic again! Liberation Down!" Itsuki carefully assessed the situation and cast the status-reducing magic again. That was a big help!

"I'm on it! Shooting Star Sword! Gravity Sword! Hundred Sword!" Ren slashed and sliced.

"Hear me roar, I say! Shooting Star Spear! Brionac! Air Strike Javelin! Second Javelin!" Motoyasu got in on the action.

"As quickly as possible! Shooting Star Bow! Bird Hunting! Spread Arrow!" Itsuki launched his own barrage, all of the other heroes firing off everything they had one after the other.

"Air Strike Throw! Second Throw! Dritte Throw! Tornado Throw!" said Rishia.

"Eight Trigrams Blade of Destiny Successive Strikes! First Formation! Section Formation! Third Formation!" Raphtalia piled on too.

"Tiger Break!" In went Fohl.

"Spiral Strike! Haikuikku!" Filo raged.

"Master Naofumi!" Atla hastened me on even as she struck at the Phoenix herself.

"Quickly—Scissor Blaze!" S'yne split up her scissors into two separate blades and sliced into the Phoenix as though she was dancing in the air.

Gaelion, now full-sized, also understood the situation. Incanting magic, he unleashed his breath toward the Phoenix!

"High Wing Slash!" With the cooperation of Wyndia, he immediately unleashed blades of wind that caused a tornado that swallowed the Phoenix. We actually lost sight of it! While that was happening, I directed life force at our foe, using Wall and Air Strike Shield to prevent it from escaping from the attacks.

"Everyone, you finished?" I asked.

"A-as best I can," Raphtalia managed. The entire team had unleashed an exhaustive barrage of attacks. Finally, the dust settled from all of that firepower . . . and the Phoenix appeared, still swelling larger, almost reaching its limit.

This damn bird! Was there no way to finish this thing off?!

I checked whether the energy blast inside the Spirit Tortoise Heart Shield could be unleashed, but it wasn't even operating. No chance of firing it now.

I stood in front of them all, ready to take the self-destruct on myself to protect them. I then activated the Gather technique created from life force.

If we took this self-destruct attack full-on, there was no chance of anyone surviving it apart from me. The heroes might be able to withstand it, but there was the coalition army and all of the slaves here too.

I couldn't give up.

In the place where the Phoenix had been, there was a concentrated ball of fire, blazing like a miniature sun. It looked ready to rip apart at any moment, unleashing fires of annihilation to burn away the entire surrounding area. In that moment, far away . . . even in Melromarc, the fire that rose into the sky was visible.

In an instant, the light from the halo passed through all of our bodies. I checked my status to see a resistance down icon . . . . Damn this thing! Just how badly did it want to kill us?!

At ground zero of the Phoenix explosion, I defended Raphtalia, of course, and then the heroes, the slaves, and the entire coalition army, from flames trying to decimate the entire vicinity.

I gave a defiant scream, taking one step and then another forward, pushing back the flames. In every direction other than the one I was defending, the flames rose higher, scorching the very ground black.

Gah . . . I could feel the blazing flames creeping through the defenses of my shield. The enhancements on this shield were pretty heavy, and it was still coming through. Just how strong was this attack?!

The only thing I could think of was to use the preparatory time for the self-destruct attack to escape. Should we have done that?

But no. The range was so wide there'd be no escape from this.

The feeling in my fingertips had surpassed simple burns and I was feeling almost nothing at all now.

My instincts whispered to me. If the fire did break through, everyone behind me was going to be turned to ash. The fire unleashed by the Phoenix was trying to burn through me and kill everyone. I was holding it back, barely, but it also felt like I didn't have five seconds of this left.

Just how long did I have to hold this for?

I'd already deployed Shooting Star Shield, and it had been destroyed instantly.

Reflect-type shields would be meaningless, and I already had Air Strike Shield and Second Shield deployed. I had a multilayer Float Shield deployed, but it was barely holding.

What the hell could I do?

"Drifa Resist Fire!" Someone was backing me up from behind . . . Ren? He sent me some magic to increase fire resistance. Motoyasu was more skilled at fire magic, but as it was the Way of the Dragon Vein, it meant Ren could also use it. He wasn't using Liberation in order to cut down on enchanting time.

It was a wise move too. It did feel like I was taking slightly less damage . . . but it was also just water on a hot stone.

I roared again, in anger and frustration. Raphtalia stood to support me, putting her hands forward and joining with my Wall and Gather.

We'd been training together, so Raphtalia could somewhat make use of them, but even then, this was going to be difficult.

However, there was still an approach we could make.

If Atla, S'yne, Raphtalia, and I all combined our strength, we might be able to direct the attack away in a safe direction.

However, almost as though reading my mind, the Phoenix increased the output of its flames, as though to say everything so far had just been a prelude. An intensely increased burst of fire attempted to burn me to ash.

Fire leaked in through a gap in my shield and burned my shoulder.

No matter how many of us teamed up, we were not going

to redirect that anywhere. The fire was so intense, so pure, I couldn't be sure if throwing all the energy and life force I possessed at it right now would even be enough to stop it, even if I didn't care what might happen afterward.

"Mr. Naofumi!" Raphtalia called to me.

"Naofumi!" Ren and the others joined in. I could only grunt in return. Some of them were using healing or support magic on me, for which I was grateful for their efforts in such a short time.

However, even then, it wasn't going to be enough to withstand this ultimate final attack from the Phoenix.

I grunted in effort, desperately trying to keep my shield-holding arm from being pushed upward. I was being buffeted by winds strong enough to blow me away at any moment. My limbs had been burnt and were about to turn to ash. The status magic HP hovering in my field of vision was slipping into the danger zone. This slow roast was about to turn into blazing BBQ.

I was pretty amazed that the Seven Star Hero from the past managed to survive against this monstrous attack. The range of the attack looked far larger than shown on the wall. I guess we had the enhanced Phoenix to thank for that.

Damn . . . a few more seconds and I really was going to be blown away.

No. There was one method. If I used it, I could save

everyone's lives—but it was definitely going to kill me.

If I didn't use it though, then I would die anyway and take everyone else with me.

"Like I have a choice!" In the same moment that I shouted, a girl appeared at my side.

"It's okay. For everyone . . . I want to realize your wish, Master Naofumi," the girl said.

"Wh—?!" Both the girl's brother and I were at a loss for words. The girl gave a curt nod and then placed her hands in front of her and jumped forward.

It only took a split-second. But from the point of view of an observer, time seemed to slow down. My heart ached so intensely. I thrust my hand futilely forward.

This was my job. My role. If I didn't do this, someone other than me was going to pay the price.

If I did this, maybe I could survive it. If anyone else did it, they seriously weren't going to.

That was the absolute power that we faced in these flames.

My hand didn't reach Atla, however. She released all of her life energy, using Gather to direct the fire entirely at herself. Then she used Wall to determine its direction, pointing it away from the people nearby.

The sparkle of her energy was multiple times greater than the amount I had been preparing to release myself.

"Atla!" At my cry, the girl gave a gentle smile. Sweat was

pouring from her forehead . . . The flesh on her hands was burning away, and yet she remained determined, using her life force to change the fire's direction . . . and the fire obeyed that incredible force of will.

There followed an explosion loud enough to burst eardrums and a flash too bright to avoid closing your eyes.

I couldn't see anything through the smoke. Spluttering, I shouted Atla's name, waving my hands around to try and clear the air. Then I turned back and asked, "Everyone! Are you okay?"

The smoke cleared, and I saw them all, looking exhausted. While the direction of the fire had been changed, some of it had still gone through and caused serious damage to the coalition army.

Rather than that though, I was now focused on Atla.

I searched for the girl who had stepped in front of me—my own focus so caught up in the flames—and literally bent that fire to her will.

Then I happened to look up into the sky. I saw something. It looked like a piece of burnt trash coming down toward me.

I put out my arms and caught it.

"Ah . . ." It felt both heavy and yet incredibly light . . . this strange burnt thing . . . It took me a few moments to realize . . . My God.

It was Atla.

"Atla!" Fohl dashed over. In the same moment, with another piercing shriek, the shapes of two massive birds appeared again in the sky.

"Naofumi! Fall back, quickly!" Ren shouted at me. I was still stunned.

"Ah . . . but . . . but if I retreat . . ." I could barely talk. Ren pointed at the enhanced Phoenix.

"They don't have those halos on their backs anymore. It looks like, immediately after reviving, the Phoenixes aren't at full strength. We've got some prep time," Ren explained. The Phoenixes' movements did look stiff. We had some recovery time then.

"You can't fight at the moment! At least get yourself healed! And . . . you need to get her treated, right away! We've got others who have been hurt too. We need you, the best among us at healing and curing, to help everyone get back on their feet!" Ren shouted. I couldn't form the words to reply. What should I do? What should I be doing? "Hurry up! We can handle things here!"

"O-okay," I finally managed.

"Raphtalia! Take Naofumi and Atla and get back from here! Fohl, you go too!" Ren said.

"O-okay! Filo!" Raphtalia replied, quite stunned.

"I'm here!" Filo responded. My own head was pure white inside, and following Ren's angry orders, I allowed myself to be taken away.

I tried to speak, but nothing came out.

Atla was close to death, mortally wounded. It wasn't just her legs that had been turned to ash. Almost her entire lower body had been burnt. It was a miracle that she was even still alive.

But she was. She was breathing, barely, as I laid her down in a tent set up at the rear of the army. Then the healers there and I all started to try and heal all the terrible injuries our forces had suffered.

The most terrible of all was Atla.

The others . . . It looked like the focus had been on bringing in those who were still alive.

My head was still white inside. I reflected on the things I had heard.

"Atla! Hang in there!" Fohl shouted to her desperately, clinging to the hand that Atla had left as she lay on the cot.

Atla was whispering something to Fohl, barely able to talk.

I needed to pull myself together. Right now, I had to focus on curing her injuries—curing everyone's injuries. As many as possible, from among those who could be saved. That was what a hero did. That was what the Shield Hero should do.

I was better than anyone else in this entire world at defense, support, and healing, after all. Those were my things, for what it was worth.

And yet I couldn't concentrate.

And yet . . . I couldn't let everyone die—let Atla die.

Desperately forcing myself to focus, I concentrated my awareness and cast some high-level healing magic.

"Liberation Heal!" The healing magic flew toward Atla. But . . . that healing light failed to restore her missing pieces.

"What? What's gone wrong?!" Healing magic could cure anything, right?

Now that I thought about it, the healing magic cast on me while we fell back had healed my wounds, but Atla had not been affected at all.

What did this mean? Did it mean that she was healing but her wounds were just far too bad?

She had unleashed all of her life energy, not worrying about any limitations.

Should we just be grateful that she was even still alive after such a feat?!

I took out an Elixir of Yggdrasil from my shield and had Atla take some. It worked even when just applied to the skin. If drunk, it could bring someone near death fully back to life. Using this in combination with everything else should definitely cure her. Some life force water should also replenish the energy she had expended when unleashing all of her life force!

And yet . . .

"Why isn't it working?" I shouted. There was no sign of Atla's injuries being cured. My tone was almost accusatory, brimming with frustration, as I questioned the healer. "Why isn't she getting better?!"

"She is simply beyond the range of injuries that can be cure—that can be healed." Rat appeared, muttering this quietly.

"What . . . what do you mean?" I was unable to process her words.

"It's an absolute miracle that Atla is even alive right now. The work of the healers, and your magic and medicines, Count, are just barely managing to keep her alive. There's nothing more—" But Rat trailed off, not wanting to have to complete that sentence.

"Rat, can't you save Atla?" Raphtalia asked.

"Yes, you must be able to do something!" I jumped in. "Anything! If you use all those devices in your lab, surely you can at least prolong her life a little? Right?!"

"Monsters and demi-humans are different. If I use homunculus technology I may be able to restore her arm and both legs perhaps, but her internal organs have been burnt too. There are some things that alchemy just can't do," Rat sadly explained.

"I can't believe this . . ." Raphtalia lamented.

"I don't have the materials. Even if I did, I couldn't save her. There's not enough time. I've heard talk of forbidden ancient magic that allows for the transfer of souls, but that's not something I can just do right now," Rat continued.

"This can't be the end!" I couldn't believe it! There had

to be a way somewhere. There had to be a way to save Atla!
Somewhere, somewhere right now, there had to be a shield that
could save her, even in this state. "Shield Hero?" Hah! What the
hell was I shielding if I couldn't even save a single girl?

"Master . . . Naofumi." Atla spoke to me. "Did I . . . defend
everyone?"

"Yes. We need to worry about—"

"Brother . . . bring Master Naofumi closer to me . . ." she
asked.

"Okay." Fohl pushed me roughly up to his sister.

"I understand the situation. There is . . . little time remaining," Atla said.

"What are you talking about? You've got all the time in the
world," I replied. That only made her shake her head, however.

"Master Naofumi. It's fine. No need to concern yourself,"
Atla managed.

"Of course I'm going to concern myself!" I replied. Of
course, of course! The problem was that I'd only used one
Elixir of Yggdrasil. If I used more of it, we'd surely be able to
keep her alive.

I'd only had two in reserve, but a few more should do it.
Surely. I called over the healer and told him to bring more Elixir
of Yggdrasil.

"Enough, Count! Like I already said, she's beyond the limits of what we can do!" Rat entreated.

"We won't know unless we try!" I countered.

"I'm saying this because I do know!" Rat came back. I ignored her and administered the second elixir to Atla.

First, I applied some to her wounds . . . but as I touched her, I realized something. The ash wasn't coming off the places that were burnt.

"I'm sorry, Atla!" I apologized. Then I took a healing knife, cut the burnt part, and applied the medicine.

There was still no sign of it regenerating. Atla's breathing remained ragged, as though she could barely draw breath. She still managed to touch my hand with her own remaining one.

"Please . . . stop this," she begged.

"No. Never!" I retorted. She shouldn't speak like that in front of me!

I'd never given up, no matter what happened to me. Even when someone I believed in betrayed me, when I was framed for a terrible crime, or when I'd almost been killed, I'd never given up.

So I wasn't about to give up now! Not in the face of this!

"Master . . . Naofumi. Please, you have to understand. I can't be saved now. I understand this . . . better than anyone. I can feel the life force draining from me . . . with every passing second," Atla breathed.

"But . . . but—" I'd thought my eyes dry long ago, but tears fell from them now.

"Your miraculous power, Master Naofumi, is the only reason we can still talk like this . . . That's all. Please . . . just try to calm down and listen to me," Atla said. She took another moment to gasp for air, stroking my cheek with strength so frail it might fail at any moment.

I was simply unable to reply.

At my silence, Atla smiled and wiped my tears away—almost like a mother consoling a crying child.

"Master Naofumi. I love you more than anyone in this world. And as I've told you before, I want to become your shield," Atla said.

"I know," I replied. So that was her explanation for doing this?! If she died protecting someone, died as their shield, did she have any idea how the people she protected would feel?!

Even as I thought this, I realized what it was that Atla was trying to tell me.

Atla had done exactly what I had been trying to do: collect the attack to her with Gather and then direct it away in a different direction. I knew better than anyone what putting such a plan into action would mean.

If Atla hadn't stepped forward . . . then I'd be where Atla was right now.

"Even so . . . this is too much," I lamented. A pathetic, scratchy voice rasped from my throat.

"I'm . . . satisfied. You saved my life, and now I've used that life to protect you, Master Naofumi," Atla explained.

"I can't allow this. You can't die. You can't die protecting me!" I said. That was my job. That was what I was meant to do.

I wasn't going to let her die. If it had been me, I might have been okay. I might have survived.

"Master Naofumi . . . I'm sorry, but . . . I don't think I can obey that order," she replied.

"Why not?!" I knew. I knew she was telling the truth. Yet all I could do was pray for a miracle.

Someone. Anyone. Any god who'll listen. I vowed to pray to them.

I don't believe in anyone, but I'll believe in you!

I knew I was being selfish. Even if the four heroes were the gods of this world, I'd throw that all away . . . if only I could save the girl in front of me . . .

"Master Naofumi . . . please accept an act of selfishness on my part," Atla continued.

"What? Whatever you want, I'll make sure of it. Just don't die on us!" I replied.

"I wished to become your shield, Master Naofumi. That wish is unchanged . . . and what's more, I don't want my blood or flesh, or my very soul, to return to this land," she stated.

"What?" I said, surprised. After gripping my hand, Atla moved it to touch my shield.

"I knew I could never become your number one, Master Naofumi," she said.

"What now—" I started.

"Yet I still wanted to be that for you. I wanted to be as close to you as possible, even if just physically," she cut me off. I remembered Atla trying to come to see me every single night.

Atla had claimed she just wanted to be at my side.

"Even if I lose my body . . . please let me stay with you, Master Naofumi," she asked. That question, though, incensed me.

"Stop joking around!" I knew what Atla was trying to say. But I still persistently shook my head. "Do you know what you're saying to me?!"

"Yes . . . I'm fully aware of everything I'm saying," Atla replied. Her expression plainly said she wasn't joking.

I turn to look at Fohl. He was standing steady, still glaring at me.

This was where I wanted him to step in, to help. So why was he silently watching? He was clenching his fists so hard his palms were bleeding. So why wasn't he speaking up?

"Please give me my further selfishness too," Atla continued.

"What—" As I turned back from Fohl to Atla, she gathered all her strength and kissed me.

Kissed me on the lips.

My first kiss from a girl . . . tasted of blood.

Then Atla's strength failed her and she collapsed.

"I've been wanting that for so long. Finally . . . finally I got it," she breathed.

"What the hell are you playing at? This is hardly the time . . ." I reacted.

"Raphtalia," Atla said.

"W-what is it?" Raphtalia replied, a little shocked herself. She had been quietly watching the exchange between Atla and me up until now.

"It seems the ongoing battle between us . . . neither side ever giving ground . . . is finally coming to an end," Atla told her.

"Not yet! It's going to continue . . . for a long time yet!" Raphtalia told her pleadingly.

"Hehe . . . to hear even you say that, Raphtalia, does make me a little bit happy. As I'm sure you already know, I've always been jealous of you, Raphtalia. I knew no matter how hard I tried, I'd never be able to become Master Naofumi's number one," she explained.

"Nothing is decided yet! Our fights are going to continue, Atla . . . into the future . . . on and on . . ." Raphtalia trailed off, tears streaming down her face. Atla smiled at her in response.

Then as though she finally understood everything, Atla continued.

"You are so kind, Raphtalia. I understand why Master Naofumi likes you so much. But there's one more thing I need to say to you."

"No need to limit it to just one! Tell me lots more things.

You can even have Mr. Naofumi once, if you have to," she pleaded.

"Raphtalia," Atla went on, "Master Naofumi . . . likes women more than you think. He's a regular guy. So please, look at Master Naofumi . . . a little more closely than you do now."

"I understand. But you'll be here with me. Don't give up!" Raphtalia said desperately, pleadingly. But Atla's life energy was already so weak she couldn't even tell where anyone was anymore.

That fact spoke the cold truth about how little time she had left.

After another moment, as though finally realizing something, she muttered a few more words, seemingly to no one at all.

"Ah . . . I know what we should have done. I should have colluded with Raphtalia and we could have shared Master Naofumi between us. Why didn't I realize such a simple thing? Thinking like this makes me . . . I want to live. I have a dream I want to achieve," she said.

"You can live! I'm sure Mr. Naofumi can heal you!" Raphtalia said.

"I can!" I said. But Atla slowly, even more weakly, shook her head.

"Please, Master Naofumi," she said. "I need you to realize something."

"What? Anything!" I replied.

"I did everything I could to become your number one, Master Naofumi. But . . . I couldn't achieve it," she said.

"What do you mean?" I asked.

"Master Naofumi, from the wounds you've suffered in the past, I'm sure you've just been trying not to think about this. But you need to be more self-aware. Raphtalia likes you, Master Naofumi . . . as a member of the opposite sex, just like I do," Atla revealed.

"This isn't the time for this!" I pleaded.

"I know . . . This is the only time you will listen, Master Naofumi. Please, believe me . . ." Then she descended into spluttering.

It was clear that Atla was weaker than before.

No! If I just used more Elixir of Yggdrasil, more Liberation Heal—

"Please . . . promise me. This is my final request, my final selfish request. Please, Master Naofumi, become aware that there are people who like you, and please . . . respond to their feelings. That's all I ask of you," Atla said.

"Okay! I get it! I understand, so please just stop pushing yourself so hard!" I exclaimed. *Oh God! Please! Save the ones who believe in me!*

I'd never prayed for a divine miracle as hard as I did in that moment.

When Witch framed me, when I was tricked and driven out, I'd never wished this hard.

"Promise . . . me. I know I'm asking a lot . . ." Atla breathed.

"Okay . . . I'll do everything you asked . . ." I responded.

"Hehe . . . having you treasure me like this, Master Naofumi . . . I'm so . . . happy . . ." For a moment I thought she had more to say, but her words cut off.

"At . . . la?" I desperately tried to keep my awareness together, but with a gentle smile on her face, Atla had finally stopped moving.

"Atla!" Raphtalia wept.

"Atla!" I shouted . . . but what remained of the girl, lying there on her cot, could never answer me again.

Epilogue: The Girl Who Became a Shield

I had no idea how long I'd been out of it.

Raphtalia had been crying the entire time, while Fohl just wordlessly glared at me.

Atla's life had ended. She wasn't with us anymore.

"You can . . . hate me," I managed. I'd failed to save his sister . . . someone he had loved and treasured more than anyone else. I could accept him hating me.

The moment I said that, Fohl grabbed the front of my clothes and his fist . . . stopped just in front of my face.

"I'm not going to hate you! I'm not going to hate you and make this any easier on you!" Fohl raged.

"What?" I could hardly comprehend.

"Let me tell you about Atla! Right up to the end, she was in love with you! She chose to sacrifice herself for you! So I can't blame you . . . I can't hate you! I didn't save her either. If I'd stopped her, when she stepped forward, none of this would have happened!" Fohl said.

"But—" My words stopped as my head filled with possibilities. Things I could have done differently to stop Atla from dying—questioning myself as to why I didn't respond to her feelings.

"If I'd never met Atla . . . then she wouldn't have died like this." In the moment I uttered these words, my whole head was rocked hard to the side.

I realized that Fohl had finally punched me.

"Don't say that to me! Never say that to me!" he raged.

"But it's the truth—" I managed around my aching jaw.

"If we hadn't met you like that, Atla would have died long ago!" Fohl countered. "I didn't have the money to buy the medicine we needed to keep Atla alive. If she had another episode, she would have simply died! Instead . . . she was able to walk around, even fight with me, which was all thanks to you! So I won't forgive you if you ever say something like that!"

"But even so . . . this is just—" I stumbled.

"Don't you dare defile Atla's pride any further!" Fohl demanded, turning his back on me. His hands were bunched so tight they were bleeding.

I was as hard as metal and he'd punched me. That was going to do more than just hurt. Droplets of his blood dripped onto the ground.

"Atla told me that she wanted me to protect everyone from the village, just as though they were her. I have to stand by her final wishes! How can I hate you, the one who should have become my brother-in-law? I can't hate you!" Fohl roared, his rage ringing out.

That shout . . . perhaps having awoken something, caused

a blinding light to rise from the temple in the castle town. That light flew toward Fohl and enveloped him.

The eyeball-burning flash lasted for just an instant before vanishing . . . and then gauntlets appeared on Fohl's hand.

"This is—" I'd seen these particular gauntlets before. Had the legendary gauntlets responded to the shout of Fohl's heart? I would have mocked this all as simple contrived coincidence up until yesterday.

But right now, I didn't have the leeway even to mock such tropes.

It was too late. Too late for anything . . .

"You'd better keep your promise to Atla! I'm going to go and do the same!" Fohl dashed away, tears streaming from his eyes.

To protect those fighting on the battlefield . . .

For my part . . . I tried to console the sobbing Raphtalia . . . and reflected on the final words of the departed girl who had so adored me.

"Can I have a moment alone?" I asked Raphtalia, Rat, and the healers, even as I held Atla's remains in my arms.

"If that's what you need. But don't forget the battle is ongoing," Rat said.

"Yes, I know," I managed. Raphtalia just gave a sob, and then the two of them nodded and left. Still stunned . . . I thought back over my memories of Atla.

I remembered that night when she first came to sleep in my room.

"I'm the Shield Hero. All I can do is protect people," I had said, playing down my own role.

"Looking at your village, Master Naofumi, it seems like everyone is being protected under your wing," Atla replied.

"Wing, huh?" I hadn't been convinced.

"I think you are protecting everyone, waiting for their moment to leave the nest," Atla had continued.

"Leaving the nest is all very well, but I still need you to defend it. I'll have to consider some punishment otherwise," I had told her.

"Everyone in the village has told me about your great deeds, Master Naofumi. I think you're doing a wonderful thing, something to be proud of. I respect you for overcoming such adversity, always carrying on," she had replied.

"I mean . . . I guess so. I'm not trying to be humble, but I guess I've made something of myself," I had admitted.

"One thing though . . . Who protects you, Master Naofumi?" she'd asked.

"Me?" I'd asked in surprise. Then I'd remembered Raphtalia saving me and the others. "I guess I do have some people."

"I've had a thought. If Raphtalia is your sword, Master Naofumi, then I want to become your shield. I want to protect you," Atla had said.

"A shield, huh? That might not be as glamorous as you think," I'd told her.

And now that wish had been fulfilled at the cost of her life.

In that case, I had to respond to her final request. I hadn't been able to protect her, so the least I could do was fulfill that final wish . . . or I wouldn't be able to forgive myself.

That was the heart of this. No matter who might take exception with what I did next, or disparage me, having failed to protect someone else so badly, I had to keep this promise—this promise above all else!

I grit my teeth, determination flowing through me. I was about to step into forbidden territory. Then I scolded myself; I was a criminal, buying people's lives, using them up, then discarding them, so what did I have to feel guilty about?

I looked at Atla's body. It looked like it would crumble at a single touch. It was all because she chose to protect our lives with her own, small, fragile body. She had certainly helped keep our casualties down. When considering it pragmatically . . . I did understand.

If it was to save the heroes, if it was to save someone you loved, people might be willing to give their lives for such things. I'd considered making that choice myself, so I could sympathize with that thought process.

But then take a look at the reality. Look at what happened to her. The kind of death so horrible it could barely be put into words. And yet, right up until the end, she had still been thinking of me.

This girl had loved me, of all people, accepting everything about me, unconditionally.

And now I was going to put her inside my shield.

Fear, terror, despair, lamentation—all kinds of emotions whirled inside me. My body couldn't stop shaking.

I still had to do this.

If nothing happened after all of my prayers, if they could just stand by and not see the injustice in this outcome . . . there surely were no gods.

No. There couldn't be a god. I wouldn't allow it! If any such god existed and allowed this to happen, I would never forgive them. I'd kill them, whatever it took.

It was all so messed up!

Everything had been going well. I'd been aware of everything, ready for anything. It was a battle we could have won without losing anyone!

If not for that light, that terrible flicker, Atla wouldn't have had to die.

Heroes? Hah. Gods? Double hah! This world . . . this unreasonable world . . . who could stand it?!

"Atla . . . I think I understand a little about what you meant when you said you didn't want to return to this world," I whispered to her. Her body was so light—the body of a girl that I would never talk to again.

I was going to keep that promise.

I couldn't possibly break it.

I wasn't going to let this shitty world take Atla.

I grunted. I gasped. The body of the girl vanished into the shield.

It sparkled in exactly the same way as when I'd put a monster or item inside in the past.

Curse Series. Shield of Wrath, blessing!
Bless Series. Shield of Compassion forcibly unlocked!
Soul Shield conditions unlocked!

Demi-Human Series forcibly unlocked! Completed!
Slave Master Series forcibly unlocked! Completed!
Companion Series forcibly unlocked! Completed!

Bless Series
The Bless Series is a powerful series of weapons only obtained by those who have overcome a terrible curse. It exists as a default shield and imbues power into the weapon it changes into.

The equip bonus depends on the shield it is changed into.

Bless Series
Shield of Compassion
<abilities unlocked> equip bonus: skills: **Change Shield (attack), Iron Maiden, Shooting Star Wall**
special effects: call of compassion, enchant, bless, all resist, spell support

Hand in hand with a blind girl . . . the Shield of Compassion was created by the mercy in two hearts.

It was an incredibly simple and yet a gentle shield. It was like sunlight through the trees on a warm day. It also had the best effects of any shield I had collected so far. I knew that "enchantment" meant the effects of this shield could be overlaid on other shields. That alone provided a massive boost to my defensive capabilities.

On top of that, it had forcibly unlocked the Demi-Human Series, Slave Master Series, and Companion Series. It also had equipment bonuses. In other words, it provided a massive boost to the stats of slaves, demi-humans, and companions.

I switched to the Spirit Tortoise Shell.

Growth up due to growing power!
Changed to Spirit Tortoise Shell Shield!

Further boosts were being triggered. I didn't have the time

right now to look in detail at everything that was happening. Those who had been getting treatment had now all been treated too. The healers were clamoring about it being some kind of miracle.

I stepped out in front of the tent and looked at the twin Phoenixes whirling in the sky. They shrieked, as though taunting me. Just like Ost, I was here fighting these birds for the sake of the world. I understood the true nature of it, that I was simply a device completing my assigned role.

Ost had known that too . . . had fought, based on that understanding . . . meaning there was only one thing I could do.

"Filo!" I shouted, calling her over. She was putting up a good fight against the Phoenixes.

"What is it?" Filo approached, clearly worried about Atla and seeing the sad expression on my face. I glimpsed a kindness in Filo in that moment that I'd never seen in her before.

I couldn't tell if that was Atla's power or the power of the Shield of Compassion.

Conflicting emotions rose inside my chest. Not just sadness, but also kindness mixed in. However, I didn't want to think this was just the influence of the shield.

"I know you won't like this, but take me over to Gaelion," I told her.

"Okay . . . we're doing this then," she replied.

"Yeah. Time to bring overtime to an end!" I stated. I

climbed onto Filo's back and sped back to the battle. When I gave a signal with my hand, Filo bunched her strength into her legs and then leapt up to Gaelion.

"Gaelion! A request from our master!" she shouted.

"Kwaa!" he replied. Gaelion, with Wyndia still on his back, caught me in midair as I launched myself off from Filo.

"One final push, Master!" Filo gave me a pseudo-thumbs-up with her wings as she plummeted back to the ground.

"I've got it!" I replied. As soon as Filo landed, she charged right back into battle with the low-altitude Phoenix.

With a shriek, the Phoenix turned its attention on me and came at us with its claws. I should have tried to retain my composure, perhaps. Just because my hated foe was before me, I couldn't let it fill my heart with darkness. But I could understand the pain. I could understand how unfair this world was.

I understood the wounds we had taken . . . and the sadness of what we had lost.

It was exactly because I could understand it that I had to get angry.

"You shut the hell up." I stopped the Phoenix's incoming claws with a single hand and hurled the bird down toward the ground.

Its only shriek now was one of surprise.

Spinning dizzily, the Phoenix recovered in midair and flew back toward me. Its expression looked like . . . one of pain? Was it weak? Then this was the moment to strike.

I immediately leapt off Gaelion's back and headed straight for the Phoenix.

"Kwaa!?" Gaelion squawked.

"Huh!?" Wyndia was surprised too, rider and steed both with shocked looks on their faces.

"I'm going to smash this overstuffed turkey into the ground. Pile on!" I shouted.

"S-sure thing," Wyndia affirmed.

"Kwaa . . ." Gaelion growled too. I let them know my plans, with suitable gravitas in my voice. Then I activated gravity field.

It hadn't had any effect when I'd tried it before, but now I could use it. I made it as heavy as I could, stopping the Phoenix from flying completely.

With more pathetic squawks, the Phoenix, unable to fly due to the weight, desperately flapped its wings. But it was completely unable to maintain its height.

It continued to fall down to where the low-altitude Phoenix was waiting below.

And then close to the ground, dust rising from the battle, I grabbed both Phoenixes and shouted a skill.

"Chain Shield!" Both birds were caught up in the chains that emerged from my shield and bound together. With those preparations in place, I shouted to everyone else in the vicinity.

"Everyone! Take them down!"

"Naofumi?!" Fohl was stunned.

"What are you doing?" I yelled. "Take them both out!"

"Okay! Tiger Break!" Fohl was also the first to act. I mean, he would be. I really felt like I could understand his feelings the best in that moment. That was how I felt. Maybe I didn't understand what it was like to lose a family member like that. But I knew exactly what Atla had been like.

"Don't worry about me. Just hurry up and defeat this thing! Make sure you kill them both at the same time!" I commanded. There were general shouts of agreement, and then special attacks started pounding in.

"Naofumi, what about Atla?" Ren asked me between attacks. I was unable to reply and just looked away. I didn't want to think about that right now.

"Damn . . ." Realizing what it meant, Ren made a painful sound. He also applied more strength to his sword.

"I feel so . . . light!" With her sword in front of her, Keel charged forward just like Filo and attacked the Phoenix.

"Yeah. I feel, like . . . totally different from before." The slaves and everyone else in my unit were definitely performing better, their attacks sharper, more on point. This was clearly a result of the boost from the Slave Series and Comrade Series being unlocked. I still hadn't checked the details yet, but the effects were clearly pretty massive.

It was all thanks to Atla.

"Faster. Finish them off faster. All the unfairness, all the sadness here . . . we have to eradicate it as quickly as possible," I shouted. Both Phoenixes were together now, attacking me one after the other, but I didn't feel a single thing.

The claws, the breath, the feathers, none of it meant a thing.

Once we had them pinned in a single place, they were just prey. All we had to do was pile on and tear them down.

"Gravity Sword!"

"Brionac!"

"Bird Hunting!"

"Tornado Throw!"

"Eight Trigrams Blade of Destiny Second Formation! Third Formation! Stardust Blade!"

"Spiral Strike!"

Everyone unleashed all of their highest-powered attacks, one after the other.

"I'm activating the Ritual Magic, Meteorite! Hero Iwatani!" the queen cautioned me, but I signaled with my eyes that she should just go ahead regardless of my position.

"Very well! Everyone other than Hero Iwatani, fall back!" she warned. As my other allies all put some distance between themselves and the target, a massive meteorite dropped from the sky to envelop both myself and the two chained birds.

A huge explosion swallowed the three of us, but I didn't take any damage at all.

"Our turn, Shildina!" Now it was Sadeena.

"I'm ready!" Shildina replied. The two of them, located toward the back of the forces, promptly completed incanting ritual magic.

"Gale and Thunder Gods!" they shouted together. The ritual magic caused a thick blast of lightning, far more powerful than Judgment, to crash down onto the Phoenixes, combined with an air-shredding tornado.

One of the two birds gave a protracted scream, and the other started to pulse in a strange fashion. It was happening again.

Self-destruct.

Of course, we weren't about to let that happen.

As the cacophony of ritual magic came to an end, my allies dashed back in.

"Attack Support!"

"Tiger Rampage!"

Fohl's special attack thundered home after he had received support magic from pretty much everyone else, and the two birds were reduced to feathers at almost exactly the same time, proceeding to vanish into nothing.

A roar of victory echoed out across the field.

Feathers drifted down like snow. And amid the blizzard I just stood, quietly, simply existing.

"Atla . . . we did it," I finally said. I lifted my shield high, reporting the victory.

We definitely could have won this without having to pay such a price.

Whoever was responsible for this . . . they would never find forgiveness from me.

"Ren! You know what needs to be done?" I shouted.

"Yeah!" he replied.

"Tell the queen too. Whoever it was who fired that flicker of light, we're going to burn them at the stake! No forgiveness!" It might have been one of the suspicious Seven Star Heroes. Or it might have been S'yne's enemies. I looked over at her, but she just shook her head, telling me that she didn't know.

A cunning move, I'd give them that. If it had been S'yne's enemies, they really had targeted the best single moment that could possibly kill the heroes.

S'yne had always warned us about that possibility.

If they were the ones, then . . . they were going to take full responsibility for everything that had happened as a result!

"Still . . . after the first explosion, the Phoenixes became a real pushover," Ren commented. I ignored him, my anger still seething. Who cared about any of that now?!

"We're moving!" I stated. I called over Filo and told her to head straight for where the light that had punched through the Phoenix had come from. Ren came too, riding Gaelion.

We searched for the remainder of the day until the sun went down but didn't find anyone who could have been the culprit.

"Dammit! Where have they run off to?!" I roared.

"This search isn't going to find anything now. Naofumi, you need to take a break." Ren chose that moment to give me what sounded like an order.

"What are you talking about?!" I fired back.

"We'll keep going and let you know if we find anything," he said. "You need to rest until then. Please."

"But—" I wanted to carry on.

"Please, Naofumi," he repeated. I wanted to debate the point, but Ren wasn't having it. His expression was a complex one, mixing sadness with anger. "You aren't the only one who's angry here. I'm filled with an incredible rage."

"Okay," I managed.

"I'm not going to forgive whoever did this either. But we need you to approach this a little more calmly," he said, which was actually quite effective at calming me down.

When I became truly angry, completely incensed, it could feel as though I was actually completely calm. My feelings in that moment . . . couldn't be easily described.

It felt like I was being controlled by a totally different type of anger from when Witch betrayed me. He was right. I should take a break. I needed to rest up well enough to be able to tell the difference again between those I needed to protect and those I needed to get angry with.

That was what my seemingly calm mind told me.

"Okay. I'm sorry. I'll leave this with you," I told him.

I sat down beside the temple, the sun slipping away.

The search was ongoing.

As I rested as Ren had told me to, I realized that I had been angrier than I'd even been before. The Shield of Compassion helped to soothe that anger, which otherwise felt as though it might burn me away. Yet beyond that, I just couldn't hope to find forgiveness for whoever had done this.

I understood the depth of the unfairness, sadness, and suffering this had caused.

As the anger faded though, I became aware of a feeling of loss, like a hole had opened in my chest. It swelled up to overtake me. Before I knew it, I was sitting in a temporary tent erected by the coalition army . . . with Raphtalia standing in front of me.

"That was a cowardly move on Atla's part. I was hoping to get you to notice me, on my own merits, Mr. Naofumi," she said.

"Okay . . . but . . . for now . . ." I could still barely speak.

"I know. I know, so please . . . stop crying." Raphtalia said, who was crying more than I was. They were tears from her heart—tears that understood the pain of others.

"I'm not crying," I replied and then realized something was running down my cheeks.

Were these . . . tears?

When I left the medical tent, I hadn't been aware that I was crying at all. But everyone else must have seen it.

I was crying.

In the moment I realized that this a feeling of emptiness had started to overtake me.

"Mr. Naofumi . . ." Raphtalia started. Without thinking, I grabbed onto her and started to sob.

After the battle in the castle, I'd decided I wasn't going to cry anymore.

Now my tears wouldn't stop.

The more I tried to stop them, the more they flowed out of me.

It was because I understood the sadness, suffering, and pain of others now. This wasn't something to be ashamed of. It was the correct thing, the right thing to do. I understood that now. For now, I just wanted to quietly cry, thinking of the girl who became a shield and who was now closer to me than anyone else.

I also made a vow, however, deep in my heart, that those responsible for this, whoever they might be, were going to be made to pay.